George Jonas

George Jonas was born in Budapest, Hungary, survived the German occupation and the Russian siege of 1945, and came to Canada in 1956. Since then he has written, produced and directed hundreds of programs for CBC radio and television, including *The Scales of Justice*. He has written librettos for two short operas and a full-length stage play, and has published three volumes of poetry. Jonas's controversial book, *Vengeance*, was a number one best-seller for many weeks in both hardcover and paperback. *By Persons Unknown* (with Barbara Amiel), published in 1977, was also a number one best-seller in Canada and won the Edgar Allan Poe Award for nonfiction in the United States.

A man of widely varied interests, George Jonas contributes articles, reviews and poetry to most major Canadian (and some American) magazines and newspapers.

FINAL
DECREE

GEORGE JONAS

FINAL DECREE

HarperPerennial
HarperCollins*PublishersLtd*

First published by Macmillan of Canada: 1981
First Totem Press, division of Collins Publishers, edition: 1985
First HarperPerennial edition: 1994

Canadian Cataloguing in Publication Data

Jonas, George, 1935-
  Final decree

ISBN 0-00-222855-6

I. Title.

PS8519.052F56 1985   C813'.54   C85-099221-4
PR9199.3.J66F56 1985

94 95 96 97 98 99 ❖ CW 10 9 8 7 6 5 4 3 2 1

Printed and bound in the United States

CONTENTS

AUTHOR'S NOTE

Recent events similar to the ones described in this book led to a well-publicized tragedy in a Toronto court-house. These events directed my mind to the possibility of a story, in the literary tradition of Dreiser's *An American Tragedy* or Dostoevski's *Crime and Punishment*, books that are in no sense "based on" the cases that inspired them. *Final Decree*, like the many books in this tradition, is a work of fiction. Its characters have existed only in my imagination and are not intended to resemble any real persons living or dead.

In my attempts to make the legal and medical aspects of the book as plausible as possible I have consulted a number of authorities. I am especially indebted to Mr. Philip Epstein, a barrister specializing in family law, and to the psychiatrist and author Andrew I. Malcolm, M.D., F.R.P.S. (C) for some source material and interpretations.

This acknowledgement of assistance does not imply that anyone else subscribes to my views or shares my responsibility for any errors.

PART ONE

THE VISITOR

THE STRANGER WHO was going to help Kazmer bring justice into the world parked his Chevrolet in front of the workshop, got out and dropped a dime into the parking meter. From where Kazmer was sitting behind his bench in the basement, all he could see was the stranger's feet and the frayed edges of his dark overcoat. It would have made no difference if he could have seen his face, for Kazmer had never laid eyes on the stranger before, nor did he know when to expect him, but in that instant he knew who he was all the same. He felt comfort, familiarity and trust. For that reason it wasn't necessary for him to look up when the little bell rang above the door and, as if he were back in his village at home, he could continue running his chisel over the block of cherry wood on the bench until the stranger stood directly in front of him.

He knew he had guessed right when the visitor began to talk, even though he spoke the first few words in English. "Are you the man they call Catfish?" the stranger asked, except for "catfish" he used the word *harcsa*, and stressed the Hungarian word with the deep, open vowels of the mountain people. This was the way good, shrewd, sober people spoke, people whose fathers never descended the steep, clean, snow-covered Carpathian slopes into the fertile, duplicitous and much too western plains of Hungary. To such a man Kazmer could reply in the same Transylvanian dialect with the sly confidence of a compatriot.

"That's what they called my uncle, so that's what they call me, I guess."

The stranger nodded and, thrusting his hand deep inside the pocket of his overcoat, brought out an object wrapped in a patterned cotton handkerchief. "They tell me if I had something to sell, you'd buy it from me," he said to Kazmer.

"That I would," replied Kazmer. He put down his chisel and moved toward the door, taking care to walk slowly and with dignity. He took down a sign that said OPEN, in elaborate hand lettering, and replaced it with one that proclaimed BACK IN 5 MINUTES. Then he double-locked the door and put the key into his pocket. Though he was stepping softly, the jars of glue on the workbench rattled slightly under his heavy stride as he ushered his visitor to the back room, separated from the main shop by a plain blue curtain.

He set out the small glasses on the rickety table underneath the unadorned black Calvinist cross. "You will take a drop," he asked the stranger politely, as custom demanded, though he knew that he would say yes even if he wasn't a drinking man. This, too, was prescribed by tradition before the bargaining would begin. The stranger pulled up a chair, and Kazmer tipped the bottle of *szilvorium* over his glass. The clear liquid filled the small room with the aroma of ripe plums.

The stranger raised his glass to him and drank, still holding the object inside the patterned handkerchief in his other hand. Then he put both the glass and the object on the table, inviting Kazmer with a gesture to unwrap the handkerchief. "Is this what you had in mind?" he asked as Kazmer looked at the black, heavy 7.65 mm Mauser, which in that instant had become as much a part of the room as if it had always been there, German, dull and reliable. Without picking up the gun, Kazmer folded the handkerchief over it.

"Yes," he said quietly, though he could feel the small vein in his temple pounding with excitement. "If I can buy bullets to go with it, this is what I want."

"It has four bullets in it," said the man. Looking at him, Kazmer thought the stranger was a man of his own age, a few years older perhaps, and he could almost see him angling for brook trout in the river Olt, down in the valley, while high up in the mountains alien batteries were lobbing artillery shells at each other. It was not the stranger's battle. "Four's too many for one rabbit," Kazmer replied in the native idiom that would use a metaphor even for the time of day, "but not enough for seven."

The other did not smile but he picked up the idiom and elaborated on it, as people would in the mountains. "Seven rabbits at one sitting," he said, "are six too many even for a man who eats with a big spoon. But let's drink to it anyway," he added as Kazmer poured more brandy in his glass.

"This is an old gun," said Kazmer. "My aunt Rosie had one like it and she used it for scaring the crows. I may not be able to get any more bullets for it."

"I remember those crows," said the visitor. "Some of them had Rumanian hats. Sure it's an old gun and that's why I'm selling it so cheap."

"How cheap?"

"Would $250 be too much?"

"It wouldn't be for someone who had it," said Kazmer, "but all I have is $175, and you're welcome to it."

The stranger cast a glance at him just to see if Kazmer was telling the truth, then, satisfied, he extended his hand. Kazmer shook it and filled the glasses with plum brandy for the third time. While he rummaged around the shop for the cash, the visitor's eyes slid over the camp bed, the unpainted chest of drawers, the table and the wooden chairs, coming to rest on a child's handsomely carved hobbyhorse. It was painted jet black, and from the proud line of its neck one could see that it was not a meek Mecklenburgian and not even a swift Arabian, but a stallion from the plains of Hortobagy, waiting for the sound of the bugle to toss its head and come to life once more. A horse like that would not have been made by a machine.

Kazmer came back and counted the money on the table, some of it in single bills and the last five dollars in silver. The stranger started recounting the tens and twenties, but after he reached a hundred he scooped up the rest and put it in his pocket, saying, "If it tallied so far, the rest shouldn't be short." Then he got up, leaving the gun and the patterned handkerchief on the table.

The visitor spoke only once more, and that was at the door while he waited for Kazmer to unlock it. The question he asked was not intrusive but courteous, showing neighborly concern for a man who had spent hard-earned money that he could ill afford on something of importance to him. "And are you going to hunt men or beasts?" the visitor asked.

Kazmer nearly told him. The stranger he had never seen and would never see again, and still one of the few who could be counted on to understand him in this city whose very name—Toronto—Kazmer still took to mean "lake upon a wake," following the ancient Mongolian syllables his own language used to share with the North American Indians who gave the city its name, although with a different meaning. To all others he would be a crazy man, here in this new metal-and-glass country on the wrong side of the Gulf Stream. Crazy—and why? For liking this fertile land and trying to preserve it from evil? For saving the new country from those who would pervert it the way they had perverted the old? In a night full of foxes, would the stranger call a hawk crazy for circling watchfully over his nest?

"Only beasts," replied Kazmer as he opened the door.

THE VILLAGE OF BUGYI

THIRTY-TWO YEARS BEFORE he bought the gun from the stranger, Kazmer was sitting on a horsehair sofa in the home of his Uncle Harcsa, who had just downed a small glass of red wine and, having carefully wiped his black mustache in both directions on the back of his hand, continued staring out of the window, deep in thought. The hillside beyond was covered by the first snow of winter. Snow in October, even in the Carpathian mountains, augured a cold birthday for Jesus in 1944.

The others in the room, including the Reverend Vegvari, whose very name brought to mind the old Lutheran hymn about our God being a mighty *fortress*—which the Reverend had never failed to point out to those who could not make the association on their own—were looking at Uncle Harcsa expectantly. Today Uncle Harcsa was going to solve a strategic problem, the only one directly involving the village of Bugyi so far in the Second World War.

The problem had to do with SS Lieutenant Baumann's sex life, or more precisely, some information that had reached the people of the village because of it. It seemed that this good commander of twenty-five men, five PzKw IVh tanks and two trucks, making up a platoon of an SS Panzer regiment—itself merely one of many mid-echelon units of a certain Volksgrenadier division—decided to defend his one-kilometer section of the front against the advancing armies of Stalin by blowing up a dike and a bridge across the river Olt. This military move, come spring, would have resulted in Old Man Toth's potato patch being flooded.

Old Man Toth, a man of advanced years and considerable influence in the village of Bugyi, learned about the tactical significance of his potato field from the Rumanian whore Lilian, whose services he shared with SS Lieutenant Baumann. This was just another unforeseen side effect of Hitler's decision to move Army Group E from the Adriatic to the Carpathians. Lilian, still an imposing figure of a woman at age forty-four, with creole skin and long black hair and eyes, possessed fine instincts. For one thing, they told her that a young officer of the Third Reich would feel more comfortable in her company if he thought that she understood no German. For another, they suggested that in spite of Old Man Toth's age he might be much longer for the world Lilian inhabited than Lieutenant Baumann. Though by nature discreet and somewhat divided in her loyalties, when the time came to choose sides, Lilian chose Old Man Toth's.

Having already lost his younger son to Germany's ambitions in the East, Old Man Toth could not contemplate with equanimity the additional loss of his potato harvest. He informed the Reverend Vegvari, and together they called on Kazmer's Uncle Harcsa. It was a time for action.

Kazmer was looking with fascination at his uncle's Adam's apple, which was still bobbing up and down tasting the wine deep in his throat, where good red wine ought to be tasted. Uncle's Adam's apple was big, as were his ears and nose, which was remarkable only because he himself was an unusually small man. He had broad shoulders, though, and a deep chest like Kazmer himself, and no strands of gray in his black hair and mustache to show that, God willing, people would drink his health on his turning sixty in a month's time. He had spent the first and the last twenty-five of his years in the village, but it was the intervening ten years that gave Uncle Harcsa his special position. Kazmer, though too shy to look at the others in the room, watched them from the corner of his eyes. It was magical being the nephew, at this momentous hour, of such an important man.

What Uncle Harcsa did in 1909 was to leave Bugyi, which in itself was more than ninety-nine out of a hundred people born there had ever done, and to leave it not for Kolozsvar, the proud capital of Transylvania, or the legendary western city of Budapest, but for Constanta, a Black Sea port in Rumania, at a distance that cost the life of a seven-hand donkey. Having in this fashion made his way out of the crook of the great elbow the Carpathians form with the Transylvanian Alps, being God's protective arms to keep the Tartars out of Europe (not that they ever did), Uncle Harcsa crossed the sea into Asia Minor, thence striking out westward like that other great conqueror, Darius. And even though his treasure, unlike the ancient Persian king's, consisted only of a few *vasgaras*— the iron coin with a hole punched in its middle, and at that time still favored as legal tender in some parts of Franz Joseph's empire—Uncle Harcsa made it to the Gates of Hercules, which King Darius never did.

After outmarching the generals of antiquity, Uncle Harcsa stopped across from Gibraltar on the yellow sands of French Morocco. It was time to take stock, and it took little time with his *vasgaras* all spent and his donkey long dead. The seashore was flat, but deep inland there were supposed to be great mountains, where the breezes would no longer be tepid and moist, and a man coming from a place where the eye could not travel a mile without seeing walls of granite and snow-topped evergreens might feel at home. Before leaving Bugyi, Uncle Harcsa had signed over his share of the twelve-acre patrimony to the younger brother who would later be Kazmer's father. When he saw two Foreign Legionnaires in Casablanca who couldn't lift together the ass-end of a wagon to replace a wheel—a job that Uncle Harcsa could have done on his own, even though he was only half their size—he decided to join up. He could handle the Legion. Any man born at the bottom of the sea, which Transylvania was before the waters receded a few millennia ago, leaving only Murder Lake locked in between four mountains, clear as crystal and more than three thousand feet deep, could handle it.

But the Legion had a few tricks of its own, and the mountains of Africa were as different from those of Uncle Harcsa's home as the mountains of the moon, which they resembled. Still he followed the tricolor, and when the war came he stopped shooting at Bedouins and supported the English instead, who were assisting the Arabs to subvert the Turks. He learned enough French to obey his sergeant's commands, and enough English to make the sailors blush in Oran. He learned no Arabic. He called the English "eels," partly because in his native language the words for this electric fish and for the island nation resembled each other, and partly because he considered them long, slippery and shocking to the touch. He touched more than one in the winding alleys behind the whorehouses of Rabat, and they took away worse scars from these encounters than he did. Once he saw a lean, blond, limp-wristed eel in a burnoose, having no idea that this man, escorted by two tribesmen on camels and treated by his captain in the officers' canteen, would later be known as Lawrence of Arabia. He might not have been impressed had he known, because Uncle Harcsa, without ever having heard of *The Merchant of Venice*, had long since come to the conclusion that if you prick them, all men bleed.

It was this knowledge, in fact, that brought his career with the Foreign Legion to a dishonorable end. One day after the war Uncle Harcsa was struck in the face by a young Zouave lieutenant for moving too slowly. The unfortunate Frenchman did not know that men born on the shores of Murder Lake always move slowly, but you don't strike them for it unless you are their mother or you mean to kill them. Uncle Harcsa, standing respectfully at attention, tried to explain this to him, but the excitable youngster struck him again. Uncle Harcsa made no further remarks, but a week later he cornered the lieutenant in front of the supply tent in the darkness and, still moving slowly, he slit him from the bladder to the solar plexus with his trench knife. People could survive such injuries after the discovery of penicillin but in 1919 they couldn't, and Uncle Harcsa, not wishing to be guillotined, shed his uniform and made his way back to Transylvania, arriving just in time to see the Rumanian army, led by its array of rouged and tightly corseted homosexual officers, occupy his homeland on their way to Budapest.

The Peace of Trianon, which ended the war for Hungary, was a sad peace for Transylvania, which instead of independence (first choice) or continued association with Hungary (second choice) became Rumanian (which was no choice at all). However, Trianon was a good peace for Uncle Harcsa, who became coachman for the old Count Talnoky *de* Borszek *et* Tusnad, who still owned three-quarters of all arable land, virgin forest, sheep, horses, oxen, brown bears, deer, timber wolves and bald eagles between Bugyi and Murder Lake. He also owned a four-in-hand, with his coat of arms painted on the yellow coach of polished brass and curtains, and an American Peerless roadster which he never used. Still, he wanted a coachman who could handle the diabolical contraption, narrowing the choice in those parts to Uncle Harcsa and one or two other local veterans of the Great War. When Uncle Harcsa cranked the vulgar machine to life, for only the second time since it had been uncrated, the old Count said, "Good, son, now

shut the damn thing off and saddle my gray mare," signifying
that Uncle Harcsa had been hired.

By the time Kazmer was born in 1928, Uncle's reputation as
the living symbol for the powers of the human brain was well
established. That was quite a position in a village that prized
quick-wittedness above all other qualities. By any applicable
test—as a world traveler, a linguist or a man who'd never draw
a knife from his boot-top unless he meant to use it—Uncle
Harcsa's sophistication had no match. As a scientific genius
Einstein might have come a close second, but then Einstein
didn't live in the village. Once the old Count, being driven
home very late at night, startled his ancient *komondor* watchdog out of its deepest sleep, and it began barking at him.
What with Transylvania lost to the damn Rumanians and the
whole damn world full of gramophones, telephones and inter-
nal combustion engines, the old Count considered this the final act of betrayal, and in a fit of blue-blooded anger ordered
Uncle Harcsa to shoot his damn dog.

"Right now, or in the morning?" asked Uncle respectfully.

"Now, dammit. And you bring his body to me in the
Weapons Hall."

An hour later, brooding underneath the lances and sabers
of his ancestors, the Count rang for Uncle Harcsa, who came
running in his nightshirt.

"Have you shot that dog yet, you scoundrel?"

"I'm just loading the gun, Excellency," the coachman
replied, and trotted off into the night. In a little while he
reappeared, bearing the lifeless body of the huge white dog,
and placed it before its master's feet. The Count looked at the
corpse darkly, and emptied another glass of apricot brandy.

"Is it shot, then?"

"Pretty much," replied Uncle Harcsa.

"Then resurrect it, goddam it," said the Count. "It's a good
dog. You get five harvesting acres and a cow if that damn dog
barks again."

Uncle walked around the animal slowly, as if wondering at which end to begin, then emptied a big pitcher of water over the limp body. The *komondor* sat up with a snort, shook itself, and escaped through the door. The Count looked at Uncle Harcsa.

"How did you do it, scoundrel?"

"Do I get the five acres and the cow?"

"Yes, but speak up."

"Well, it took half a gallon of corn whiskey," said Uncle Harcsa, "seeing as it is a very big dog."

When Kazmer's parents both died—of the Spanish flu which arrived, as all things good or bad, in Transylvania a decade after the rest of the world—Uncle Harcsa adopted the orphan by the simple expedient of taking Kazmer, crib and all, and depositing him in his wife Rosie's kitchen, uttering only the word: "Here!" Nothing more needed to be said about the matter, since Rosie, a bright-eyed, buxom, pretty woman, couldn't very well expect to have a longer discussion on any subject with Uncle Harcsa than she'd had on the subject of her own marriage, which consisted of the following exchange: "All right, then, Rosie, we see the preacher the first Sunday after the harvest," and "All right, then, if you say so." It was a very good marriage.

Though just as ardent a nationalist as any other Transylvanian, Uncle was far more pragmatic. Shortly after Hitler came to power, a conflict arose with some local Saxons. Emboldened by the fact that, far-flung as they were from Germany proper, the new order considered them *Reichsdeutschen* or German nationals, they disputed the ownership of a herd of pigs that the people of Bugyi thought of as their own. The death toll in the ensuing battle was eighteen German nationals to only five Transylvanians; and one of the old Count's houseguests, an ultranationalist intellectual from the University of Kolozsvar, or Cluj as it was called in Rumanian, toasted the results of the epic encounter with moist eyes and trembling lips. Serving the drinks, Uncle Harcsa sighed deeply and cleared his throat, whereupon the Count, who

despised intellectuals on principle, asked him if there was anything he wanted to add to the discussion. "Only this, with
respect," said Uncle Harcsa, "that seeing as there are seventy
million Germans and less than three million of us, if the
Professor wins us many more such battles there won't be
none of us left to drive him back to Cluj."

Uncle Harcsa was right of course, but not too right, for the
same number of Transylvanians who stayed alive by not fighting the Germans came to their deaths by helping the Germans fight the Russians between 1941 and 1944. Preference
had nothing to do with it, for Transylvanians preferred only
each other and tolerated maybe the Hungarians, but they certainly wanted no part of the Rumanians, and it so happened
that in that particular corner of the world it was Adolf Hitler
who allowed this little bit of national self-determination to
occur. If the people of Bugyi knew that Hitler meant to be evil
to the Jews, they gave the matter very little thought. There
were maybe half a dozen Jews in the entire region. As for the
rest of the world, well, the eels and the frogs were just getting
what was coming to them for putting the Rumanian yoke
around the neck of the good mountain people at Trianon.

Still, these were abstract matters, while Old Man Toth's
potatoes were the here and now. Uncle Harcsa's eyes left the
snow-covered hills, roamed past the anxious faces of Kazmer,
Old Man Toth and the Reverend Vegvari, and came to rest on
Lilian who, not being offered a seat, was standing in the doorway. "Speak up, you," said Uncle Harcsa encouragingly, ad-
dressing the breasts of the village's only working girl. "What's
the thing that worries him the most?"

"Who?"

"Why, Tancred the Conqueror," said Uncle Harcsa, who
never thought much of the tank commander's martial virtues.
"What's he really afraid of?"

Lilian thought for a second. "The clap, I think," she said,
"and the partisans."

This was a joke, because Lilian never had the clap, only syphilis back in her youth until a friendly doctor from Cluj cured her with a series of Salvarsan shots free of charge, nor were there any partisans between the Olt and Murder Lake. Around Bugyi the villagers were ready to fight, but they preferred to put their lives at risk for private causes. It was like the story when, some centuries ago, a Saxon and a Transylvanian sat down in a rare moment of armistice to smoke a pipe together. "Why are *you* fighting?" asked the Saxon. "Why, for loot and plunder," replied the startled mountain-dweller. "But why are you fighting?" The Saxon drew himself up and said, "I'm fighting for virtue and honor, of course." The Transylvanian smoked his pipe in silence for a while. "Well, I guess we're each fighting for what we haven't got."

The people of Bugyi did not want for honor, but they had no potatoes to spare for the greater glory of Germany. This being the point of the matter, Uncle Harcsa said to Lilian, "You tell him, girl, the partisans are ready to strike across the ice on Murder Lake."

"Are there," asked the Reverend Vegvari, who, having much faith, had less need for wits than the others in the village, "are there partisans at Murder Lake?"

"There will be," replied Uncle comfortably.

"But they can't strike across the ice because it's too thin."

"That," said Uncle Harcsa, "is what we call a *ruse de guerre.*"

This was the start of Operation Rosedigger. Receiving Lilian's intelligence, Lieutenant Baumann smelled a coup, a promotion and perhaps even a week's furlough in France. Being a cautious soldier, however, he first summoned Uncle Harcsa to his headquarters in the village school. It was not remotely because he trusted the old ex-legionnaire but, except for Lilian's few words of French, he seemed to be the only person in the village with whom it was possible to communicate in any European language.

"Are there partisans," asked the SS commander, "in the

woods behind Murder Lake? You know, partisans? Boom-boom? *Franc-tireurs?*"

"Ah!" said Uncle Harcsa. "Partisans. I don't know. *Je ne sais pas. Das weiss ich nicht.*"

"Oh, for sure," said the onetime Hitler Youth sarcastically. "You don't know. But do you know if the ice on the lake will support a truck?"

"I don't know," replied Uncle without batting an eye. "But that's how we drive the steers to market right up till May." Like Goebbels, Uncle knew that the best lie is a big one and he flirted with the idea of saying June before he thought better of it. It was just as well, for May had done the trick.

Lieutenant Baumann's expeditionary force set out at the crack of dawn the next day in a classic operation of encirclement that was a joy to behold. Two panzers approached the woods behind Murder Lake on a loggers' road, cutting off all avenues of escape for the family of wild pigs and one solitary stag that resided in the forest, while the main force of two trucks and a tank struck across the ice for a frontal assault. The remaining two tanks were wisely held in reserve. Much to the surprise of the villagers the first truck actually made it across the ice, for the winter of '44 was unusually early and cold. Emboldened, the tank pulled up on the near shore and started laying down a proper barrage under the cover of which the soldiers from the successful truck started advancing into the forest. Lieutenant Baumann gave the signal for the second truck to move forward.

Luckily for the warriors in this vehicle, the ice cracked under them when they were hardly more than fifteen yards from the shore. A beautiful crevice appeared noiselessly along the entire length of the lake, sliding truck and driver in slow motion to its bottom of three thousand feet. The rest of the soldiers made it back to shore, though in no condition to pursue the battle.

Meanwhile the two panzers, encountering little opposition from the wild pigs, met the advancing infantrymen from the first truck and halted without killing anyone except a lance corporal. This was the point at which Uncle Harcsa, who had been quietly smoking on an outcropping of rock overlooking the theater of operations, handed his pipe to Kazmer, saying, "All right, son, now you shake a few embers on that there fuse."

Trembling with excitement, Kazmer held the bowl of the pipe to the end of the thinly braided candle-string and watched the sparkles from the old Count's duck-shot shells run down the mountainside to the logging road, under which his uncle had buried the small crate of dynamite the night before. Nothing happened for a while and Uncle Harcsa, sensing Kazmer's disappointment, said, "Well, hell, it's old stuff, from the time His Excellency wanted to build that fish hatchery in '25." The old Count had had many such piscicultural plans. Then the logging road blew up.

The two lips of the chasm rose silently at first, then with a thump like a gigantic heartbeat that shook the snow from the trees half a kilometer away, a crater opened up through which a truck could drop four floors to the serpentine below. The pigs, the stag and Lieutenant Baumann's forces were trapped in the woods, unless they made their way five kilometers east to the Russian front lines, a course of action open only to the stag and the pigs. Abandoning their tanks and truck and the corporal's body, the soldiers made their way back to the Axis side of the logging road, and that only because Uncle Harcsa sent Kazmer to fetch a ladder from the village to help them across the fissure. "*Verschwunden*," he explained to the soldiers, who were anxious to know where the partisans had got to, without taking the pipe out of his mouth. But if the partisans had disappeared and Old Man Toth's potatoes were safe for the time being, SS Lieutenant Baumann was still in the village, contemplating his crippled forces and thirsting for revenge.

It had pleased God to make Lieutenant Baumann a cruel man. During an earlier stint with the military police he earned the nickname of Lieutenant "*Das macht mich noch nicht krank*." Baumann, for ordering the continued torture of a prisoner whose sufferings, as he put it, had not yet made him sick. Now he ordered his sergeant to bring Lilian to him. He received the creole-skinned lady, as usual, in his bedroom and dressed in his pajamas, but with two soldiers in attendance.

Lilian was apprehensive but tried not to show it. *"Travail d'amour, non?"* she asked in her best French, flirtatiously. The Lieutenant smiled. *"Mais non, ma petite,"* he answered, "at least not until you tell us nicely just where you heard all about those *franc-tireurs*. You will tell us, won't you?"

Still smiling, Lieutenant Baumann opened a bottle of cognac and filled up two tiny glasses. He drank one, then blew Lilian a kiss and motioned to the two soldiers to take her to the cellar. It would serve no purpose to describe what the soldiers did to her there but, dropping by after three-quarters of an hour, Lieutenant Baumann declared that it had not yet made him sick. So the soldiers went to work again and, though the Lieutenant would still be feeling quite well after his second inspection, Lilian was already dead. Whether she said nothing out of heroism or because her combined French and German were inadequate for an act of betrayal must forever remain a mystery.

The next day Lieutenant Baumann withdrew the remnants of his platoon to a point west of Bugyi and established a defensive position by blowing up the neighboring village's dam. This enabled him to hold his sector against the Russian T-34s for nearly an hour and a half when the Red Army reached the Olt ten days later. But Lilian was buried long before that, and in sacred ground, too, though not without some misgivings on the part of the Reverend Vegvari, who thought that the line ought to be drawn somewhere. It took Uncle Harcsa a good ten minutes of shouting into the old Count's ear trumpet before he understood and summoned the pastor to the great Weapons Hall, where at eighty-seven he was still sitting in his bath chair with a bearskin rug over his knees. "You bury the damn girl, you hear," said the Count, who knew how to influence the clergy, "and remember that I mean to come to *your* funeral even if you are a bigger whore than she ever was."

A week after Lilian's funeral the feudal era in Bugyi came to an end. The dawn of the modern age was heralded by a cheerful detachment of soldiers from the Second Ukrainian Army, who to Uncle Harcsa's expert eyes seemed so drunk it was a miracle they didn't fall off the tanks on which they were sitting, holding their submachine guns strapped around their necks much the same way Elvis Presley was to hold his guitar a decade or so later. Their effect on the women of the village, however, was the opposite of the rock'n'roll idol's, and they ran screaming from their houses and courtyards to hide in any barn or wine cellar that was handy. This seemed not to offend the Russians, who never meant to rely on personal charm for their sexual conquests, nor—like their American GI counterparts—on cigarettes, chocolate and tins of corned beef. The Red Army raped, in a matter-of-fact and thorough fashion. The front-line soldiers exhibited not a whit of malice toward the objects of their passion. They used all the force necessary but no more, and never killed a woman who survived the experience itself.

At any rate, the people of Uncle Harcsa's village soon concluded that this brave new postfeudal period was not going to be very different from the ordinary old days. This brought a certain sense of relief to a community that, after the comings and goings of foreign soldiers for centuries, could once again be satisfied that the more things change, the more they remain the same. Aunt Rosie was past the age at which one needed to worry about rape, unless, as Uncle Harcsa remarked in her presence, she initiated some action on her own. (He would have caught Aunt Rosie's milking stool in the kneecap, too, if he hadn't slammed the kitchen door quickly after his *bon mot*.) Kazmer hid out in the barn for a short while, not because his virtue was in danger, but because the occupying forces were fond of borrowing strapping young men to load wagons or work on the roads. The official words of invitation for such services were *malinko robot*—"a little work"—and they could mean just that or, if fortune decreed otherwise, fifteen years in Siberia. It was all a matter of luck.

Up to that point Kazmer seemed to have had his fair share of luck in the world. True, he needn't have been orphaned but, having been, he could have grown up in a house far worse than Uncle Harcsa's. The worst thing about it, for Kazmer, was being called "the orphan" throughout his childhood, not maliciously but descriptively, as in "Tell the orphan to fetch the saw!" He would have liked to have been able to whistle through his teeth like the blacksmith's son Johnny, but he didn't brood about the fact that he couldn't. He was strong, healthy and, at sixteen, already a head taller than his uncle. When he worked with wood, the shavings sizzled under his fingers and silver birch trunks became as pliant as plasticine. Uncle Harcsa said nothing, but one day he had a brief talk with Görény the carpenter, who was in need of an apprentice. Soon Kazmer was permitted to fetch water and sweep the floor in Mr. Görény's workshop, and it didn't cost his uncle more than a suckling pig for the entire year.

All things considered, it was normal for Kazmer to fall in love in due course, and he did so just around the time when, in another part of the world, Harry Truman astonished all pundits by winning the presidential elections against Governor Tom Dewey, with a leftist candidate named Wallace running a distant third. Kazmer, having never heard of Harry Truman, let alone Messrs. Wallace and Dewey, was not in the least astonished. What amazed Kazmer in 1948 was Katika, a long-legged maiden with thickly braided dark blond hair, and eyes that were the color of amber, like a mountain cat's. The miraculous thing about it was that Katika's eyes, presumably, were the same color the year before, and perhaps throughout all the years she had been growing up alongside Kazmer in the village, but Kazmer never noticed them. Now he did, and in a way that filled him with longing and ecstasy. These sublime feelings, however, could have been noted only by an electrocardiograph, for while Kazmer's pulse quickened whenever Katika happened to walk by him in the street, he only looked past her and said or did nothing. Still Katika did not remain ignorant of Kazmer's feelings, because one evening in September when the villagers, as usual, were husking corn in a circle, the boy sitting next to her whispered something that made her giggle and blush. Sitting opposite, Kazmer only looked at the floor, but after all the corn had been stacked he waited for the other boy by the riverside and, still without a word, grabbed him by the shirt and pushed him into the water. "What the hell?" the boy asked him after clambering back to shore, mainly to save face.

"Just don't talk to her again, that's all," replied Kazmer darkly.

When word reached Katika the next day, she considered it the official beginning of Kazmer's courtship, which it was, for in Bugyi you could not expect a man to humiliate himself by coming right out and speaking to a girl in whom he had an interest. Not that some didn't, for all men are not cut from the same cloth, but you couldn't expect them to. Mostly they initiated courtship by pulling your five-gallon pail up from the well in the village square (ordinarily they would not be so polite) or maybe by knocking another fellow down. The rest was up to you.

Katika did her best. She began with a bit of stage business, much favored in commedia dell'arte in the sixteenth century and still in vogue in Bugyi, which consisted of dropping her hankie on the road the next time she saw Kazmer, then emitting a little scream to make sure the accident did not escape the passing gallant's notice. The trick accomplished the first half of the desired effect, for Kazmer stopped and remarked, before continuing on his way:

"You dropped your hankie."

But Katika was not discouraged, and a week later she took her old mousing cat out of the barn and deposited it in the front garden, the exclusive domain of the *komondor* watchdog. This was such a gross territorial effrontery that, on seeing the cat, the dog did what can only be described as a double-take before coming to its senses and treeing the feline intruder. The cat still sat on the topmost branch, hissing and spitting, half an hour later when Kazmer walked by on his way to the carpenter's shop.

"That's my cat up in the tree," Katika said to him.

"Looks like a worried old cat," said Kazmer politely, after examining the situation.

"What would you do to get it down?"

"I would," replied Kazmer, "tie up that dog."

"And I would climb that tree and bring it down," said Katika with flashing eyes, "if I was a man."

Kazmer could no more resist such a challenge than the *komondor* could resist chasing the cat, for both commands had their sources in the same ancient part of the brain. The sinewy old cat obeyed a few commands of its own, and, sitting in a position of great tactical advantage, it clipped Kazmer smartly on the cheek four times before he could pry it loose from the limb.

"Lord Jesus," said Katika. "I could bandage that for you."

"Hell, no," said Kazmer, "but I heard there will be music at the school on Sunday."

"I know that," said Katika, her heart skipping a beat. "It's the gypsy fiddlers from Tusnad."

"Well, I wasn't going to go," said Kazmer, "because I'm not much for dancing. But now I think maybe I will."

"Come to think of it," Katika replied, "maybe I'll be there myself."

This was the way in which Kazmer's first date with a girl came about, and if he had been the kind of person who reflects on omens he might have noted, while wiping his cheek, that it had already cost him a few drops of blood. But the sober, practical people of the mountains were not given to such reflections, and had they known that it was their country, of all places, that the imagination of the English writer Bram Stoker had populated with vampires, they would have been greatly amused. Kazmer's people had, in fact, remarkably few superstitions, which is not to say that they were without religion or legends. The most popular legend regarded the Milky Way— called the Avenue of the Hosts—a great military high road, upon which the avenging armies of Prince Csaba would ride to the rescue of all Transylvanians in times of danger. And in 1948, on clear nights, the people of Bugyi had as much reason as ever to scan the brilliant skies for a sign.

For while Kazmer was polishing his best boots for Sunday and Katika's little sisters were carefully braiding her hair, the times continued taking their big leap from the Middle Ages to the age of scientific socialism in Bugyi, trying to touch the in-between land of liberal democracy as little as possible on the way. That was the reason why, while dancing the *csárdás* with Katika, Kazmer could say:

"Well, manna is falling from heaven once again."

"Is it?" asked Katika, surprised, for she hadn't seen any.

"They're giving away the old Count's land. My uncle's getting some, too. No less than three acres, even to Juicing Abel on Trashpit Row."

"Why to Juicing Abel?"

"Because he never had any, I guess," replied Kazmer.

This answer expressed as well as any other the spirit of the great land reform that came to every country in east-central Europe in the wake of the conquering Red Army, nor would many people have called it right that Count Talnoky should own 75,000 acres while Juicing Abel, that other child of the Calvinist God, owned none. And considering that for every Count there were a hundred thousand Juicing Abels, none would protest as long as it was only the Count whose ox was being gored, especially when every table might expect a piece or two of its flesh. Such new laws might even be mistaken for equity, at least until Juicing Abel would come to be deprived of his three acres by the same piece of paper bearing the same stamp that had taken away the Count's 75,000 the year before. But it takes a toad to sense rain on a sunny day. The Russians just wanted to do away with counts as the Germans just wanted to do away with Jews, and why should that concern the good people of Bugyi, who were neither? Even the Reverend Vegvari took a cosmic view of the matter and bellowed some soothing words into the old Count's ear trumpet about a camel and the eye of a needle, before hastily removing himself from the reach of the old gentleman's cane.

Much less happily for the majority of Transylvanians, Rumania came back again to rule in the footsteps of the Soviets, possibly as a reward for abandoning Hitler's tottering Reich a smart few months before Hungary—and as a little compensation for Moldavia being sliced off by the USSR. Whether it was more or less of a bad thing to be a Hungarian minority in Greater Rumania than to be a Rumanian minority in Greater Hungary was something historians could debate forever without changing the minds of the minorities themselves. Uncle Harcsa tended to be philosophical about the whole thing. "Yesterday it was the *Szekely*'s turn," he explained to some weeping fellow-*Szekelys* at the inn, "and today it is the *Olah*'s. Tomorrow it will be our turn again."

But tomorrow was slow in coming, and what came instead was a notice requesting Uncle Harcsa to present himself at the local schoolhouse for an interview with the Party Secretary. By the time the notice came people could save themselves the trouble of asking which party, there being only one left, the Communist. In the village, Juicing Abel and a few of his cronies belonged to it.

Juicing Abel was in the schoolhouse, too, sitting next to a thin Rumanian, who looked like a consumptive dry-goods salesman and got up to shake Uncle Harcsa's hand. There was a third man sitting behind the table, thickset and morose.

"So you are the famous Harcsa," said the Rumanian. "Well,

well. This is Comrade Panciu from the District Secretariat, and I expect you know Comrade Abel."

"Him I know all right," said Uncle Harcsa pleasantly, "and now I know Comrade Panciu. I guess the only comrade in this room I don't know is you."

The thin Rumanian smiled, thinly. "My name is Lei," he said, "and I'm being sent to you by the Party."

"I call that a good idea," said Uncle Harcsa, *lei* being the official currency of Rumania, "and I hope they'll send us many more like you."

"I'm glad you have a sense of humor," said Comrade Lei, seriously. "The Party approves of humor and satire as weapons in the class struggle. Today, however, our main weapon in the class struggle is land."

"Land, eh?" said Uncle Harcsa cautiously.

Comrade Lei changed the subject. "I'm told by Comrade Abel here that you have played a significant part in the local resistance," he said. "He tells me your role was instrumental in the destruction of a Nazi unit opposing the glorious Red Army of liberation."

"Yes, well," said Uncle Harcsa modestly, "except it didn't help the potatoes much."

"The potatoes?" Comrade Lei seemed confused.

"In July they got took anyway."

"Who took them?" asked Comrade Lei, although something told him he shouldn't.

"Why, the glorious Red Army of liberation," said Uncle Harcsa innocently. "The same time when they took the barley. On trucks."

Comrade Lei cleared his throat. "I'm also told by Comrade Abel," he said, "that you own twenty acres of land."

"That I do," replied Uncle Harcsa with dignity. "Twelve after my late brother, may he rest in peace, five from the Count because of the dog, and the last three that the new laws gave me from the estate. And that's twenty."

The morose Comrade Panciu raised his head for the first time. "You are," he said to Uncle Harcsa accusingly, "a middle peasant."

The accusation was true enough, though Uncle Harcsa, not being well versed in Marxist mythology had no way of knowing it. According to the Communist Party's view of the world, people were divided into classes and subclasses along very precise economic and occupational lines, their own as well as their fathers'. The exact details of this could fill a book (and did fill many), but in rural areas it meant titled landowners and rich peasants who were cast in the role of the damned, and poor peasants or agricultural laborers who were sainted. Between the two, in a kind of purgatory, were the middle peasants, who could achieve salvation through good acts but would go to perdition otherwise. The acreage that would put a person into one or another of these categories varied according to region, but around Bugyi anything over eighteen acres would be enough to exclude a man from paradise. Unless.

"Unless, of course," said Comrade Lei, "he shows a good example and signs his land over to the collective."

"You mean the extra three acres?" asked Uncle Harcsa.

"No."

"The five I got from the Count, then?"

"He means the whole damn thing," said Comrade Panciu, who had no patience for bedside manners.

Uncle Harcsa thought the matter over. "Well," he said finally, "I see what you mean. It makes sense, I guess. It's just that I was a poor peasant myself until you gave me the extra three acres, wasn't I?"

"Hell, yes," said Comrade Panciu. "That's why we gave it to you. You don't suppose we give land to capitalistic middle-peasant pigs."

"You mean, if you hadn't given me the three acres, now I could keep my own seventeen?"

"Poor peasants," said Comrade Panciu decisively, "can do whatever they damn well like."

"For the time being, anyway," added Comrade Lei.

"All right," said Uncle Harcsa. "I just wanted to be clear about it, that's all. Now, where do I sign?"

To create the impression that everyone was as philosophical as Uncle Harcsa about joining the collective would be misleading. To be given the land they had been dreaming about for centuries only to have it snatched back from them a year or two later was for the peasants of Eastern Europe the cruelest joke a state could play on its subjects. They didn't care whether the tiny plots most of them ended up with after the great land reform were economically viable or not. For the sake of private ownership they were ready to take their chances with poverty and hardship, which, after all, were no news to them. They didn't care if the land they were once again excluded from owning went back to some aristocrat or forward to the People's Democracy. They resisted collectivization the way wild animals resist capture, and for the same reason. "You hear those wolves?" Uncle Harcsa asked Juicing Abel as they were leaving the schoolhouse. "They are starving. Maybe you and your comrades should tell them they'd be better off in the Bucharest Zoo."

But if both wolves and people preferred hungry liberty in the woods to regular meals in collective cages (where the meals were not so regular anyway), both wolves and people also knew when they were licked, though people knew this a lot sooner than wolves. It was one thing to savage a few Nazi trucks or tanks, with the Germans in full retreat from the Russians five kilometers away and the Allies well on their way to the Rhine, and quite another to snipe at the Marxist deity with a triumphant Red Army in the backyard, and the great democracies washing their hands like Pontius Pilate in the distant West. Only a fool would use up his matches trying to light a fire in a rainstorm, and whatever else the people of Bugyi might have been, they were no fools.

Anyway, it wasn't as though the whimsies of power came as a shock to anyone around the banks of the river Olt. "The

Lord giveth and the Lord taketh away," murmured the Reverend Vegvari to his distraught collectivized parishioners, dutifully rendering unto Caesar what was Caesar's in the hope that, as ever before, Caesar would render unto the Reverend Vegvari what was God's. And "what the hell," Juicing Abel could say to Uncle Harcsa, with some justification, "it's not as if you didn't tip your hat to the bloody Count all these years. So what if you're gonna tip it to Comrade Lei?"

"Yeah, well," replied Uncle Harcsa, "so long as you're not trying to get me to tip it to *you*." It wasn't a very good answer, but it was the best a man could think of when fighting a rearguard action for his dignity. It certainly served as a warning to Juicing Abel that a new membership card in the Party, for the time being at any rate, would not entirely upset the traditional pecking order in the village.

Because when everything was said and done, the dignity of a man among his fellows mattered more than anything else; and in this one sense Bugyi was no different from greater communities. For even though Uncle Harcsa had no medals and tucked his pants into his boots like everyone else, when he walked down the main street, people would know that this man was to borrow from rather than to lend to, and to be advised by rather than to advise. His hands, they knew, might be for hire, but not his tongue or his heart. He might, like a brown bear, shuffle out of harm's way whenever possible but, like a brown bear, he would make any fool pay a price who mistook his wisdom for weakness. Such a man would expect his due, though he would give others theirs, and his wife would not be at the neighbors, gossiping, when he came home for supper.

And Kazmer grew up wishing that he were like him and hoping that one day he would be.

THE BLUE PANEL TRUCK

BUT ALL THE twenty-eight years that had meandered by since 1948 had not brought that day any closer, though they had brought some amazing things, like the blue Dodge that Kazmer was backing slowly out of the laneway, being careful as always to keep the engine in low revs and not to slip the clutch. "You be good to your tools and your tools will be good to you," Mr. Görény the carpenter used to say, even though back in Bugyi he would never have dreamed of tools the like of which Kazmer had in his workshop now, nor of a vehicle of such proud luxury as the blue Dodge panel truck. But what use was it, and what use was the electric power saw, the snowblowing machine in the driveway, or the color television set that brought Johnny Carson with his loose talk into the living room—speaking bad words, to judge by the way his wife would giggle and blush, though Kazmer could not understand half of it. And how was it possible that all these miraculous things—not a single one of which was needed for Uncle Harcsa to command respect, though he would have commanded even more if he had had them—only served to humiliate a husband in front of his wife. That Johnny Carson! Or the beautiful blue truck: "Just park it down the block when you're picking me up. I don't want people to see."

It would have been smarter to buy a gun perhaps, if that was the way it had to be, not that a gun would ever command respect which only a fool would believe, but for protection. Because a gun could provide protection for a man and his children and, if not that, at least justice. And it wasn't as though Kazmer would blame anyone who looked to the law for both, because that was the way he started out, too, until he learned better. Better, though not as quickly as a dumb animal, for he had burned himself many times when even a cat wouldn't jump on a hot stove twice. And maybe the cup was not meant to pass from his lips yet, blasphemous as it was to compare his own misery with Christ's.

He thought that he saw his wife's face peering out from behind the curtain for a moment as the children were coming out of the door. Petrona hadn't changed, not that there would have been any reason for her to change in the four years that she and Kazmer had been separated, but she hadn't changed in all the ten years before. Not since the day they were married. The little girl, now clambering into the truck, had her cheekbones; Johnny, the boy, had her eyes—black, black as the night.

"You been good, Borbala, honey?" Kazmer asked. The little girl looked at him coldly.

"My name's Barbara," she replied. "Mommy says so."

It was another deal that Petrona had gone back on, because Kazmer had agreed to his firstborn being named Johnny—after Johnny Carson, he suspected, although Petrona had said, don't be stupid—on condition that if the next child were a girl they'd name her after Kazmer's late mother. Well, a girl it was, and Kazmer's mother had been called Borbala, there was no doubt about that. Of course Petrona had right away started bringing out some big book she said was a dictionary, which had Borbala as "Barbara" in English. True, Kazmer had silenced her at the time by pointing out that the book also said *harcsa* was "catfish." Petrona would not have liked to be called "Mrs. Catfish" even in private.

But these were little things, not worth remembering. A person could go through life hurting, if he remembered little things. It was no worse than being called a Big Mac Daddy, which is what that bald young Mr. Perkins called Kazmer when Kazmer told him that on Sundays he was picking up the kids. "Me, too," he had said. "You and I are Big Mac Daddies." It was the "you and I" that did it, for while Kazmer liked Mr. Perkins, who was a steady customer and paid his bills promptly, he was mortified to think that he could be compared to him in any other way. Mr. Perkins wore blue denims and worked at City Hall in a job that had something to do with how the streets were going to be laid out in the suburbs. He was Kazmer's customer because he fancied old Canadian pine chairs and benches and would always start restoring them, but could never finish the job. He had a squeaky voice and kept nodding his head in the fussy way of a hen. When Mrs. Perkins had left him, Kazmer remembered saying to Petrona— when they were still living together, it was the customers in the shop she liked hearing about—that he wasn't surprised. "Nice sort, but not much of a man. Only his mother would take him for a hero."

"That's a funny thing to say," Petrona had replied, as she often did, jutting out her chin in an offended kind of way.

But now Kazmer and unheroic Mr. Perkins were Big Mac Daddies both, with their wives gone and their children waiting for them on the porch on Sundays. It seemed to make no difference whether a person held his head in the way of a man or of a hen. If pieces of wood obeyed him or jumped out of his hands. If his voice boomed or squeaked. What Uncle Harcsa maintained could only happen to a mother's hero had happened to Kazmer. "When the devil gets into your wife, he won't come out for the asking," the men in the village used to say, by way of apology, if anybody saw them carrying a whip from the stable into the house. In spite of his barrel chest and booming voice, Kazmer was a mother's hero himself. Like Mr. Perkins.

He stole a glance at the children, now that the road was straight and wide and he didn't have to mind the traffic much. The blue Dodge purred along sweetly, much like the day four years earlier when he had brought it home from the show-room, and little Johnny had proudly pointed it out to the other kids on the street as "Daddy's tluck." Borbala was then too lit-tle to notice anything farther than arm's length away from her crib. But if a man could care for a blue truck so that a thou-sand days or more should leave no mark upon it, how was he to do the same for his children? Not that they were not both clean and neat, Johnny in his jeans and checkered shirt and the girl in her velvet frock, Kazmer could never fault Petrona for that, but who could know what was going on in their heads? The way Johnny was sitting, stiffly, hands grasping the edge of the seat and not looking at Kazmer working the steer-ing wheel and the gearshift, he might not even have been his son. Nor silent Borbala his daughter.

A man's mind works in curious ways. He remembers, he for-gets, and he seems to have no good reason for either. Children would forget even more easily, Kazmer supposed, but perhaps they would also remember longer. Who could tell? They would only nod, shake their heads and say nothing.

The scene was etched in *his* memory, for instance, and the children were part of it, but maybe it was like nothing to them now, a day among other days that they could not even recall. Or was it worse for them than it was for him? At the time they cried, of course, Borbala like a waterfall and little Johnny with his lips squeezed tight, but they were only four and six, they'd cry over a broken toy, Kazmer couldn't go by that. His own concern then was only that they shouldn't get hurt. Not by the emotion of the moment, either, but simply by the rush-hour trucks whizzing by.

Because it was April and the pavement was covered with slick slush, as always in Toronto. Petrona had left maybe a month earlier, leaving a note on the kitchen table that said, "I took the TV, the standing lamp, the sofa and the children." It wasn't a very helpful note because Kazmer could see for himself that the TV, the lamp, the sofa and the children were gone (and the $600 cash money was also gone from the linen closet, which the note did not disclose), but it told him nothing about how it had come to this or what was now going to happen to his life. Later that night he phoned the police and they said, well, there was a note, wasn't there, Petrona left of her own free will, there was no law against a wife leaving her husband. Maybe one day she'd be back, there was no law against that either.

No, but if a thief grabbed Kazmer's wallet, and there *was* a law against that, he'd try to grab it back, nor was a wallet as important to a man as his wife and children. Kazmer got up early next morning, cut himself shaving, then went to stand in front of Johnny's school. He didn't come. He didn't come the next morning, either, or the morning after that. The teachers in the school knew nothing, they said maybe the School Board. But all Miss School Board knew was to ask Kazmer to write her a letter.

"What I write you a letter for?" asked Kazmer, in English of course. "Now you tell me you don't know nothing. Maybe if I write, you write me that you don't know nothing, too?"

But he left School Board his name and address, which she took down in a little book. It was a good thing he did, because less than three weeks later she did write a letter to him, saying that Johnny's records had been sent to some Catholic school in Rexdale. A Catholic school, well, that was all right, Petrona being a Catholic herself, not that Kazmer had ever seen her pray in church, but Rexdale? That was the other end of town from the Beaches, where they had the house, and the shop, too, not very far away, and Kazmer had to buy one of those little map-books for $2.50 to find out exactly where. Three weeks, and a man's children were going to school in Rexdale. Well, the policeman on the phone had said it happened all the time.

Another good thing was that the letter from School Board came on a Thursday, and the toy shop at the downtown Simpsons was open late. For Johnny, Kazmer bought one of those plastic underwater boats you have to load with a fizzy capsule, like a soda bottle, and then the jet of escaping air drives it as nicely as anything. Kazmer tried it out in the bathtub, just at periscope level. Borbala got a doll with blue eyes who could wet herself just like a real baby, though Kazmer, not having bothered making out the instructions, did not know that. The next morning he roused himself at five-thirty. Outside it was still completely dark.

It was not just a matter of anxiety, though it was that, too, but Kazmer thought it wiser to leave the blue truck at home. The bus would take longer to Rexdale, wherever it was, but who knew which route Petrona would use to walk the children to school? If she recognized the truck, and she would if she saw it, maybe she'd turn back before he even noticed them. Though God alone knew why she should turn back, she'd know he wouldn't hurt a hair on their heads, but then God alone knew why Petrona would do anything. It was better not to take a chance.

But Petrona did not show up at all in the slick, slushy April morning as Kazmer waited near the school, only Johnny and Borbala, walking hand in hand on the other side of the street. They were making for the school crossing guard farther down the block, and Kazmer could only snatch sight of them now and again through the thundering traffic. If they caught sight of him, God, they'd dash to his side of the road and be killed for sure. They were only toddlers, and how could Petrona send them to school by themselves with no protection?

So Kazmer crouched down between two parked cars, careful to keep the gift-wrapped parcels out of the slush, watched them cross to his side and even let the children walk by him before he rose and called their names, softly. Oh, how they turned! Oh, how the two of them jumped into his arms, knocking their gifts and his hat into the wet snow. And the way Borbala took a quick breath, with her eyes and mouth wide open, before the tears came and she was clutching his neck strongly enough to hurt him, and she a four-year-old girl! Oh, Petrona, Petrona.

But that was four years ago, maybe only yesterday for Kazmer, but half a lifetime for such little children. Would they still remember it? Children get used to everything, or seem to. Their pains come big and pass quickly. Like piglets that had to be neutered, and back in Bugyi it would be Kazmer's job to catch and hold them for the butcher, while their bloodcurdling squeals filled the street. The piglets would suffer with no dignity, but when the knife had done its job and the bloody bits were squeezed out and thrown into the bucket, a dab of grease and a minute later the piglets would be charging across the courtyard as though nothing had happened. See, silly, Kazmer would chide before catching the next one, was it such a big thing worth making all that fuss about? Yet even if the pain lasted only for a minute, a piglet would still stay neutered for all time. A knife was a knife, whether it severed bits of flesh or feelings, and were children any different?

Maybe Johnny and Borbala didn't hurt anymore, couldn't even recall that they ever did, but were still walking around with some vital part missing from them. If so, was it not worse even than hurting? Pain is not the worst thing, or wouldn't anyone prefer a sore arm to an arm cut off? Maybe they were sitting in the cab of his blue Dodge now like two little alien beings from the moon, because they were no one's children anymore. His children, no one's. Not a whit of pain, only a strange man with a barrel chest and a black mustache in whose truck they were obliged to sit every Sunday for some reason. Orphans, with both parents living. Wouldn't orphans be better off with both parents dead?

Another thing that had been bothering Kazmer lately was that his thoughts seemed to be such a jumble. Suppose something happened, and somebody asked him to tell about everything that led up to it, could he tell his story straight? Could he tell it from the beginning, and where was the beginning, if there was one at all? Was it when he came to this country? Was it when he met Petrona?

Or was it much later, when things started to go wrong? Did it begin only after he found her note, watched his children crossing the slushy street in April, or much later still, when he got that first letter from the Court or heard the name of that lawyer Mr. Loeblich for the first time?

Wouldn't it be foolish if something happened, and they'd ask him and he couldn't tell them why? They'd take him for a demented crazy person. They would shut him up in some place where they kept people who did things for no reason, and rightly, too, for even a sheep isn't worth the shearing once it begins to go around and around. A man is no better. He's best forgotten. Feed him water and bread.

Though even if he could tell his own reasons, it would be less than the half of it, for how could he tell anybody else's? How could he tell Petrona's? He couldn't, Kazmer supposed, because if he could the two of them would still be married. If he could only understand what she wanted. Or, more to the point, why she wanted it so badly, whatever it was, more than her home and family where she belonged, more than the husband to whom she had once said, "Till death do us part." Well, later she'd stop a long way short of death. An itch would do it.

But perhaps it wasn't necessary to go that far. If he could give his own sense of what happened, it would be enough. People would understand him. Why others did what they did would only be guessing, anyway. Like why did Comrade Lei want to bring that combine to the collective in Bugyi, because perhaps that was the real beginning. If it hadn't been for the combine, who knows? Maybe none of it would have come to pass.

There was no denying that the combine was a dignified machine, with its covered parts painted a thick bubbly blue, and the rest shiny metal. A real harvester, such as no one had ever seen in those parts. The old Count had a tractor for the estate, not that he'd ever allow it to be used, because the noise would frighten the horses and the fumes spoil the taste of the apricot brandy. But a tractor was just a tractor, anyway; a harvester-combine was something else.

Only the old-timers grumbled, as old-timers always do, because they understand nothing about the great spirit of progress. They know, perhaps, that for them, progress only consists of taking one step closer to the grave. It was the land they muttered about, and how harvesters were designed for the plains, the great western *puszta* of Hungary, but not for the little twisting parcels of stony soil running up the mountains around Bugyi. What would a harvester do in the potato patches? As for a few hundred acres of barley, why, didn't they have the oxen and even the three teams of sooty-nosed white buffalo? A harvester was just a waste of good, expensive diesel oil.

But socialism didn't come to Bugyi just so that old-timers could do things the way they did them before, as Comrade Lei pointed out to Uncle Harcsa, or else what would have been the point of socialism in the first place? Every poster in the schoolhouse had a smiling lad sitting at the controls of a combine, with a windblown lass feeding golden sheaves into its great iron mouth. And that was the way it had to be in Bugyi, especially since the collective was getting a no-interest loan for the machine from the Workers' State itself.

Kazmer took no part in the controversy, having better things on his mind, for by that time he had already proposed

to Katika or, to be more accurate, walked up to her one Saturday and told her that he intended to have their wedding in
the fall. It was like Uncle Harcsa's own proposal many years
earlier, and Katika's assent followed the pattern of Aunt
Rosie's pretty closely. "If you say so," she said, averting her
mountain-cat eyes.

Even Uncle Harcsa had better things to do than worry about
the harvester-combine—besides which, he didn't mind machin-
ery as much as other old-timers did—because he was preoccupied
by the menu for Kazmer's and Katika's wedding. In the village,
as elsewhere, women did the everyday cooking, but cooking for
festive occasions was too important a thing to be trusted to
women. Aunt Rosie wouldn't know how to make a proper bridal
cake tree—the famous *menyasszonykalácsfa*—or even a simple
csörögefánk. Uncle Harcsa did, and for the right occasion he'd
even lend his services to the neighbors if people asked him politely. Nor did Kazmer ever grow up thinkng that cooking was
women's work. Food was important and everything was a man's
work if it was important enough. Except giving birth, as Aunt
Rosie once remarked rather pointedly to Uncle Harcsa.

But for proper food you needed proper ingredients, because
even the best chef couldn't make a pudding out of air and water.
The lean years had come to Bugyi once again, five years after
the war, for which the Communists blamed the American im-
perialists, while the people preferred to blame the Communists
themselves. Whoever was right, to make Uncle Harcsa's famous
fried bowknots—because that's how *csöröge* would appear on
the menu at the St. Moritz in New York—you wanted egg
yolks, vanilla sugar and a thimbleful of rum, the first of which
was scarce and the last two not to be had even for the love of
God in Bugyi. But at least the bridal cake tree had to be made,
and Kazmer would spend hours in the woods with Uncle Harcsa, selecting the right branch, from which thin twigs had to rise
heavenward, and which would eventually be dipped in pancake
dough and dry-roasted in the oven. The base of the tree would

be a large cake, and the final product would be hung with sweetmeats, a live frog or two, and little sacks into which the wedding guests could put money for the bride.

Still, the tree gave Uncle Harcsa fewer problems than the feast itself, the main dishes of which should have been pork, with some mutton, lamb and a fattened goose or two thrown in for good measure. But with the flocks and herds of the district killed off or just plain mismanaged by Comrade Lei and his fellows, tradition had to yield to necessity, and not for the first time in history, either. Luckily socialism was a bit slower coming to the forests of Transylvania than to the cultivated parts, and the woods still sheltered plenty of fallow deer and roebuck, nor was it impossible to harvest some snipe, grouse, field fare, ortolan and even that species of bustard plover, the *tüzök*: a big, tasty bird, of which the proverb held that a sparrow in the hand was to be preferred to it as long as the *tüzök* was still in the bush. Kazmer could test the truth of this ancient bit of wisdom himself, as he nearly broke his leg trying to chase one to the ground across the rocky valley. But he could console himself with the thought that catching a sparrow would have been easier for anyone who had nothing to shoot it with.

For no guns could be held in private hands anymore, the Workers' State having forbidden all weapons of aggression or of defence, as a sign that both were to be its own monopoly from now on. This was said to promote the public peace, though private citizens could still slaughter each other with soda bottles or kitchen knives; and they did, too, more or less at the same rate at which they used to shoot each other before. True, the police had it much easier, it being one thing to go with a sickle at your neighbor, who had nothing much better to defend himself with, or at the militia, which certainly had.

But snaring snipe was smarter than shooting them anyway, and even a roebuck could be trapped by people who knew how. Uncle Harcsa's partridge with quinces was something to look forward to, and he could make even his famous smothered cutlets with venison instead of wild boar, as you would not have wanted to trap a wild boar if you valued your life. The way preparations for the feast were coming along, the Harcsa wedding would be nothing to be ashamed of even in these hard times.

Katika's own parents took no part in the proceedings, for the good reason that by that time they were no longer alive. Nor did she have any sisters except two younger ones, which according to Aunt Rosie wasn't a bad way for a girl to prepare for motherhood. As the saying had it in the village, work simply burned under Katika's fingers and she would go through her chores like a conflagration fanned by high winds. She even made the honor roll of the collective twice for planting her long legs firmly on the side of the new harvester-combine and feeding more golden sheaves into its gaping lips than any other girl in her work brigade. She looked, as Uncle Harcsa remarked, exactly like that girl on the poster in the schoolhouse, right down to the last detail of her thick, dark blond braids, except of course that her eyes were not blue but amber. Kazmer, not that he did not merit a girl like Katika, was considered lucky. The two orphans, and didn't they go hand in glove. It must have been ordained.

But other things must have been ordained, too, because Uncle Harcsa walked unexpectedly into the carpenter Mr. Görény's workshop, where Kazmer was running his chisel across a block of cherry wood on the bench. It was high noon, a day before the wedding.

"There's trouble," said Uncle Harcsa to Kazmer.

Kazmer put down the chisel.

"Well, you know that machine the collective has," said Uncle Harcsa. "That big harvester."

Kazmer nodded.

"That's the machine your girl was working on," said Uncle Harcsa, clearly hating to come to the point. "Katika was working on it, see."

Kazmer said nothing. Mr. Görény spoke instead, starting to untie his blue canvas apron.

"When?"

"Well, maybe an hour ago," said Uncle Harcsa, looking away. "When it tipped."

Kazmer got up. "When it tipped?" he asked. He started walking out of the door, but Uncle Harcsa held him by the arm. "They stopped it so it didn't go over," he said. "But she fell into it. She fell into the gears. So there is nothing for you to do now."

It was true, for even if Katika hadn't bled to death, she would have had no lower arms left by the time the harvester's gears had wound down. The old-timers said they should never have taken the big machine up on the hillside, but they had taken it up before and with no trouble. It was nothing but bad luck that, in Bugyi, long-legged Katika had to become the first victim of progress.

There was no telling who its second victim would have become if Uncle Harcsa and Mr. Görény hadn't locked Kazmer into the toolshed for the day. Comrade Lei certainly seemed like a good candidate. Raging in the toolshed, Kazmer did the villagers proud—they liked to see grief properly expressed—for he not only yelled the most bloodcurdling threats but nearly hacked his way through the five-inch-thick hardwood by nightfall. But of course all of this would have done little for Katika, who by that time lay between two candles in the parlor where she ought to have appeared in her bridal gown the following day.

"Do you want to see her, then?" asked Uncle Harcsa in the evening, unlocking the door that Kazmer in a little while would have broken down anyway.

Kazmer was twenty-two. He held a small ax in his hand and his chest was heaving like the blacksmith's bellows while Uncle Harcsa looked at him, as it seemed, without emotion. After a few seconds the boy put down the hatchet and nodded.

"Let's go, then."

They looked at Katika, who was laid out under an immaculate white sheet, her dark blond braids neatly arranged on a white pillow, and with not a mark on her face. She was very pale, though, and her amber eyes were closed. Kazmer stood looking at her for a very long time, alone, for his uncle had ushered the keening women out of the room. Then he walked back in the darkness to the carpenter's shop where Mr. Görény had been laying out some white birch planks by the light of a lantern.

"I'll make the coffin," Kazmer said quietly.

So she was laid to rest in his coffin the next day, which was more than nothing, and all he could do for her in any case. Though their engagement had lasted nearly a year, they had never been in bed together, for in 1950 that new custom still had a little ways to go before it would reach Bugyi, nor had they been in the hayloft more than twice. On the last occasion Kazmer had unbuttoned Katika's blouse and rested his hand on her breast, but never moved his fingers as far as her nipple. There would be, as it then appeared, time enough for that. Marriages might not have been made in heaven in the village any more than anywhere else, but they did last a lifetime.

Comrade Lei at first thought it proper that he should appear at the funeral dressed in a black suit and just a small Party emblem in his buttonhole, but then he took Uncle Harcsa's advice, conveyed through Juicing Abel, and stayed away. He could have come with no trouble, for Kazmer stood quietly at the graveside and looked at no one. Later at home he took the bridal cake tree and chopped it up for firewood. It was just as well, for winter came early and hard into the mountains that year.

"We got far to go, Dad?"

That was Johnny speaking, looking at the rust and gold of the Ontario autumn surrounding them on the way to the Moon River or, more likely, at the hamburger stand at the roadside, to judge by what little Borbala said next:

"I'm hungry."

Kazmer glanced into the mirror and pulled the blue truck over on the soft shoulder, engine idling. "See, in a little while,

when we get there," he said. "I was going to make you a fish
fry." He would have, too, out of fresh perch and walleye,
which he could catch in a minute at a spot he knew, not that
Georgian Bay fish were to be compared to the brown trout in
the Olt River back home, but they were still a long way from
the bone meal and gristle they'd sell you for good money in a
restaurant. "Wouldn't you like that?" He spoke in Hungarian
to them, knowing that they'd reply in English, as always.

"What if I just had a hamburger, Dad?"

"Me too. And chips."

In the old days he would have argued, of course, or even
forced them to feed his way, but that was when he was a father, not a Big Mac Daddy. A Big Mac Daddy buys Big Macs,
that's all, because he is there to please his children, not to
raise them. And selfishly, too, because he knows that if he
raised them they'd remember him or it anyway, but if a drop-
in visitor doesn't please, he is easily forgotten.

Like that tug-of-war, Kazmer thought, sipping his coffee and
watching the children stuff their healthy little faces. Are they
still burdened with remembering *that*? Because that must have
been four years ago, too, just a little while after their first
meeting at the Catholic school, when Borbala told him their
new address, and in the evening he went to have a talk with
Petrona. It seemed that she would see reason, back then.

She spoke to him in English, just like the children, except
he never resented that. After all, Petrona had been born on
this English-speaking continent, somewhere in New Jersey,
and only her mother was a decent *Szekely* girl, her late father
having been some kind of a Ruthenian Pole. That was how
she came to be a Catholic, after her father, and it was a miracle she could speak any Hungarian at all, but she could, her
mother had seen to that. Except she didn't like to, nor did she
teach it to her children. Kazmer had no objection to the English language, of course, he spoke it himself after a fashion, as
it was the language of the eels and this was the eels' country.

He was the guest here; he could not expect people to change their mother tongue, or their children's, for his sake. But he'd be damned if he would speak English to his own wife and children. Kazmer wasn't much for taking a lot of words into his mouth, chewing them and spitting them out again, which to his mind was the way the natives did it. But let Petrona speak to him in English if it made her happy.

She stood in the doorway of the house after he rang the bell and the landlord had called her. For it was a rooming house or such, and not a patch on her own lovely home, but that was Petrona's business if that was the way she wanted to live. Kazmer only came because of the children. Still, he couldn't help feeling a pang of pain as he stood there looking at her, not that he would have shown it in any way. There was no denying it that at thirty-three Petrona was still an eyeful, maybe even better looking than when he had first seen her, though now she wasn't even dressed up in proper clothes. A woman to make a man proud when he walked down the street with her on his arm. But in the end that was nothing, less than nothing. Kazmer himself could draw a glance or two from women passing by, with his deep chest, his rich black hair and mustache, even now that he was forty-five. But he still slept in an empty bed, and she, well, Kazmer preferred not to think about how empty or how filled up Petrona's bed might have become. Not right then, anyway.

"I would have called you," she said. "I wasn't hiding from you, or anything. I knew you could find me. I just thought we both needed a little time before we could, you know, talk things over."

Kazmer only nodded, or shrugged perhaps, for what could a man reply to that? Walking through the door to find a note and a spotlessly vacuumed empty space where your life used to be, and then your wife telling you that you needed time before you could talk about it! Well, it sounded like something on the color TV, not that he ever watched it. Petrona did, though, she would watch it in the afternoon and in the evening, and now she even talked like the TV set. About her own life and about his. And the children's.

"I didn't need time," he said finally, "but that's okay. Maybe you did."

"Well, I have to find myself," she said, looking at her slippers. "I told you that before."

It was on the tip of Kazmer's tongue to say that if she needed any finding, it was he who did all of it, or maybe the School Board, but he held his peace. "You do what you want, Petrona," he said. "I'm going to take the children."

"No," she said. "Please don't make trouble."

"A rooming house," said Kazmer. "That's no way for them to live."

"I'll move," she replied. "I'll be moving soon. I'll let you see them whenever you want, don't worry."

"When?"

"Well, Sundays. Every Sunday if you like. Saturdays too, I don't care, except you work Saturdays. What would you do with them in the shop?"

It was true. Kazmer hesitated. "I could just pick up and take them right now," he said, but he said it without conviction and Petrona knew it. "Well—you need some money?" he asked finally.

"No." She shook her head. "Not a penny. I took some."

"You took," Kazmer replied, "all there was to take. But, hell, I wasn't keeping it for drink, Petrona, I made it for you and the children."

"I know," she said serenely. "That's why I took it."

He was silent for a few seconds after that, Kazmer remembered, because Petrona's reply set him to thinking that if he had been a drinking man, or had begrudged his wife the money he earned, he would now be $600 richer, for she would have left it all in the linen closet. At least, that was the sense of what she said. But how was he to understand whatever she said? Or how was he to make any sense of her last words, as he started walking down the steps and she came after him and put her hand on his arm, saying, "I'm real sorry, because you are a good man. A fine human being"? For if he was, if she thought that he was, why did she ever leave him? He wouldn't have left her, and he hadn't been so sure that she was a fine human being, either. He was sure though that she was his *wife*.

But seeing the children was no trouble after that, not for a whole month. They would come out of that rooming house by themselves, every Sunday at noon, and always clean and neatly dressed, too, so that it would be a joy walking down with them half a block to the blue truck. It was curious how he would still park a little distance away, as if it still mattered that Petrona used to be embarrassed by them driving a truck, a thing that Kazmer could never understand anyway. But habit was stronger than good sense, or else why would he still sit down sometimes in the empty spot where the sofa used to be at home? Or reach deep into the closet for his coat, expecting to push aside Petrona's clothes?

It was all right with him that Petrona never came out with the children. He didn't want to see her that badly himself, there was nothing much to talk about anymore. She was going her way, and he, his. But coming back at night was different, for you wouldn't just push a couple of innocents into some cavernous rooming house, almost like an inn and filled with strangers. Children should be delivered to their mother's hands, if they have a mother; and if he could put up with that little quickening of the heart on seeing her, which a person couldn't help, then so could she. It was not as if the life they were now forced to lead hadn't been her choice.

It was on the fourth Sunday that he pulled up, as usual, at a few minutes to nine, bringing the children back to what was now their home. He rang the bell, and it was the landlord who answered, not Petrona.

"You call my wife, please," said Kazmer politely.

The man, though it might have been only his imagination, smirked.

"She ain't home."

Kazmer looked at the children, little Borbala half asleep and leaning against her brother, as they had spent the whole afternoon in the new zoo, the big one, feeding the monkeys when the keepers weren't looking. It was the other end of the earth, and Kazmer had urged on the blue Dodge faster than he liked to, not to keep Petrona waiting for them. And now she wasn't even at home.

"Where she is, you know?" asked Kazmer.

The man shrugged.

"Went shopping," he said.

That was funny shopping to Kazmer, Sunday at nine, and he said so. The man invited him to leave the children, his wife would look after them, he said, but Kazmer thanked him and took Borbala and Johnny back to the truck. They waited until nearly ten, the little girl sound asleep in Kazmer's lap, and then he put the blue Dodge in gear, grinding it for the first time since he'd had it, and drove them back home. He washed the girl's face, gave Johnny a glass of milk, and put them both to bed. He himself sat in the armchair afterward, looking at the wall against which the TV used to stand. It was not until midnight that Petrona started knocking on the door.

"What you want?" Kamer asked through the door, speaking in English himself, which, as Petrona ought to have known, was not a good sign.

"You've got the children. Let me in!"

Kazmer opened the door wide.

"They sleep," he said. "You bad mother. Now you stay away."

She tried to push past him, but it was like trying to push away a granite wall, and after a second the wall began to move, crowding her out of the doorway while she beat her fist against it, and then Kazmer closed the door again. Petrona hammered at it until her hands hurt and the banging echoed down their quiet street, but no lights came on in any of the windows. The neighbors slept or heard nothing, or didn't want to. The only person who came up to her was the taxi driver, and all he said was; "You staying or what, Miss?" And so Petrona got back into the cab.

But she was at the house again the next morning, as Kazmer knew she would be, not too early, just around the time he'd be taking the truck over to the shop. That was at nine-thirty, or quarter to ten at the latest, it never varied. By ten the first customers would be showing up, mainly with their old chests and chesterfields. But small fishes, good fishes: it was all business. Petrona knew he couldn't afford to waste a morning, and wouldn't if he could. God took care of everything, except the mortgage. For that He expected a man to look after himself.

So there she was, standing on the sidewalk, prettily dressed but with her black eyes rimmed with red, not even daring to step on the porch. There she stood, waiting; with the same snow that had fallen on the day she would still have had the right to walk through the front door not even having melted from the ground. And though Kazmer's heart nearly broke looking at her, what could he do but walk past her holding the children's hands firmly in his own.

"Please," Petrona said as they were walking by her, Kazmer looking stonily ahead and the children frightened and ready to cry, "please, can we talk?"

Kazmer stopped. A little while ago Petrona said she needed time before she could talk. Time to think things over. Now that he had the children in his hands, she seemed ready. He didn't have to go over half the town looking for her: there she was, standing on his doorstep. But he said nothing.

"Perhaps I did wrong," said Petrona, "and I don't mean last night, because that wasn't my fault. I could tell you exactly what happened last night, but you wouldn't listen because you never do."

Kazmer made a move as if he was going to walk on with the children, and Petrona started to speak rapidly. "But I'm not going to talk about that," she said, "all I'm going to say is that maybe you're right to be mad at me and maybe I did wrong, but they're my children and I'm their mother. They're little children, Kazmer. They need me."

Kazmer stopped and spoke to her in English. "So you mother in a hurry," he said, with heavy sarcasm, "and children need you. Maybe, maybe no. Maybe you need children. Maybe I'm father and children need me, too. Is not true? Color TV not talk about that?"

"You wouldn't even know what to do with the children," said Petrona. "You just want to get at me, that's all."

He became angry at that, with the old fury rising to his lips like a red fog, the searing fire only she could kindle. She, who'd buy meat from a freezer, old meat, because she couldn't feel the plumpness of a duck under the feathers, nor kill and clean even a chicken. She, who'd serve corn mush and peeled potatoes floating in a tin. Would he not know what to do with the children, he who had to show her how to fry a little flour and chopped onions, so the soup wouldn't taste like water? She, who wouldn't even take baby Johnny to her breast, the one thing he couldn't do for her, because of something she had read in a magazine. At the hairdresser's, under the electric dryer!

But how could he say all this in one breath? Maybe a woman could, some were pretty good at giving their mind a tongue, but men's tongues didn't work that way. His tongue would only jumble it, trying to say it all at once, so that he wouldn't make sense even to himself. He could speak all right when he was happy, relaxed with a glass of good red wine, he could joust with other men, sling two shots at them for every one, or sometimes even say soft, quiet words of kindness. But speaking in anger, that wasn't for men. When a man was angry he would walk away if he could, and hit out with his fist if he could not. But only a low kind of man would hit a mother in front of her children.

"What you try me for, Petrona?" Kazmer said. "When you go away, who come after you, like lots of husband? I say nothing. I leave you peace, now you leave me peace, too."

"You bastard," she replied. "I didn't walk away from my children. I walked away from *you*. Now just let me have my kids back."

It was Johnny who began to cry first, and of course Borbala followed. Shaking his head helplessly, his face turning red in embarrassment and shame, Kazmer asked the little girl first. "Who you want to go with, honey?" he asked her. "You go with Mommy or Dad?"

"With Mommy," Borbala whimpered. "And with Daddy, too."

Kazmer let go of her hand, and Petrona snatched her up so quickly it seemed as if she was afraid the little girl would change her mind, and she her own daughter! Kazmer looked at Johnny, who had stopped crying, then back at Petrona, who stood with wide red streaks running down her face and her black eyes on fire. For judgment was about to be passed on her and Kazmer, astonished, caught himself hoping that it would not be too harsh. But it was, because Johnny said, holding Kazmer's hand firmly, "I'm staying with my Dad." And that should have been all there was to it, but there was more, because Petrona grabbed hold of Johnny's other hand and started pulling him away, so that the boy cried out in pain, and even the passersby turned their heads. The silent tug-of-war lasted only for half a minute, maybe even less, but it seemed to last forever before Kazmer removed Petrona's hand and walked Johnny away from her. It was, as it turned out, more than a year before Petrona saw her son again, or Kazmer, his daughter.

But the world was longer than a year, as the saying went, and it was true, for here were the children sitting together again, as brother and sister should be, relaxing after that cheap bribe of french fries and ginger beer. That year passed, Kazmer thought, turning the truck onto the old Bala highway toward the Moon River, and the year that followed was better and worse, and so were the years that came after that. As for the years still to come, who knows? God does, but He won't tell. It would stop people from praying.

And praying wasn't the end of it, either, for how was a man to know what to pray for? It wasn't as if many of Kazmer's wishes hadn't been granted, only an ungrateful person could say that, nor was it those prayers that went unanswered that troubled him now. It was when God listened that misfortune followed. Because, as the Reverend Vegvari had it, God had set a price for every gift a person would get in a lifetime, and then it was just a matter of that person asking and paying for it dearly. Not all Christians knew that, but all Calvinists did. The word they had for it was predestination, and Kazmer had plenty of trouble in Bible school for not being able to remember it. Well, he'd never forget it now, the passing years had seen to that.

It took nearly seven of them to pass between that autumn day they had lowered Katika's coffin into the ground and the spring of 1957 for Kazmer to come to his big decision, perhaps the first one of his life. And it wasn't as though he had brooded much about it, because he hadn't. But one evening, coming home from the carpenter's shop, he sat down to the table at which Uncle Harcsa was preparing a soft bed for his red wine with a thick slice of fresh white bread. Kazmer was just about thirty then and his uncle, not that anyone could tell by looking at him, was seventy-three. He suddenly seemed older, though, when Kazmer said to him, after a few minutes of polite silence:

"Well, I'll be going myself in a little while now."

Uncle Harcsa knew what Kazmer was talking about, of course. By that time the rumors had been filtering into Bugyi for months about the big doings next door in Hungary, which for the people of the mountains was still their own country, if they had a country at all, and never mind that their names were written in Rumanian on their identity cards. And even if the radio in the schoolhouse wouldn't say a word about it, and not a line printed in the newspaper either, how could they mistake the endless columns of trucks on the highway, filled with soldiers in battle dress, going first one way then the other, or the flatcars on the railway line with the long guns under the tarpaulin? There was trouble in Hungary, and people in Bugyi could find out about trouble long before the radio and the newspapers were ever invented.

Soon word would come of young men crossing quietly into Hungary, first from this village and then the next one, not to help their Hungarian cousins fight the Russians—for there wasn't much fighting to be done since the first snows of 1956, the tanks and the long guns had seen to that—but because even the mice know how to have the run of the pantry when the cat's away. Slipping across one border is bad enough, and only a crazy person would try for two, but that second border between Hungary and Austria was almost undefended for a few months, just long enough for a brown bear to get his winter's sleep or a young man his liberty. And what was to keep Kazmer in Bugyi, what with the white birches of Katika's coffin still bending in the wind, but not a girl in the village to measure up to her memory?

Uncle Harcsa knew that, but what he said was this:

"There isn't much to see in the world."

"Is that the truth? You spent ten long years looking at it."

"That I did," said Uncle Harcsa with dignity, "and that's why I'm telling you."

"Well, if I look at it myself," replied Kazmer, "I can come back and be a witness for you."

That was a good reply, and it wouldn't have made much difference even if it hadn't been, for when a young man had to go he went, unless somebody stopped him with a gun. And since there were many to try between Bugyi and Austria, and not being sure that Kazmer knew how best to avoid them, Uncle Harcsa asked him where he planned to cross the first border.

"Black Creek, where else?" said Kazmer.

"How?"

"Well, in the dark, I guess," replied Kazmer uncertainly.

"That's smart," said Uncle Harcsa, "but I'd still take along a lantern and a stick."

"A lantern?" asked Kazmer, surprised. "I'll take along a stick, but anybody can see a lantern from miles."

"From the end of the world," replied Uncle Harcsa, "if you're lucky."

With that he explained another one of his old Foreign Legion *ruses de guerre* to Kazmer, a good one, and before the week was out Kazmer was ready to put it into effect. His Aunt Rosie baked him a dozen crackling biscuits in hot ashes, which, if he had fresh water to drink with them, could keep a young man walking from Bugyi to Cluj, and she even scored the top of the biscuits in her special lattice pattern with a knife. She needed no salt because, according to Uncle Harcsa, her tears in the flour were sufficient condiment; and as neither he nor Kazmer could stand the sound of women wailing, they would not take her along to the fork in the road, though she'd try to follow them from a distance. At the fork it was already dark, with only a few uncertain stars glimmering in the February sky.

"I'll write when I can," said Kazmer.

"I don't mind, if you have the time," replied Uncle Harcsa, "though my eyes are not what they used to be. But don't get into more trouble than you can help, even if you have to take a little shit sometimes."

"Well, I won't take too much, either," said Kazmer.

"Hell, boy," said Uncle Harcsa contemptuously, aiming a little pipejuice at the ground, "no Harcsa ever has."

There being nothing more to say, Kazmer nodded and started walking, but then to lighten the moment he turned back and pointed at the outline of the Milky Way overhead. "Well, anyway," he said, "Prince Csaba's nowhere near riding the Avenue of the Hosts tonight."

"And why should he?" replied Uncle Harcsa. "We are in no trouble yet."

Kazmer chuckled, for this was the kind of thing a Transylvanian would say at the age of seventy-three, with his few acres only a memory and his only male relation on his way to becoming another, and who between the Russians and the Rumanians didn't even have a country anymore. And confident that things were as they should be and would forever remain so, by midnight Kazmer had walked the ten miles separating Bugyi from the Hungarian border.

As soon as he could discern the silhouettes of the darkened watchtowers against the barely lighter sky, Kazmer lit his lantern and, stick in hand, struck boldly across the mile-wide strip of plowed land between the two countries, one of his citizenship and the other of his native language. And the sentries saw the pinpoint of light, as it was visible for miles in the night, and they fired their submachine guns in the air, amazed at the stupidity of anyone trying to sneak across the border with a lantern. They fired their guns, but turned on no searchlights, nor did they unleash any dogs, for the light of the fugitive was as plain as it could be, moving across the field, and all they had to do was to bellow into their loudspeakers ordering him to stop. And in a moment or two the light did stop, and waited, and seemed to be getting brighter and brighter as the cursing border patrol stumbled toward it, with their guns at the ready. Not having long to walk, maybe a mile at most, it took the soldiers less than seven minutes to reach the swaying lantern.

It was the lantern that they reached, swaying gently from the stick planted in the soft earth, for by that time Kazmer himself was long gone. And the memory of watching the border guards from a clump of bushes on the other side, smashing the light and breaking the stick into pieces, was still as sweet as if it had been separated from him by neither time nor distance. For Kazmer knew, as much as the ancient Greeks did, that victory is sweet because it means that a person is being favored by the gods. But if men and women are fickle, which young people learn soon enough, they can't imagine that the same is true of the gods even when Homer tells them so, and Kazmer had never heard of Homer, anyway.

What Kazmer had heard of was the great city of New York, for it, like Rome two thousand years earlier, cast a gigantic shadow around the earth, filling the imagination of people even in remote places that no New Yorker would ever have heard of, like Bugyi. It would have been a foolish question to ask what Kazmer thought he'd find in New York, as foolish as asking what a person might expect to find in heaven. As for the difficulty involved in getting there, he never gave it a thought after he had crossed the second border into Austria. In a way he was right, too, because for anybody in jail the only real distance is the few yards separating his cell from the roadway outside. Once he can make that, New York, India and Rio de Janeiro seem only next door. And Kazmer's luck held, though he hadn't counted on it, for in 1957 traveling in the world was an easy matter for any refugee claiming to be Hungarian, at least for a few months. And when the rickety Icelandic turboprop rented by the Americans for ferrying displaced persons landed him at Idlewild Airport, as it was then called, Kazmer believed that in this new world miracles could be taken for granted. A fool, but let those who can blame him cast the first stone.

"Is it far, Dad?"

"Dad, I've got to go to the bathroom."

No, this wasn't the time to think of New York and Petrona, Kazmer couldn't face that. Not, at least, as she was back in those days. Riding with her children now, trying to make a little sense of their lives, trying to salvage a bit of their future, if they were to have one at all, it was simpler to think of Petrona only as she had been in the last four years since their separation. *That* Petrona in New York would have been too painful, like looking at snapshots of a dead person, only worse.

"Half an hour, maybe, no more," he said to the children, and Johnny made a face, Borbala imitating him, as always. "Stop fidgeting, honey." He made a face back then, too, the little boy did, when they had been living together for about a year, after Johnny had chosen Kazmer over Petrona, and coming home from the shop one day he had asked the boy if he had no more homework to do. Johnny had been moody in those days, brooding, short-tempered, not doing too well in school.

"Naw, Dad. I'm all finished."

"And what about the fiddle? You practiced that, too?" The violin teacher lived only on the next block with a very nice sign in his window saying PROF. FISCHER MUSICOLOGIST. Kazmer had subscribed to half a year's lessons in advance, not that he could afford them, and rented the violin that the boy would need. They didn't give violins away for nothing, either, but Prof. Fischer said that you couldn't learn the fiddle, not just from playing it at his house for an hour a week, and Johnny needed to practice if the music was to do him any good. And it was a beautiful violin, too, with highly polished thin wood that must have taken somebody many weeks to shape, but Johnny only pulled a face.

"It's your future," said Kazmer, hating to see such an expression of disrespect. If he had made a face like that when he was Johnny's age, he would have got a good hiding for it, too, and maybe it was time to give Petrona's son a taste of the same medicine. "You're doing me no favor. I could save the money, if I was thinking about myself."

"Dad, none of the other kids have to play that dumb violin," replied Johnny morosely.

Well, that might have been true, Kazmer knew nothing about that, but he wanted Johnny to have the best, the best that the little money he had in those days could buy, nor did he want to expose himself to Petrona's wicked tongue if he didn't. Not that they were talking to one another that year, after that tug-of-war, because they weren't, but word would filter back of Petrona saying, "God alone knows how my poor boy is faring under *his* hands!" Well, and couldn't he throw the violin lessons in her face if she ever said such things again! If she had made up her mind that he wasn't good enough, for not having watched that color TV day and night, as if that took anything except money for the monthly payments. But how many people could play the fiddle like Johnny?

It was something else, though, to explain all this to a boy who had not yet spent a full eight years on this earth. And if some people could, Kazmer could not. Or maybe he could have, with his life intact and a doting wife hanging on his words, nodding her assent to the children, instead of the wolf howling outside his door. But as it was, all Kazmer could do was to check his hand halfway before it would fetch Johnny a smart slap on the cheek, then send him to bed without supper.

But that was not doing much, because all it did was to send Johnny into his shop the next day after school instead of going straight home as he did on Thursdays when Kazmer had to keep the business open late. And not only that, but the boy even had a suitcase in his hand.

"What are you doing here?"

"Please, Dad, don't be angry."

"I'm not angry," said Kazmer, lowering his voice because there were customers in the shop. "Why didn't you go home after school?"

"Well," said Johnny, turning red in the face but looking Kazmer straight in the eye, "I just thought it would be better if I stayed with my mother. You know, like for a while."

The shop did half a turn in front of Kazmer's eyes but he did nothing. "We'll talk about it at home," he said finally, and his voice seemed to come from somewhere outside him, deep and hollow. But the boy shook his head.

"No, Dad. Mommy's picking me up here. I phoned her from school."

A boy not yet eight, but didn't people say back home that trouble's children grow up quickly? "Where did you get her number?" Kazmer asked, as if it mattered, though in truth he didn't have Petrona's new telephone number himself. Earlier that year she used to wait outside the school, hoping to catch Johnny alone, but Kazmer was careful, he'd always take and pick up the boy himself, so nothing came of that. He even spoke to the principal, had Petrona barred from the school grounds, just in case she'd try something when he wasn't around. Then she stopped showing up, but she had sent a note with her phone number in to Johnny through one of the teachers, to say he could call her if he ever needed anything, but not to show the note to Daddy, promise. Nor did the boy tell him about it—to his credit, Kazmer had to admit—until today.

And soon Petrona swept into the shop, flushed and pretty, and dressed to the hilt, too, and she would have picked Johnny up and gone out again without even a look at him, if he hadn't stopped her. "How are you, Petrona?" he asked.

She looked at him suspiciously for a second.

"I'm fine," she said finally. Then, after another moment of hesitation, she added, "And you?"

"I have no trouble," Kazmer said, speaking in Hungarian. "And I don't want to give you any, either. Maybe Johnny's better off with you for a while, you being his mother and all. He misses you, and no wonder. But maybe Borbala misses me, too."

She nodded, for it was true, then raised her head suspiciously again. "But I won't let her live with you now, no way. She stays where she is, Kazmer."

He almost smiled, in spite of himself, for it had come to a man bargaining with his own wife in the way of strangers, and ones who couldn't trust each other either, like two horse traders at the fair. "Come to your senses, woman," he said, like in the old days. "I want brother and sister to be together. I just want to see them once in a while, that's all, if it has to be this way."

"Oh, I don't know, Kazmer," she said, "there'll only be trouble again. I say the wrong word, or maybe I'm a minute late, and you'll just hit the roof. We never got along, not for a long time."

"Getting along?" said Kazmer. "I'm not asking to get along with you, Petrona. I just want to see the children."

"Well, all right," she replied, holding out Johnny's coat for him to take, "I don't mind if you pick up the children Sundays, like before. But I don't want to talk with you, Kazmer, because it doesn't work. Maybe, one day, after we get the divorce, but not now."

He almost missed the word, divorce, because he was listening to what she was saying about Sundays and the children. But it was a bitter word, even now, and it stuck in his throat. "You want a divorce, then," he asked. "You want a divorce, Petrona?"

"Well, you don't have to do anything about it," she said. "The lawyer will send you the papers, that's all. They say it'll take months, anyway, maybe even a year. The doctor says perhaps we'll get along better afterward, you and I."

Doctor—what was the woman talking about, what kind of doctor would have anything to do with a divorce? But then he decided to ask nothing. Maybe she only meant the lawyer. They were talking in a mixture of Hungarian and English, as usual, and lawyers were often called "Doctor" in Hungarian. Anyway, he was glad the two of them were talking again, it was unnatural for two people who had shared the same pillow for ten years to be like strangers. Man and wife, and if he closed his eyes he would still know the skin on her back, every inch of it, as she could remember his. No lawyer has invented the piece of paper yet to wipe this away from a person's mind.

"How are you fixed for money, then?" he asked, forgetting about the doctor.

"I'm okay," Petrona said. "Well, the lawyer will tell you about that, too, it'll be in his letter. Or maybe it will come from the Court, you know, the Family Court, I don't know which. I'm working again, but inflation's murder and the children need new shoes and things."

It was true, of course, but the inflation cut both ways; he couldn't stretch his dollar any further than she could stretch hers. Whenever he'd raise his prices to match the cost of the wood or paint, a customer would drop away, so that he would be no better off than before. All the same, he didn't pay much heed to business in the last year, having other things on his mind. Perhaps he'd do better now that he had pretty much got over the hurt, and maybe his own wife wasn't his enemy anymore. That, and no worry over the children.

"Looks like I won't be feeding Johnny, I guess," he offered, "so maybe I'll slip him twenty dollars every Sunday to give to you. Would you like that?"

Petrona averted her eyes.

"Don't worry about it now," she said uncertainly. "Just let's have no more trouble, you and I, that's all I ask."

And she took Johnny, letting the boy kiss him before they left.

Soon Kazmer would know that Petrona had been lying, in divorce no less than in marriage, but at least she did not go back on her word about the children. Johnny and Borbala would be there for him to pick up every Sunday, all scrubbed and dressed, and he would even take them for holidays, once to Disneyland and once as far as the Rocky Mountains. No fights, either, no tugs-of-war anymore, and if his kids grew stranger and stranger, moonchildren, orphans, well, maybe it was only his eyes, he'd try not to notice. Until he could not help it anymore. God, Petrona, Petrona!

And opening the passenger door of the blue panel truck, Kazmer sat back for a moment, watching Johnny and Borbala as they stood casting their small shadows over the rippling surface of the Moon River.

PART TWO

THE LETTER OF
THE LAW

THE MAIL COMING to the house was mostly for Petrona still, the envelopes said "Mrs. K. Harcsa," lots of catalogs and the like, and even one for fur coats. Kazmer was never much for getting letters, or for writing them, either, and what was the use of looking at pictures of fur coats that you could never buy anyway. Not that he minded if they gave Petrona pleasure, catalogs cost nothing. He himself wrote to his uncle and aunt once, that was years ago in New York, and a few months later received a postcard back that he still had, on which Uncle Harcsa had written, "Your letter found us in good health, your aunt read it too, and she says for you to take care of yourself. Here everything is the same, except the plague got into the potatoes, your loving Uncle." Then when he came to Toronto he wrote again, twice, but he got no reply, so who could tell if they received his letters? If, God willing, they were alive, they wished him well anyway—Kazmer knew that, just as he knew that he wished his own children well, it was nature. Even a goose loved its young. She would turn on a goshawk for them, but wouldn't waste time writing them letters.

So Kazmer mostly got the mail heads of families get, which is bills. And if the family is long gone, small difference, the bills still keep coming. Petrona only a picture on the mantel-piece, but the mortgage, the taxes, the insurance, the electricity would slip through the front door come the first of the month, and the worry of them might even get into bed with Kazmer at night to keep him from being too lonely. Except the letter he held in his hand was no bill, unless it was a very big one. It was thick and stiff, and the deep black print on the envelope said it came from the Supreme Court of Ontario.

That was maybe four months after Petrona had picked Johnny up from the shop, and for three or four days Kazmer didn't even bother opening the envelope. The morning it arrived he was in a hurry to get to work, and when he came home he just forgot, which was funny only because he had been thinking about the letter all day. He wondered what could be in it, not that he expected a gift of frankincense and myrrh.

When he finally opened the envelope, in the evening while the *puliszka* was simmering in the double boiler, he tried to read it quickly so as to get the gist of it, but he couldn't. There were a lot of long words, but there was no point in letting good cornmeal mush go to waste over those, so he put the letter down and didn't go back to it until the mush was all layered with ricotta and a sizzling cup of bacon drippings poured over the lot. Then he picked it up again, and he even put on the new reading glasses the doctor gave him a couple of years back, for maybe they would help to make sense of whatever it was the Supreme Court wanted to tell him. And help they did, for Kazmer was slowly turning red in the face as he kept staring at the letter of the law, until the mush congealed into a hard lump on his plate, cold and inedible.

That he had been acting badly to Petrona? That he had been cruel to her? That he had failed to provide for her and for the children, and was not a proper husband, nor the kind of father to deserve his own children? And it wasn't just people saying it, willy-nilly, because that was what the Supreme Court thought of him, too, and would make a judgment to say so unless he answered that it was wrong, in twenty-one days. Or only fifteen, because of the four days Kazmer took opening the letter, and the two it had spent in the mail.

He couldn't sleep that night, for only the second time in his life, the first being the night after he had found Petrona's note. Around two in the morning he would have taken one of those little pills she'd take sometimes to help her sleep, except they were not on the bathroom shelf anymore. And it wasn't the letter or what they would do to him, for letters were easy to write for people who knew how, and Kazmer was not afraid of them; they were just dogs barking while the caravan marched on. But that it was untrue, what the Supreme Court was saying. The Supreme Court had it all wrong. If they had said about Petrona all the things they were saying about him, well, that might have been closer to the truth, not that Kazmer would ever have said such things about her to strangers, he would sooner have let his tongue rot. He breathed no word, only shook his head when people asked him, not that many did, for he was not the kind of man people would question unless he offered to speak first anyway. But while he asked for no one's sympathy, in his own mind he knew he had done nothing to deserve the blow Petrona had dealt him by breaking up his life. And if it was a sin to be self-righteous, well, God could punish him for that; but even so Kazmer felt as innocent about his misfortune as a man falling into a pit that wasn't on the road the day before. But not if you asked the Supreme Court of Ontario. No, he had brought it all on himself, and on his wife and children, too.

But Petrona would not say untrue things about him. Kazmer wouldn't say anything about her, not even the truth, and not just out of kindness but because she was his wife, and what kind of a testimonial would it be to him to have married a bad woman? But how would it speak of her to have married such a bad man as the letter said he was? Nor was Petrona a liar, not in this way, in ten years of marriage it would have come out of her if she had been. No, somebody must have put her up to it.

That must have been it, for it was easy to put Petrona up to things—well, not that she was different from other women in that, they were like flocking birds: if one flew up, all the others started flapping their wings. Buy this, buy that, paint your eyes blue. And with Petrona, she'd say things she had heard on the color TV the night before, or read in the hairdresser magazine. She'd say them as though they had been the Word made Flesh, even if she herself had never heard of them the week before or remembered them the week after. And, Kazmer thought, in the days when he was courting her she used to repeat the things she had heard from *him* in much the same way. But that was long ago.

And it made little difference now who put her up to it, and how or why, there would be time enough to think about that later, for first he had to clear his own name and set the Supreme Court right about these things they were saying about him, as if he were some kind of an animal. Nor would they have to wait twenty-one days for him to answer them, or fifteen, or even one day. He'd tell them come morning, and they wouldn't put his answer in the window, either.

The girl behind the desk at the courthouse on Queen Street seemed scared when he thrust the letter in front of her, Kazmer saw that, so he repeated his question in a quieter voice: "Is it you who write me this letter, please tell me?" And when she looked at the envelope and just nodded, as if she had lost her voice, Kazmer even felt sorry for her, because it was one thing to send off a piece of paper with bad words on it and something else again to look the person you sent it to in the eye. "You nice young girl, why you write me such lies?" asked Kazmer, but not angrily.

The girl found her voice at that, not that it helped Kazmer much, because she used words that made no sense to him. She was saying nothing about Petrona, or how he was supposed to be cruel to her or why he had suddenly become a bad father, only about somebody called *Ex-party* and how his children didn't have any *custody*, if that's what it was, and then she said something about *interim relief*. She said a lot of other things, but these were the words Kazmer remembered because they were in the letter, too, mixed in with all the other words about how bad he had been to Petrona and the children. And she said that there was no use complaining to her because she only wrote down what the Court ordered, that was her job, and there was nobody else there to complain to, either. The Court never talked to people, she said, only to lawyers. But that was no worry because anybody could get a lawyer to talk to the Court for him. All it would cost was some money, and not even that if he was poor. If he was poor, other people would pay for his lawyer, and all Kazmer had to do was to ask.

Well, the girl didn't have to worry about him asking other people to pay for his lawyer, he wouldn't be poor enough for that if he was starving, which thank God he wasn't, or anywhere near it. Though it wasn't right that anybody could just lie about him, and then it would cost him money to put it right with the Court. But it wasn't the girl's fault, Kazmer could see that easily. There was a first time for everything, and let it be a lawyer, if it had to be.

"I sorry I yell on you," said Kazmer to the girl, "and maybe you show me where lawyer is, please? I got money to pay."

"Oh, I can't do that," said the girl, and Kazmer could see her blush, in a nice way, though, and he didn't understand why. "Look, there are lawyers all over Queen Street where we are, and on Bay and Richmond, too. If you made an appointment, they'd see you. Any one of them would."

"They all good lawyers?" asked Kazmer, shrewdly, for the girl and he had become friends now in a way.

"Oh yeah, sure," said the girl. "Well, you know."

He thanked her, then stood in the foyer of the courthouse for a few minutes, looking at the lawyers hurrying by in three-piece suits or all dressed up in black gowns, carrying papers, though some of the older lawyers had younger ones to carry their briefcases for them. But most of the lawyers were not so old. In fact they seemed to be half Kazmer's age, if that. They were decent enough to look at, not the beady-eyed pale stamp-lickers that the word "lawyer" brought to Kazmer's mind, but broad-shouldered men with open, ruddy faces. They looked as if they would be at home in a hockey rink, some of them. Kazmer began to like the thought of a lawyer taking up his case. He was only after the truth, but even the truth was like rolling a rock downhill, first it needed a little push. Less trouble than Petrona's lawyer, whoever he was, for he'd have to be pushing it uphill all the way.

There was one lawyer he particularly liked, an older man with short, iron gray hair, who stood talking with a woman in the corridor for a long time, a very sad woman, but the way the lawyer was talking to her she started smiling through her tears, and she even laughed by the time he shook her hand to say goodbye. Kazmer was fascinated by this and after the cry-ing-smiling lady left he almost walked up to the lawyer; but it was no use, his feet wouldn't take him. A person couldn't just go up to an important man like that, what would he think, that Kazmer didn't know any better? No, he'd do the proper thing, even if it had to be another lawyer. A man wasn't like a horse, anyway, that you'd buy him for his looks. Though, Kazmer supposed, you *would* buy him for that sometimes, and sometimes you'd buy a woman that way, too. Oh, Petrona!

So it was to balding, timid Mr. Perkins that Kazmer turned the next day, even if he hated to do it, for it put him in the same boat with Mr. Perkins all the more, and it was too much of a personal thing, besides. But, just the same, Mr. Perkins had been through a divorce himself, and who would know the lie of the land better than a man who'd been through it? And it wasn't as if Kazmer had known a lot of people who had been divorced, even if the policeman on the telephone that night had said that it happened all the time.

But a nosebleed is no big thing to a doctor, nor even an ulcer perhaps, for everybody who walks through his door has one, and it was the same thing with Mr. Schuldig, Marvin Schuldig B.A. LL.D., as it said on his letterhead, the lawyer Mr. Perkins said Kazmer should see. Because as soon as he looked up from the Supreme Court's lying letter, he said, "Well, Kazmer—you don't mind if I call you Kazmer?—don't worry, you've come to the right place for help."

But Kazmer was a little worried, not because of Mr. Schuldig, who seemed a nice enough young man, with a firm handshake and a firm jaw and a firm deep voice; short, but dressed very neatly in gray pants and a gray vest, like those color advertisements in Petrona's magazines. It was only Mr. Schuldig's office that worried Kazmer a little. There were at least five ladies sitting outside, each with her own typewriter, and the fabric on the armchairs and couches would have run fifteen dollars a yard, wholesale. Then, two strong men would have had to spend the better part of a day to shake the fleas out of the hard-twist broadloom, which ran all the way from the elevators back to Mr. Schuldig's corner office, from which one could see the whole of Yonge Street stretching north through the immaculate floor-to-ceiling glass. No wonder, for it was on the twenty-ninth floor and only one of the elevators in the huge marble building would take you up to it, the rest didn't even bother going so high.

"You please tell me now how much this law going to cost me?" asked Kazmer prudently.

"Well," said Mr. Schuldig, "I generally don't charge for the first interview. A retainer, do you know what a retainer is—well,

I don't normally take a retainer. I don't take any instructions. First time, I don't even take any notes, you know."

Mr. Schuldig seemed to say this with some pride, and Kazmer nodded, though he didn't quite understand why a young man would want to brag about all the things he didn't do. But Mr. Schuldig explained, raising a cautionary finger:

"You'd be surprised, Kazmer, how many people walk through this door the first time and then change their minds later. A little quarrel, a few angry words, tempers flare, and here they come, knocking on my door. Well, that's fine, I tell them their rights, tell them what's involved. Maybe I recommend counseling. But if they change their minds, I'm all the happier. Lawyers don't break up marriages, you know, people do that all by themselves. And," Mr. Schuldig continued, "if they do, we are here to see that everybody's treated fairly."

Well, that was fine, there was nothing wrong with that, fairness was all Kazmer was looking for; but something Mr. Schuldig said earlier caught on a small branch of his mind, and he asked, "Maybe you think Petrona change her mind, too?" It was not anything Kazmer himself would have thought, but who could tell? The young lawyer must have known something about wives and husbands, it was his job, even if Kazmer understood nothing anymore. He never thought a woman could call a man her husband, accept his ring in church, then turn around and lie about him to strangers. But it had happened.

Mr. Schuldig cleared his throat.

"Well, she's your wife, Kazmer, you must know her better than I," he said. "From this letter I'd say they mean business. How long have you been separated now?"

April, well, that would have been just about a year and a month since he came back to the empty house and Petrona's note, though from the sting of it in his heart, it could have been yesterday. But Kazmer just said a year and a month, for the rest wasn't the young man's business.

The lawyer nodded.

"Okay, so she hasn't just walked out in a huff. Well, fine. You see, the thing I said earlier about not taking a retainer and instructions at the first meeting, Kazmer, applies more to people who want to start an action themselves, but in your case it looks like they're starting the action against you. Well, do you want to defend it?"

Now Mr. Schuldig had a very quick way of talking, Kazmer wasn't even sure he understood all of the words he used, and the ones he understood made little sense to him at first. How would any man not want to defend himself against such lies? And why, if he didn't, would he have come to a lawyer, anyway? The old chairs and cupboards in his shop wouldn't fix themselves while he was sitting here, and nobody would pay good money for furniture that didn't get fixed. But then Mr. Schuldig explained that if Petrona wanted a divorce, well, he didn't have to give her one; the Court didn't just hand them out for the asking, not even in this day and age. At least not for five years or so, or sometimes three years. People could have a divorce right away only if they had a reason.

"What reason?" Kazmer asked. "Petrona, she don't have no reason."

Well, that was the point, because Mr. Loeblich, that was Petrona's lawyer (and Mr. Schuldig knew him, too, he said, "Oh, she went to Garry Loeblich, eh?"), in any case Mr. Loeblich thought that Petrona did have a reason. The reason was that Kazmer had been cruel to her. That's why he had no right to his children, either, except to send Petrona money for them; and that's what all the lies in the Supreme Court's letter were about.

"Is not true," said Kazmer, red in the face. "I defend."

Well, that was fine, Mr. Schuldig said, if he didn't want to give Petrona a divorce, it was his business. Though if a marriage was down the drain, it was down the drain, and even crazy glue couldn't hold it together. Some people, Mr. Schuldig said, chose not to bother about defending a divorce one way or the other, there was enough trouble about who was to get the money and the property and maybe the children. Kazmer understood that easily, for it was true enough, and let Petrona have her divorce if she wanted it, he didn't care anymore. But not all the lies, no. He would defend himself against every one of them.

But Mr. Schuldig smiled at that, and he glanced at his watch, and said that Kazmer couldn't do it that way. The only way the law would have it was that Kazmer had been cruel to Petrona, and then she could have her divorce. If he wasn't, she couldn't, not unless the Court took her word against his. And while he wouldn't tell Kazmer what to do, as his lawyer he would certainly defend him against all her lies if that was his choice.

"No way to say," asked Kazmer, "to hell with this cruel business, you just take divorce?"

No way, Mr. Schuldig replied, not according to the law. The Court wouldn't give them a divorce if they both said they wanted one, not for three years; and if Petrona said, well, I walked out on him, the Court wouldn't give *her* a divorce for five. Kazmer could get one in three, though, because it was she who deserted by leaving the note, but then he'd have to ask for a divorce himself. Of course, either of them could get one right away if there had been another man or woman, that was called *adultery* in law, but Mr. Schuldig imagined Petrona had no grounds for that or she would have used them, it was better than cruelty. Did Kazmer have any grounds?

"What you mean?" asked Kazmer, though he knew well enough, for shame.

"Well, did she have another man?"

The blood rushed to his head, it had come to that, now there would be strangers walking into his bedroom, he'd have to show them the stains on his linen, and say thank you into the bargain, for the strangers were only trying to help. And that Petrona couldn't just leave quietly, as if leaving hadn't been bad enough, but no, she also had to drag his name through the mud.

Perhaps she didn't mean to, for she never had any evil in her, but neither could she see any farther than her own nose, that woman, and it was no use trying to explain anything to her, she was so stubborn. It was only to garbage that she'd listen, on the color TV and in magazines, or maybe her new woman friends. She'd swallow what they told her quickly enough, but talking sense to her was like trying to turn a mule.

And she was like that long before the real trouble started between them, Kazmer remembered, because she'd say things like "Well, that's *my* way" or "What is it to you, if I like it?" and there was no use trying to tell her that they were one person now, the two of them, as man and wife, and neither could do anything without inviting judgment for it on the other. "If I came home drunk," he'd say to her, "you think the neighbors won't hold it against you?" But she'd only laugh: "Oh, Kazmer, you worry so much about what people think. People don't care what size sweater I wear when I go out shopping, it's not like the old country, nobody'll think any the less of *you* for that."

But she was wrong, Kazmer knew that, because this new country wasn't so different from the old. People didn't say much, that was true enough, but they noticed, they saw what was what, they could make up their minds and maybe even tell right from wrong quickly enough. Of course people noticed, or else why would a woman wear those tight sweaters or short skirts or put that blue paint around her eyes in the first place, unless she knew that people would notice? Even Petrona would have walked around in an old sack, it would have been cheaper, if she had really thought that in this country people were blind. And if she was trying to tell him that they meant something different, those tight sweaters and short skirts, from what they would have meant back home—well, Kazmer didn't believe that, either, for one thing leads to another, even on the moon. Or wasn't he sitting in a glass office now on the twenty-ninth floor, and that young lawyer, still friendly but a little impatient, urging him:

"Well, Kazmer, did she? Did your wife have another man?"

And what answer could he give to his oldest friend, let alone a stranger he had met for the first time, even if he was to be his lawyer, except to shake his head and shrug his shoulder at the same time. Let Mr. Schuldig make whatever he wanted of that, for Kazmer wasn't going to talk about his shame and the destruction of his good name to anyone, not unless he carved his answer into their flesh with a knife. But there was no call for such a thing. Mr. Schuldig meant no harm, and even a doctor couldn't help causing pain cleaning up a wound, Kazmer understood that. But he couldn't answer, the words just wouldn't get past his lips; and Mr. Schuldig saw that, too, and started talking about how they would defend Kazmer against all the lies, for he could see that this was what Kazmer wanted. He'd defend Kazmer's property and business, by which he meant the house and the shop, because the Supreme Court had written that Petrona also had a claim on those from him; and then Mr. Schuldig said that he'd accept a check for $1,000 from Kazmer for a start. A thousand and not a penny less, oh Petrona, Petrona! But it felt right, for you couldn't cover a long cut with a short bandage.

Kazmer went home with a sheaf of printed papers Mr. Schuldig gave him to fill out for when he would have to come to see him next. They had to do with what he owned and earned and spent, right down to the cost of his haircuts and laundry, as if it was anybody's business, but Mr. Schuldig said that Petrona had a right to demand this so the Court could see if it tallied with what she said he earned and spent. And Kazmer stared at the papers at home, but his mind kept going back to that other thing, that other question his lawyer wanted to know, the one he couldn't answer. Adultery, which means sleeping with another man, Kazmer, and did your wife do it? Because we can defend you better if we know.

And a question is just a question, but how to answer one that poured like molten lead into his ears and sent his fist crashing down on the kitchen table so that the wood split from end to end under the chiming plates and glasses. And it wasn't just sleeping with another man, either, for *that* was not invented in Toronto or New York, the flesh was weak even back in Bugyi, and many a good woman yielded to mortal temptation and many a good man yielded to it, too. But between him and Petrona it was a thousand times worse, Kazmer knew that, even if he couldn't say how. He couldn't say, and not only to his lawyer, for that didn't matter a pinch of salt, but to himself.

For a wife might cheat on her husband, and perhaps even go to hell for it if the Reverend Vegvari had his way; but she would still know that the man she cheated on was her husband, and she, his wife. But with Petrona, she would be talking to him as though he wasn't her husband at all, and years before she'd ever have cheated on him, as far as Kazmer could tell. Like the time—and that wasn't so long after they were married, for even Johnny wasn't born then—when she'd keep switching on the light after he had turned it off in the bedroom.

"Oh, come on, then, Petrona," Kazmer remembered saying, smiling, for he could take a joke, but a little put out all the same.

"Come on yourself," she replied, and she was laughing, too, but there was a bold challenge in her voice.

Now Petrona had always been a playful sort, even on their honeymoon or earlier still, when they were courting; and Kazmer put up with it because that's what she was like. You don't take a gray mare home from the fair only to paint it black. He even tried to play along with her, as much as he could, pretending to himself that he enjoyed it, but it wasn't in his nature, and that was the truth. Making love was not a game, not some kind of sport, nor was it anything for two people to talk about. Making love to your sweetheart was a serious matter, and to your wife, more serious still, even sacred. It was a gift, or a command you obeyed, in which you gave no lessons and took none, for a single word would make it less and two words might make it vanish altogether.

But if making love for Kazmer was only done in the shy, silent, mysterious way of a man, it wasn't Petrona's way. Or, as she'd have him believe, any woman's. What Petrona said women wanted—and what she herself did want, there was no doubt about that—was all kinds of games and gropings and words. Some of them, well, *dirty* was the only way Kazmer could think about them. She wanted bright lights, where he would have been happier in the dark. She wanted to look and touch and talk about it, and she wanted him to look and touch and talk about it as well. Right in the very beginning she'd say in an urgent whisper, "Fuck me, oh fuck me," as if that wasn't what he was doing to her anyway, and why couldn't the damn woman keep her mouth shut. She was like a witch, Petrona was, she could cast a spell like no woman Kazmer had ever known could, but a wicked witch for all that because she would then break her own spell and, worse, blame him for the magic draining away. "Oh, you're so *crude*," she'd say. "Don't you like making love to me?"

He did, though, that was the bad part of it, but the good part of it, too, back when. Bad, for if he hadn't liked making love to her, he wouldn't have, and a cow you never tried milking has never kicked you in the head, either. But good, because he liked making love to her so much in the beginning that he could even do it her way, which he could never do to any other woman, not that he would ever have tried; and he could do it so that she loved it and whimpered in delight, even if for him it was half pretend. "Oh, I can come any time you tell me to," she'd moan, "if you only put your hand on my nipples. Tell me, tell me," and he'd tell her, feeling proud and stupid and ashamed, all at the same time, for what kind of a woman would twist in sweet pain at the mere sound of his voice? It wasn't right and it wasn't decent somehow, but that was what Petrona wanted and Kazmer knew that he wanted Petrona, if that was the only way to have her.

And have her he did; but even while she was going on about how much he did have her, for she'd say it again and again, he'd feel uneasy, even scared a little, the same way he'd feel handling a treacherous tool or a skittish horse. He'd mount her and ride her, but without confidence and maybe even without pleasure in the end, for he'd be doing it her way instead of his own. Nor was it just a matter of letting her run at her own pace, Kazmer would have let her anyway, for tight reins showed a foolish rider, as the saying had it, or a bad horse. But, as Kazmer remembered thinking even at the time, maybe it was his own fault. Petrona was his wife, not a horse, and what was wrong with him to be thinking of her like that?

But what else, when it was Petrona who wanted it this way. She wanted to be ridden and mastered, even while she was making it hell for him to ride and master her. Did she not make it as plain as daylight, even back in the best days, the days when she had nothing but praise for him, that she was eating out of his hand only because he could control her *that* way? It was even the word she used once, control. And didn't she say in the first week of their marriage—true, she might have been joking, at least that's what Kazmer put it down to at the time—"Well, Mr. Harcsa, if it wasn't for your touch, I'd bolt back to New York faster than you could shake a stick at"? His touch, except it wasn't his touch at all. It was only his hands. Moved, like a puppet's, by what he could divine of her fancy.

And what if he divined it wrong, as he easily might, since he was following her instincts instead of his own, and a woman's instincts weren't labeled like switches in a car. And even if the touch had been really his, which it wasn't, should a touch control another person so? "You have the key to my heart, Mr. Harcsa," she'd say to him in those days, curling her long, slim legs around his in bed, which was all very well; but if the key to Petrona's heart was a man's touch, well, there would be many keys to fit *her* heart, and Kazmer's might not even have been the best fit. A key is easy to make, anybody can do it. Or, as the saying went back home, a ruby is worth more than a sheepdog, but it won't bite a thief.

And he came to think of her that way, a ruby, a precious stone, but no more to be relied on, for she'd belong to whoever could touch her and pick her up. Except worse, for you could lock away a precious stone or bury it, and the law would give it back to you if somebody took it. Thinking of your wife as a ruby, well, at least it was better than thinking of her as a horse. Better still to think of her as your wife, but she wouldn't let you, not Petrona.

Soon it got so that he became afraid to touch her at all, for what if he touched her the wrong way? He would lie next to her in bed, look at her raven hair tangled on the white pillow, and do nothing. He'd do nothing while she lay twisting in her sleep, for Petrona was a restless sleeper, and not because he didn't have the notion, as she might have thought, but for fear that he would only upset her in some way. His own wife, and that was in the best days; but Petrona always had a way of making him feel clumsy, awkward, even unwanted. Her very praise for his touch came with a warning, a set of instructions, like fine print. "Oh good, don't stop. Don't you like coming up behind me anymore? Then do it from above, like the last time." And "Can't you make your mouth real hard when you kiss, the way you used to?"

She also had a way of looking at him, with praise on her lips, true, but still as though he had been a gift somebody bought for her at a department store and now she was wondering whether to keep it or take it back. It was always "Your arms, look at all that black hair on your arms," or "You have such a funny big bone there, I've never seen anything like it," and even "Don't put on your pants yet, let me look at it from below." Kazmer would still shake his head in embarrassment, just thinking about it. And it was hard to say what it was, because in those days everything she said was fine and good and aren't you beautiful, but praise was still judgment, and what kind of a woman would pass judgment on her man? What if his chest had no hair or he couldn't make his mouth real hard when he kissed her? He'd still be her husband.

But maybe he wouldn't be, not when you listened to Petrona, though she never said it in so many words. Except what else could a man think when everything he did was graded by his wife, the way the teacher would grade a boy in school, and not only what he did but what he was, even the way the hair grew on his chest. Then it wasn't so much the money he made or the way he spoke or whether or not he watched enough of the color TV; that only came later, Petrona wasn't so particular about those things at first, and maybe it would have been better if she had been. For money is only money and the color TV is even less, but that woman would test him for the way he smelled to her, or for the way he made her feel in bed. If it was a relief that he made her feel good, it was a worry and a humiliation all the same. "Well, you passed me today, Petrona," he'd say to her as a joke, "and maybe you'll fail me tomorrow." And she'd laugh and slap him on his belly muscles, which were tight and firm, though even back then he was thirty-six, and she'd say, "You bet."

But that wasn't all, for maybe the things she said would have been nothing without that look of challenge in her black eyes, and another woman who said them differently could have said all her words with no trouble. For whatever was on her lips, Petrona's eyes always seemed to add, at least as Kazmer read them, that she would only belong to a man who tamed her, and more fool he for thinking that he had tamed her yet or that he ever would. As for that wedding ring on her finger, well, anyone with a hundred dollars to spend could buy one of those at Macy's in Queens, and taking it off would be no more hardship than putting it on had been, and maybe less.

And when Kazmer would put it to her, as he did now and then, after a glass or two of red wine, that "It's not what you're saying to me, my treasure, but what your eyes are saying," she'd just deny it, reply that he was dreaming, or use her favorite word, *paranoid*, but her black eyes would mock and challenge him even worse while her mouth pleaded innocence. It never went much farther than that, for Kazmer's mind believed her words, but his heart still believed her eyes. Except the heart, well, maybe the heart knows everything, but it can prove nothing. What if it was only his imagination? It would take a crazy person to reproach his wife for a look.

Or what could he say when Petrona started noticing that two nights would go by, even maybe a whole week of nights, with him keeping his hands to himself in the marriage bed? For not reproaching someone with words was easy enough, but a man couldn't tell his hands to stop doubting, they wouldn't obey him. Hands listen to no reason except their own. And it wouldn't be too long before Petrona would come right out and say, "Hey, Mr. Harcsa, what's wrong? The way you go to sleep these days, anybody'd think that one of us is getting old."

Yes, and the one wasn't Petrona, not at twenty-five or twenty-six, while he was getting on to forty. Not that Kazmer had too many worries on that score, there was fire enough in the furnace to keep a lot of women warm, and no fear of it going out for a long time yet. But what if the fire did burn down slowly, as all fires must, what then? Would that make any difference between a man and his wife? You marry for life, and life means getting old, unless people die before their time. Young as Petrona was, her years of firm flesh and sweet breath were numbered, too, but as far as Kazmer was concerned she could count on people calling her Mrs. Harcsa, and never mind that she had long traded in her high heels for a pair of shuffling slippers. But as for him, let alone a set of false teeth or a walking cane, could he count on being her husband if he stopped touching her the way she liked it? And if he couldn't, what kind of marriage did they have, if a person could call it a marriage at all? How could he reach out safely for a woman who might say to him, as Petrona did one night, in a flash of anger, "Oh shit, couldn't you wait for me?"

He said nothing, not then, for how can you reply to something no wife should ever say to her husband? But when she was still sulky the next morning, he put his hand on hers, saying, "You told the priest 'Till death do us part,' Petrona. Maybe you meant 'As long as both of us play the fiddle together.'"

Then she came right out with it, true, starting kind of slowly at first, that she was sorry and she didn't mean to offend him, but there it was: her friends had warned her that there would be a problem about that if she married someone from the old country, the men were all selfish bastards, most of them, they'd behave like kings in bed, thinking only of themselves. And not only that, but you couldn't even talk about it, they'd stand on their dignity, women were not supposed to mention such things to men because their mothers and sisters never did, and if you as much as breathed a word, well, all the big hulking strutting cocksure stallions became as shocked and shy as seminary priests, for God's sake. And that was because for all their strutting they were *repressed*, if Kamzer knew what *that* meant; sex was supposed to be some kind of big secret, even dirty, and not just a normal, healthy thing men and women did for their pleasure, and you had to go to school in America to know that. Because men from the old country didn't even know that women were supposed to be different, they never had any biology classes, no, that would have been immoral or something. All men knew was how to ask for the things *they* wanted, they were never too shy for that, but let a woman drop a hint, a whisper, and they'd look at her as if she was some kind of nymphomaniac, okay? And Petrona didn't care that Kazmer was a good provider and all that, she never said he wasn't, but in this one thing he was like all the rest, self-centered, and everything had to be his way just because he was a man. Well, she was sorry, and she loved him, and she'd be a good wife to him, but she wasn't going to just stand there and let him talk to her as if she were the whore of Babylon, when all she was asking for was her due. And if Kazmer thought that she'd stop demanding it just because it shocked him, well, he had better think again, fast.

He was so quiet when she finished, and for such a long time, that it must have scared her a little because, Kazmer remembered, she ended up by sitting next to him on the sofa and putting her arm around his neck. She was mistaken about his silence, though, because he wasn't even hurt, let alone angry, and was quiet only because he was thinking about what she had said. It was the truth of it that surprised Kazmer most, and how accurate she was about the way he felt, when he never said anything to her before. Was it so plain that, much as he wanted her, he always worried that her kind of loving wasn't modest enough for a woman? Was it so plain that, well, if he hadn't felt the way he did about her, she would have scared and disgusted him? That even as it was, he did think of her ways as dirty? How would she know, when he had never said a word to her about it? There she was, having these thoughts in her mind, while Kazmer thought that he had been doing everything to her fancy all along, just as if he wanted it the same way, too.

"Listen," he said to her after a long silence, "you always said you liked it, the way I was with you. You always said that."

She was glad then that he was talking to her, or relieved anyway, and showed it by going into a pout, like a little girl. "Well, I used to," she said, shrugging her shoulder. "I mean, you used to be different. Oh, I don't know. You used to . . . well, maybe your heart wasn't in it, even then."

"We've been married for three years, Petrona," he said, slowly.

That made her angry again, three years; why, was it supposed to be all over in three years, is that what it was all about, three years, and she still a young woman, though she might as well be dead and buried. "I didn't marry you for your money, you know," she said, black eyes flashing, "or for your schooling, either, because I had more of it than you. You didn't even speak English much, and you still don't. I married you because you made me feel good, and nobody told me it was only for three years, Mr. Harcsa."

And how could he explain to her that he didn't mean it that way, the three years, only that, well, the *hunger* of it came only once, for him as well as for her, it was always short, and it had nothing to do with marriage. First the flames, then the warm glow of embers, and that's how it was with all good fire and love. But Petrona, she'd forever mistake the flame for the fire, expect a solid log to burn like a piece of straw, and it was that that made him grow colder and turned his fire to ashes in his heart. She dampened it when she meant to kindle it, oh Petrona, for all her raven hair and coal black eyes. But how could he ever put that into words?

So he took her into his arms instead, which was a good thing, for it was what she wanted, and he wanted it, too, right until she was lying on her back, her eyes searching his, full white breasts popping out of her silk blouse, and she spoke to him:

"Fuck me, oh fuck me," Petrona said. "Tell me to come, make your mouth real hard. Oh Mr. Harcsa, you have the key to my heart."

But Kazmer knew then that he didn't and perhaps never would, no matter how much he would have liked to. They didn't talk any more about it, either, at least not for a year and not in so many words, except that Petrona took to switching the channels on the color TV to all those men in turtleneck sweaters who had more hair on their faces than their heads, and women, too, with big silver jewelry, who would talk about what men and women should be doing with each other, not that Kazmer understood half of what they were saying. But Petrona would listen to them. Anybody would think she was in church from the way she'd listen. And she would try to make Kazmer listen, too, except he wasn't interested in all that off-color talk, even if it was supposed to be scien*tific*. Nor was he going to learn how a man should be with his wife from color TV, which was always showing pictures that a five-year-old child wouldn't believe, one man fighting off ten with his bare fists, or jumping off a sixty-foot bridge and not getting hurt.

Wives and husbands knew how to get along before TV talks were ever invented; and if he had wanted to listen to the gabbing woman with the silver earrings, he would have married *her*, and maybe Petrona should have married that bald TV man who was blinking all the time. And late in the evening, when Petrona said it wasn't for education, only for fun, well, she could watch that Johnny Carson if she thought that he was so funny, but for Kazmer it was only more of the same. Maybe he didn't understand English so well, but he could tell a wink and what it meant, when it was dirty, or else why would they have put him on only after all the children had gone to bed?

But Kazmer and Petrona had no children to put to bed yet, not then, for Petrona was still working the switchboard for the government, where they gave out driver's licences and such, and Kazmer had just rented the shop for his own business, because there was no future in that job at the furniture factory, where they would be laid off half the time and had to go on strike the other half. Nor should a man bring his children into the world, not without a proper roof to put over their heads. Let the Pope do it himself if he wanted to, and even though Petrona was a Catholic she had always agreed with Kazmer about that. But with the new shop open, the customers ringing the bell and most of the down payment sitting in the Toronto-Dominion Bank, there was no reason to wait any longer. Perhaps a family was all Petrona needed, anyway, to understand why people would put on a ring in church instead of just groping for each other in the bushes.

But perhaps she needed something else to understand it, because it was on one of those nights that she'd be switching on the light in the bedroom every time Kazmer would turn it off, saying "Come on yourself!" to him with that cold glance of challenge in her eyes. And she'd pull away when Kazmer tried to embrace her, though not with a look of wanting less, but wanting more. He didn't understand her, what was that woman playing at now?

She came out with it finally, and it was bolder than any-thing yet. "You don't like me," she said, "and you never did. Ever since we said children, and sure, I want children, too, but I don't want you to breed me like a cow. How come you never do it to me with your mouth?"

"Petrona, don't," he said, but she just turned away from him and buried her face into the pillow. Her shoulders were shak-ing, but Kazmer couldn't tell whether from crying or rage. "That I'd have to be asking for it from you," she muttered into the pillow, "when anybody. . . . Oh, I'm so ashamed. What kind of a man are you?"

He could still remember the red-hot cloud of fury coming over him at that, not over what she wanted him to do, even if it wasn't his nature, but that a wife should tell her husband what to do in bed, that she would dare to judge him in his ways, teach him his own sacred duty, *that* was not only against his nature, but against nature itself. A woman, who should cleave unto her husband, not that he ever tried to be her mas-ter. But Petrona wanted him to be her slave, and it was time to do what he ought to have done to her a long time ago.

He could feel her cheekbone crack under his fist, even though he pulled his punch, but his hand had always been heavy and working with wood had made it heavier still. There was such a surprise in her eyes, he would never forget it if he had five lives, and then she fainted, though only for a few sec-onds. It was enough to scare him out of his wits, he ran to the bathroom for towels drenched in cold water, not that he could stop the swelling but at least the wet cloth started her whim-pering, so he knew that she was all right. "What happened?" she kept asking, clinging to him, and when he embraced her she broke into tears and buried her head in his chest. And in the morning she was up before him, when it was more often the other way around, and she must have been to the store for fresh pumpernickel, because a big slice of it was on his plate to go with his fried bacon for breakfast. But the real wonder of it was that Petrona had dark glasses on, and when she lifted them to show off her bruises, she did it with such pride as if it had been a medal won in battle. "See what you did to me, Mr. Harcsa?" she said with more affection in her voice than Kazmer had heard for a long time. "It's turning black and I can hardly open my mouth, see?"

There was peace after that, and a fool might have thought that it would last forever, and there's no denying that Kazmer was such a fool. And if worse was to come, it didn't come for some time, for first they bought the house and then Johnny was born, and two years later, Borbala. And Petrona, well, there was no way that Kazmer could breathe a word of complaint about the kind of mother she was, except that she wouldn't give Johnny the milk from her breast because of something she had read in a magazine. But she was what she was, she was still his wife, and many a man had married worse, even back in Bugyi, where they hadn't crammed a girl's head full of foolishness with American schools and color television. And the way Kazmer was figuring it then, no more being able to see the future than any other mortal, Petrona was getting on to thirty herself, and you can't judge a woman much, or a man either, by what they do before turning thirty. And perhaps cracking her one across the face was the smartest thing, even if Kazmer would still wince with pain thinking about it, because didn't the song back home tell about the woman who wouldn't say "husband" to the man she married, not for all the treasure and kind words he could lavish on her, but she called him husband in a hurry when he laid a stick across her backside. And if it was a very old song, well, God made men and women a very long time ago, too, and He didn't start making them all over again when color TV came to America. Or didn't Petrona herself say, even after Johnny was born, nuzzling Kazmer's cheek and putting her sweet-smelling arms around his neck, "Well, maybe I was asking for it, Mr. Harcsa, but did you have to hit me so hard? It's been a year now and, oh, I can still feel the pain when I yawn!"

But who would burden a stranger like Mr. Schuldig with any of this? Kazmer would have died of the shame of it, even if he had a right to talk, and $1,000 should buy a big piece of anybody's ear. Maybe some people could tell a priest about such things, though not Kazmer, not even to a priest, let alone a lawyer, and one who didn't even have a gray hair in his head. And if Mr. Schuldig knew all about the law, as he ought to, with all those flashing telephone lights and hard-twist broadloom, that should be enough. A man wasn't going to the Court to ask some judge to handle his wife for him, if he wasn't man enough to handle her himself, as Kazmer hadn't been, not with Petrona, and what was the use of denying it? If he had been it wouldn't have come to the lawyers and judges in the first place. Whatever was wrong with him, or maybe her, no court could put it right. Once you cut the wood and made the chair, it was what it was, and if it wasn't right, there was still nothing to do but sweep the shavings off the floor and start again with another piece of wood. If you had the strength, that is, and if it wasn't too late in the day.

Because the woman in that song back home may have called her man husband after he had laid the stick across her bottom, but the song didn't say whether she kept calling him husband forever. And that woman had no magazines to read that would tell her different, either, but Petrona did, she had the magazines and the TV, and she had those other women in the government office, too, and she'd keep going back to them even after she had quit her job. Kazmer said nothing, it wasn't as if the work around the new house hadn't been done or the children hadn't been looked after. What harm was there in a few women getting together once in a while, talking or listening to people talk to them? Like that young man Petrona even dragged Kazmer along to listen to once, not that he had heard much of whatever the young man was saying, because he fell asleep halfway through it. And she was mortified, Petrona was,

and started another bad argument at home about it, all having
to do with how Kazmer was pulling her down in the world. For
she had all kinds of *interests*, Petrona said, but Kazmer didn't,
all he cared about was making things out of wood and stuffing
himself full of blood pudding afterward. And that awful blue
truck, yes, he'd care about that, too, he'd wash it twice a day, as
if it made any difference to the way it looked.

And pretty soon she'd start in on that old thing again, about
his selfish habits as a man, and how other couples could think
of ways to make their love life *varied*, and there were some who
did not even think of *monogamania* as the only way, at least
that's how the word sounded to Kazmer. She wouldn't go that
far, though, Petrona said, *monogamania* was good enough for
her, and she knew anyway that Kazmer would hit the roof if she
thought otherwise. Worse still, Petrona said, he'd hit her, for he
had done it once before, that was the kind of man he was, the
kind who'd fall asleep at an interesting *lecture* but be wide
awake when it was time to use his wife for a punching bag.

There was no fear of that, though, for Kazmer was not very
quick to anger. He had heard that old tune before, and
Petrona would have to think of a new one before she could
reach the end of his patience. Besides, any man might kick a
dog expecting it to learn, but only a fool would kick a tree to
teach it a lesson. And if your wife had the nature of a tree,
what could you do to her? Nothing, except marvel at the way
she was growing and spreading her branches farther and farther away from you in the blue sky. Be thankful, maybe, that
at least she bore you some fruit, Kazmer would think, glancing
at Johnny and Borbala.

But being silent, withdrawing into his thoughts, would only
make Petrona angry. Also, well, *worried*, in some peculiar way
Kazmer could never understand. Hitting her would have been
a kindness, she wasn't half as disturbed at the time he cracked
her face, but now that he was just sitting quietly with his
hands folded in his lap she'd go on the boil again and again.

Was she daring him? Was she, God knows, maybe even begging him to do it to her once more? Well, to hell with it, he
would not be commanded in anger anymore than he would be
in love. A man made love in his own time, and that was the
way he would hit someone, too, and not when she wanted it.
And let her storm at him, Kazmer didn't mind that, but pretty
soon Petrona took to storming right out of the house.

That was a different thing, when she first started doing
that, and Kazmer didn't properly know what to do about it.

Any man might quarrel with his wife inside the house, or
she with him, for even in anger or in silence they would still
be together, the two of them. But when the door closes behind
one at the end of a fight, it is another thing again, for the
longest step is always the one that takes a person across the
threshold. Compared to that first step all steps are short and
easy, as Kazmer tried explaining to Petrona, even if other steps
took her to the end of the world.

"I don't care," she would reply. "Make a big thing out of it if
you like. I just want to clear my head."

It was another way for Petrona to make him feel foolish,
whenever she'd answer him like that, because Kazmer would
be put in the wrong, and never mind that he would still be
right. For what is the big fuss about a man's wife taking a walk
around the block? Kazmer never doubted that that was all
Petrona was doing, at least in the beginning, and he couldn't
explain why he would be so angry with her if he didn't doubt
it himself. It wasn't as if she was running off to her lover.

"I'm not running off to my lover," she'd say to him as he
stood in the doorway, blocking it. "I'm not even mad at you,
Kazmer. I just need my private space for a few minutes. I'm a
person, too, you know."

So in the end he would stand aside, against his better judgment, because there was no replying to words like "private
space" and "person" whatever they meant and wherever
Petrona might have picked them up. Though Kazmer had a

pretty shrewd idea where Petrona might have come up with all her funny words, and he knew for certain when, after a few months, she no longer needed the excuse of a fight to go out of the house two or three evenings a week. He didn't have to guess, either, because Petrona told him. She said, "You see, Kazmer, I can work through our problems much better now that I'm in the group."

"What you do in group?"

"You wouldn't understand," she replied. "Like, we have our consciousness raised."

"Now is ten, maybe when you conscious some more, you not home till twelve?" Kazmer remembered asking in English. "Is conscious maybe color TV word for a little screwing?"

"You don't even make any bones about it, do you?" she replied, turning crimson. "I'm married to a chauvinist."

And from the righteousness of her voice Kazmer knew that "consciousness" didn't mean screwing around, but he only spoke in anger, anyway, for he didn't really think that the government women in the group were teaching Petrona to take a lover, whatever they *were* teaching her, and the bald blinking TV man wasn't teaching her to do that, either. But Kazmer was still right, for what difference did it make what "consciousness" meant? What difference did it make what all those groups and magazines were teaching Petrona to do, when what she did was to stay away at night from her husband and children two, three times a week? And maybe she stayed away alone at first, but she didn't stay away alone forever. Or wasn't that the young lecture man, the one Kazmer fell asleep listening to, behind the wheel of that beat-up little car dropping Petrona off in front of her very house, hers and her husband's, at ten minutes before eleven? And the first two times Kazmer only watched them from behind the window, but the third time he waited on the sidewalk for them. Not that they seemed worried when they saw him waiting there, because they did not. The young man even extended his hand to him.

"Well, I brought home your wife, Mr. Harcsa," he said to Kazmer cheerfully.

"I thank you that you bring her," Kazmer replied, keeping his own hands in his pocket, "but I tell you, next time you bring her it's big trouble."

The young man's smile faded. "I'm sorry you feel this way about it," he said. "And I feel sorry for your wife. We're not in the Middle Ages, you know."

"You in young ages, I know," said Kazmer gravely, "that's why I'm telling you. Now you please go before everybody in street feel sorry for you."

But it was little satisfaction that Petrona, for once, could think of nothing to say or that the young man got back into his car very quickly and left a good month's supply of rubber on the asphalt driving away. Because Petrona recovered her tongue as soon as they were inside the house and Kazmer had let go of her arm, and there were no thanks in her words. Her words were like water over the head of a drowning man, a relentless echo, and all Kazmer could do was to grope for a miracle of solid ground under his feet.

Because she wasn't Kazmer's *property*, Petrona said, like his goddam blue truck, that he could drive her or put her up on blocks in the garage or turn her on and off whenever he wanted. She wasn't an *object*, a sex object or any other kind of object, but she was a person in her own right. And if it did not suit his old-world male *fantasies* of what a woman should be like—well, it was just too bad, because times have changed, not that somebody like Kazmer would have noticed, but times have changed all the same. People were *liberated* now, men, too, not only women, and if Kazmer wanted to be left behind like some old *fossil*, that was fine, but she was not going to be left behind herself. And she wasn't going to play the *role* of the wife, thank you, or fit into some stereotype. She did not want to hurt Kazmer, Petrona said, but from now on she would come and go as she had a mind to, and she would work or study any way she pleased. She would grow as a person, yes, and she would fulfill her *potential*. And, said Petrona, not that she gave two hoots about the young man Kazmer was so rude to— that'd be the day—but that young man understood those things, and the girl he'd marry would be lucky, not like Petrona, married to some *patriarch* living in the Middle Ages!

Kazmer said nothing, not even when he heard Petrona use the young man's words, though he knew what that meant well enough, and never mind what "Middle Ages" meant, let the devil take them. And he didn't move a muscle, either, though his fists tightened, for long words or short ones, she was telling him that she was not going to be his wife anymore. Because it made no difference if he was a "fossil" or a "patriarch," he was what he was, she was still supposed to be his wife. For if she had been lazy or scatterbrained or even a hussy, Kazmer would still have been her husband. Because what was "for better or worse" all about if it wasn't about that? They didn't say to the priest, "Till he turns out to be a fossil" or "Till she turns out to be a fool," they said, "Till death do us part"!

And if "consciousness" wasn't about screwing around and "liberated" didn't mean sitting in young men's cars, what did it all mean? What would Petrona do with herself if she became her own person? What would she do that she couldn't do now, run for president of the United States? Would she work with wood like Kazmer, when she couldn't even pluck a chicken with her own hands? Would she look after the business, quarrel with the suppliers or collect on the bad accounts? Well, she could do that today if she wanted to, he would be happy to let her, it was always Petrona who said she had no head for business. Work, hell, lots of women worked, even back in the village, where everybody knew that Mrs. Agyagos ran the butcher shop better than her drunk of a husband. But with Petrona, not that Kazmer minded, but what could she do except dress up nicely, so that your heart would break just looking at her, and smell so good you'd like to pick her up in your arms? Then, well, she'd watch some color TV or go and sit in some man's car, if not in her husband's, then somebody else's. And sure, maybe she'd also listen to long words from a man who could make his mouth real hard when he kissed her. Fuck me, conscious or not, that was Kazmer's wife. Oh, Petrona.

But if he said nothing to Petrona then, how could he say anything to young Mr. Schuldig now, who looked even younger in his black gown, walking in front of Kazmer along the narrow corridor of the Supreme Court. For it was finally the day to put things right and explain to the Court how it really was, and not the way they put it in that letter. True, Mr. Schuldig had warned Kazmer that it would not be so simple; Petrona would be there, too, with her lawyer. And Garry Loeblich was a man to reckon with, Mr. Schuldig knew, he told Kazmer the two of them had gone to law school together. "I don't want any surprises, Kazmer," Mr. Schuldig had said before they started out for Court, "if there was anything more I should know about what went on between your wife and yourself, perhaps you'd better tell me now." But Kazmer only shrugged, for it would be a lie to say he had ever caught Petrona in bed with anyone, there might have been murder if he had. As for the rest, well, how could a man put the rest into words? He had a fine marriage with two lovely children, until one day he came home to find Petrona's note on the kitchen table, explaining why the sofa, the standing lamp, the TV and his children were no longer in his house. The note said nothing about the $600 cash money in the linen closet. Then, only the Supreme Court's letter saying that he was a cruel husband. And if that was all—well, as Mr. Schuldig put it, that would have to be the case for the defence.

NO-FAULT DIVORCE

KAZMER WAS A LITTLE surprised as he followed Mr. Schuldig all the way down the twisting corridor of the Supreme Court, because they kept passing big courtrooms, one after another. Some had their doors closed but some were half open, and Kazmer could see people sitting on padded teak benches. Once he even caught a glimpse of a judge with a wide pink sash across his black robes, and an older judge in the next court had a red sash. But Mr. Schuldig kept walking on, while Kazmer thought, well, maybe the next one. But it wasn't until they reached an ordinary room, with only a single door at the very end of the hallway, that Mr. Schuldig finally stopped, motioning Kazmer to enter. And while it was a nice room, no denying it, with dark oak paneling on three sides and heavy, floor-to-ceiling shelves all filled with books along the fourth wall, it was still only a room, like an office. There were no benches in it and no dais for the judge, only a long table and some chairs around it, made of walnut and leather. And right across from where Mr. Schuldig pulled out a chair for Kazmer to sit on, there was Petrona. She had her raven hair pulled back more tightly than Kazmer had ever seen it, and what she was wearing was some kind of a black skirt and a long-sleeved blouse underneath a knitted jacket. Kazmer liked the way she looked, he had to admit, she was more like Johnny's Sunday school teacher Miss Helen in this blouse, and not at all like Petrona.

The young man sitting next to Petrona had a briefcase filled with papers, and there were more papers on the table in front of him. Kazmer knew well enough that he must be that Mr. Loeblich, Petrona's lawyer, though he had not laid eyes on him before. Still, he looked so much like Mr. Schuldig that Kazmer couldn't help looking behind himself to see if his own lawyer was still standing there. He was, though, and no trouble, as he was just closing the door. Mr. Loeblich's three-piece suit was a lighter color with thinner stripes, and his tie was gray-blue, not gray-green like Mr. Schuldig's. Another difference was that Petrona's lawyer wore no black gown over his suit, and as he shook hands with Mr. Schuldig he even asked him, pointing at the other young man's garb, "Are you due in court?"

"In half an hour," Kazmer's lawyer answered, glancing at his watch.

"Well, this shouldn't take long," replied Mr. Loeblich.

Petrona and Kazmer didn't know where to look while this was going on, but in a minute Mr. Schuldig introduced himself to her and got Kazmer to shake hands with Mr. Loeblich. Then Mr. Loeblich said to Mr. Schuldig, "By the way . . . " and they were off talking about something in a low voice, while Kazmer glanced at Petrona, who first averted her eyes, then half smiled at him, then only shrugged her shoulder. Kazmer nodded at that, for she was right, if they had anything to say to each other they should have said it a long time ago.

He couldn't help wondering, though, if a man or his wife ever tried to undo whatever it was that put them into this oak-paneled office. The two young lawyers seemed busy talking, and if Petrona would only slip her hand into his, maybe he could lead her out of this Supreme Court house before any-body noticed. Maybe the lawyers wouldn't even try to stop them, if they just walked away hand in hand. It was nobody's business but their own. And if it was a foolish thought, Kazmer tried it anyway; he put his hand on the table only inches away from Petrona's, because there was a time when it would have been enough. It was the warmth of his hand that guided her fingers, that's what she used to say, and she could feel it even when she wasn't looking.

"I know what it is, Mr. Harcsa," he remembered Petrona telling him once, "you've got a magnet up your sleeve. It makes my fingers skip to yours like sewing needles."

They couldn't have been married longer than six months the day she said this, because they were still living in Manhattan, back in that rented apartment on Second Avenue. Nor could he buy her all the fine things then that ought to make a woman proud of her man and show the world how much he cared for her. In those days they had none of the beautiful Corning kitchenware, the plates that wouldn't break even if you dropped them on the floor; and never mind a color TV, because they didn't even have the ordinary kind. Only a clock-radio, so Petrona could wake up to music in the morning, like the angels.

Yet it was back then that she'd dust the chair before she'd let him sit on it, that woman! She'd cling to him in the street, or sneak up from behind when he was coming home from work and put her hands over his eyes. "Guess who, Mr. Harcsa?" Kazmer's eyelids could still remember her touch; and for a sec-ond it seemed to him that Petrona's fingers remembered it, too, because her hand was sliding closer to his on the table. But then, as Mr. Loeblich happened to glance at them, Petrona's hand just reached into her bag for a paper tissue, and who could tell if that's what she had been reaching for all along? It was a foolish thought anyway. Kazmer stopped wondering about it, whatever it was, whether the magnet had gone from his sleeve or her hand had turned into a lump of clay.

He kept wondering, though, what the four of them were doing in this office. Perhaps they were just waiting for their turn to come up in court. Still, it was funny that they should all wait in the same room, not that Kazmer minded sitting across from Petrona—he didn't, not even after everything that had passed between them. She was still his children's mother and the bride he had promised to cherish. For he had made no such promise about anybody else, not even Uncle Harcsa or Aunt Rosie, not even Johnny and Borbala; and Katika, may she rest in peace, no husband had had time to make any promises about *her*. Perhaps it would have been better, she might have taken her promise to Kazmer more seriously than Petrona had, though who was to know? His vows in church had nothing to do with what Petrona was going to do about her own, anyway. That was something for Petrona's conscience, and if the Reverend Vegvari had read God's mind only half as well as he always said he did, it was nothing to envy Petrona about.

But perhaps his own conscience wasn't as clear as he would have liked to believe, Kazmer thought, so maybe he was sitting on his walnut chair feeling smug about nothing. Because wasn't it a husband's duty to protect his wife against evil influence, just as it was to protect her against cold or hunger? If a man was to look out for his children, guard them against bad friends, bad advice, or even against their own nature, was he not to do the same for his wife? Petrona always said that he was old-fashioned, that things were different nowadays; but if women were not frail vessels, why would the law require men to support and look after them, as the law did, all over the world? If Petrona had ordered a fur coat from one of her catalogs, they would have come after Kazmer to pay for it, perhaps even today, and it would have been no good for him to say that he had nothing to do with it. He was responsible, and if he was responsible for her fur coats, he could also be accountable for what she got out of the color TV, for which he had been making the monthly payments. For maybe he shouldn't have, not if it led to the destruction of her marriage and to their children's lives. And progress, it was easy to say progress, but when progress took the big harvester-combine up on the hillside in Bugyi, it was still Kazmer who had to nail together the white birch planks for Katika's coffin.

And thinking such thoughts put Kazmer in a different mood, nor did it help much that Mr. Schuldig was sharing a joke just then with that Mr. Loeblich, who probably invented all the lies for the Court about Kazmer being a cruel husband, because Petrona wouldn't have thought all that up on her own. It wasn't as though two such young men couldn't laugh at a shared joke together, it wasn't their own grief that they were taking before the judge. But would priests have giggled at a graveside even if it wasn't their funeral? If Mr. Schuldig had to put them together in this room to wait, he should have more sense than to be telling jokes to Petrona's lawyer.

But at that moment the hinges creaked, and from the way the two lawyers got up to say good morning to the short, white-haired man coming through the door, Kazmer understood that it was not for waiting that they had been all put together around the walnut table. For this white-haired man was a judge, even if he was not wearing any robes, and he was now going to hear what they had to say.

But again it was not as Kazmer expected, because Judge Winkler did not seem to be there to listen, only to talk. And even though he spoke very kindly, and slowly, too, so that Kazmer could understand every word, Kazmer felt ungrateful, he felt angry with himself for not liking this kind old man, who was only putting himself out for them when there was no call for him to go to all that trouble. Why couldn't Kazmer sit there the way Petrona did, nodding, listening, with that awestruck look as if she had been watching the color TV? All he could do was to keep his eyes on the walnut tabletop in front of him.

For Judge Winkler was explaining to them that this was a new thing, what they were doing here, this sitting around the table, which they were calling a pre-trial conference. It was, well, relatively *experimental*, he said. It was to make things more simple, so that people could understand what the law expected of them, and to put a human face, as he said with a little smile, upon the administration of justice. It was to make them feel less *nervous*, because surely (and here Petrona nodded her head up and down, like a little girl) they both must have felt nervous to begin with. And, said Judge Winkler raising his finger, so that they shouldn't feel like enemies, which is to say *adversaries* or *litigants* as it was called in law, but two mature adults who have come here to settle their differences. A lot of lawyers and judges decided to do things this way, he added, on account of this being progress.

There was no way Kazmer could have explained what made him feel so bad about all this, though perhaps it was when Judge Winkler said "new" first, and then when he said "progress." Because that word, even if he knew it was foolish, reminded him of the harvester-combine with its bubbly blue paint and blades of shiny metal underneath. Anyway, what was so new about bad wives, or bad husbands, if that was what Kazmer was supposed to be, that the old judge would want a new medicine for them? Men and women did nothing very new since the first five books of Moses.

But when Kazmer thought "Moses" he knew that he didn't mean it, not as the Holy Writ had it anyway, for he wasn't looking to Judge Winkler to stone Petrona for him, he would have been the first to stay his hand if he had tried. He was looking for justice, though, not for this talk about being a mature adult. For hadn't he earned his own bread since the age of sixteen? Had he not traveled halfway around the world, raising a good roof even in this strange land over the heads of a woman and two children? Kazmer knew he was a mature adult, he had never doubted it for thirty years or more, nor did the government doubt it when it was time to collect the taxes. As for settling his differences with Petrona—well, he had settled all that was up to him to settle a long time ago. No mature adult could have done more than to let her break up his life, and his children's, for no good reason, no reason at all, and without once raising a finger to stop her. No mature adult could have done more than to let her go, if that was what she wanted, and even let her take the children in the end, slipping them as much money as he could spare, while working the business and paying the mortgage for what was going to be their house and their business, anyway, after he was dead and buried. For who else would inherit it but the children?

But the way the old judge was talking, it was as if he was afraid that Kazmer didn't care for the children, or didn't know how to care for them. The judge seemed to think that, but for him, Kazmer and Petrona would be at each other's throats, with two cold and hungry children cowering in some dark corner. Well, maybe that's how it was with a lot of divorcing parents, and who could blame Judge Winkler for thinking so, but it wasn't that way with Kazmer and Petrona. The way it was with them—true, not without a lot of tears and heartache and harsh words, but in the end—they needed no one's help to pick up the pieces. Everybody had enough bread, milk and fresh vegetables, there was a roof over everybody's head, and Johnny was doing okay in school. The shop and the house, well, Kazmer could look after both on his own. If Petrona had to work herself, or if little Borbala would not speak for minutes, just look at Kazmer with big sad eyes whenever he came to pick her up, nobody could help that. Only time could, if there was enough of it. Yet there was this old judge talking about being mature adults, as if their lives hadn't been on the mend, as much as they could ever be mended, until the Supreme Court's letter! If there was trouble, it was the law that was stirring it up, and that was the truth.

But sometimes even the truth is better left unspoken, and Kazmer was careful not to say half of what was on his mind when Judge Winkler had finally finished. All he said, after respectfully clearing his throat, just as if he were talking to the preacher at the church door on Sunday, was:

"Thank you for nice sermon, Judge, but is no trouble for me. And Petrona, she pretty good with children, too."

But even that morsel of the truth might have been too much, for Mr. Schuldig jabbed Kazmer in the side, quite openly, and the old judge went red in the face, though he continued smiling. As for Mr. Loeblich, he looked very cheerful and said, as if making a joke, that he hoped that Kazmer's admission about Petrona being a good mother would be noted if custody became an issue, not that he imagined that it ever would. The way Mr. Loeblich said this put everybody in a good mood, even if a little at Kazmer's expense, and it prompted Judge Winkler to make some remark about brass tacks.

"Well, what *are* the issues, gentlemen?" he asked.

At this Kazmer's and Petrona's lawyers looked at each other, then Mr. Loeblich led off, saying that he might as well. Leaving aside the dissolution of the marriage for the moment, he said, the issues were straightforward, and he only wished that they were as simple and straightforward in every one of his cases. The only question in Mr. Loeblich's mind, as far as Kazmer understood it, was how much money Kazmer owed Petrona for having been Kazmer's wife. Because, as it was, she was not getting any benefit from the house she had left behind nor from the shop, yet she still had the expense of looking after herself and the children. If they could agree on how much money Kazmer owed her for the house, the shop, Johnny, Borbala and herself, they could all walk away from the judge's office, happy.

The way Mr. Loeblich said this made it sound so sensible that it invited people to nod their heads, and they did, both Petrona and Judge Winkler. Kazmer looked at his own lawyer, and saw that Mr. Schuldig was nodding, too. "More or less," he added, when he saw Kazmer looking at him.

"Well?" asked the judge.

Well, Mr. Schuldig said, it wasn't as if Kazmer had given Petrona no money for the children, because he gave for Borbala, and when Johnny decided to live with his mother again, Kazmer offered to slip the boy twenty dollars every week. He wanted to point this out, Mr. Schuldig said, to show that his client was in no way unmindful of his responsibilities. As for the house, they had bought it for $30,000 and Kazmer had offered Petrona $15,000 for her share of it, as his friend, meaning Mr. Loeblich, no doubt remembered. And if Mr. Loeblich and his client didn't think this was a fair offer, perhaps they could now tell the judge what they thought a fair offer would be.

At this Mr. Loeblich smiled and said that even though the case was simple, as he had said himself, maybe it wasn't as simple as *that*. The house would have to be evaluated, as even Mr. Schuldig and his client might have heard that houses were going up in value in Toronto. Then there was the shop that was acquired during the marriage, and the question of how Petrona was supposed to make a living herself, never mind the children. Mr. Schuldig cut in at this and said that they should talk about these things one by one, and Mr. Loeblich said no, before they could say anything about the house, which was the *matrimonial* home anyway, they would have to know what the package deal would be worth; and Mr. Schuldig said package deal, what package deal—which Kazmer wouldn't have minded knowing himself—and Mr. Loeblich replied that pretending that these issues were not joined would not make pre-trial negotiations any easier. And pretty soon both lawyers were raising their voices, Mr. Loeblich saying "package deal" and Mr. Schuldig retorting "no package deal," while Judge Winkler kept himself busy making notes in his calendar, and Kazmer and Petrona were glancing at each other, though only from the corners of their eyes. It was not until five minutes of this had gone by, or maybe more, that Kazmer spoke himself, and everyone fell silent at the sound of his voice.

"Is only question, my money?" asked Kazmer, turning to Judge Winkler. "My wife's lawyer, he wants to give away more my money; my own lawyer, he wants to give away less. But Mr. Judge, only question not my money. I say other good question, why cruel husband like this letter says? This pretty good question to me."

Nobody spoke after that for a while, though Mr. Schuldig put his hand on Kazmer's arm. He might have been right, too, for what Kazmer said did nothing except set Mr. Loeblich off on a long speech, after he recovered his voice. If His Honor permitted, Mr. Loeblich said, he would be glad to answer *that* question, once his friend chose to let his client ask it, which Mr. Loeblich thought Mr. Schuldig would have been better advised not to, but it was Mr. Schuldig's business; and for his part Mr. Loeblich was quite prepared to explain to Kazmer what the Supreme Court's letter meant. Or did perhaps Kazmer think that it was all right for a wife to be deprived of *cultural amenities*? To be restricted in her *legitimate social ambitions*? What about the mental and emotional anguish of a woman frustrated in her desire to upgrade her *skills*? And in case Kazmer could not understand what Mr. Loeblich was talking about because of the words he used, he'd be glad to use words Kazmer could understand. When he was talking about cruelty, said Mr. Loeblich, he was talking about a wife having to live with breast-feeding and blue trucks and blood pudding. He was talking about what Kazmer would do to her if she dared to go out of the house. A woman put down if she tried to improve her mind with magazines or television, that was what Mr. Loeblich was talking about.

And it was true, this young lawyer must have known about his life with Petrona, or at least some of it, but Kazmer could still not believe his ears. Could the way she felt about a truck or her television or the kind of things her husband liked to eat for his supper be more important to a woman than her family, and if they were, did that put him in the wrong? "Petrona, she wife," said Kazmer, astonished. "I'm husband. Is cruel to be husband to wife?"

Mr. Loeblich spread his arms wide. "I think Your Honor can appreciate our problem," he said.

Mr. Schuldig and Judge Winkler began talking almost together at this, the judge saying that they were not here to judge the merits of the case, that would be up to another judge and another court, they were just here to see if they could avoid going to that kind of court altogether, to see if maybe they could settle their differences like mature adults, in this new progressive way. And Mr. Schuldig said yes, that's why he wanted to go one by one, very maturely, first about the house, then the children, then Petrona's maintenance, instead of all this immature talk about trucks and blood pudding—which, incidentally, his client was not admitting in any case, of course.

But Kazmer could not leave it at that. "My lawyer, maybe he no admit blood pudding," he explained carefully. "Me, I admit blood pudding. I admit blue truck. Petrona, she leave maybe a year and a half ago, she no like blood pudding, she no like blue truck. She like Johnny Carson on TV. I no need kind of court tell me how much for house, how much for children. I need kind of court who tell me, after year and a half, why I cruel for blue truck?"

Mr. Loeblich smiled and said that this was very cute, but when he said "a blue truck" he was not talking about a blue truck, of course, only about a *symbol* for *conjugal affection*. In any case, said Mr. Loeblich, that was not the worst of it, he'd save the worst of it for that other kind of court they had all been trying to avoid, mainly to spare Kazmer the aggravation and money, if Kazmer would only let them. But if not, it was all the same for Mr. Loeblich, he didn't mind going to court, going to court was his business.

Judge Winkler said, well, yes, there was no point in trying to negotiate like mature adults if the parties were not ready for it, if there was bitterness, or their *egos* were more important to them than their children. It was sad, of course, but they would be perfectly free to fight it out to the end, Kazmer could contest the divorce, the charge of cruelty and the rest, it was his right, and certainly his money, though once a marriage was dead it was simpler and *much* more mature to just give it a decent burial, which Judge Winkler said he liked to tell every couple who appeared before him. But some listened and some didn't, added Judge Winkler, and it was up to Kazmer.

The meeting broke up after that, the judge saying that perhaps it would be useful if counsel, meaning the two young lawyers, would talk separately with their clients now, and if they needed him again he'd be available in his chambers. Mr. Loeblich got up and took Petrona away someplace, holding her by the arm so that she could not even glance at Kazmer from the doorway, though who could tell if she would have wanted to. Mr. Schuldig and Kazmer remained in the conference room, and for a while neither of them spoke. The young lawyer was angry at him, Kazmer could tell, but it was all right because he was not so happy with Mr. Schuldig either.

Then Mr. Schuldig turned to Kazmer and asked him if he thought it was smart to keep a dog and bark himself. It was a fine expression, which Kazmer had never heard before, and it raised Mr. Schuldig in his estimation, only why couldn't he come out with such good sayings while the judge was still in the room? And it was true, he should have kept his mouth shut and let his lawyer do the talking, that's what he was paying him for. But when a man's wife broke up his home and took away his children, was there nothing else to talk about but how much money she would get for it? "Why I pay you to ask Petrona how much I pay her?" asked Kazmer. "Cheaper I ask her myself."

But Mr. Schuldig had a perfect reply to that because, as he put it, if Petrona answered "the earth," would Kazmer prefer to pay the earth or have a lawyer handy to settle for maybe half of it? And, Mr. Schuldig continued, he was hoping that Kazmer had not been thinking that he would get away paying nothing, cruelty or no cruelty. It would be foolish to expect a judge to worry too much about whose *fault* it all was, especially if there were children involved, because it certainly wasn't *their* fault but they still had to eat and wear shoes and go to school. And anyway, said Mr. Schuldig, Kazmer was lucky that his case was coming up just then and not, say, in a year's time, because the law was soon to be changed for people like Kazmer to have much more to complain about. The law was to be changed so as to pay no attention to "fault" at all, or hardly any, for who could tell which side was at fault in a divorce, anyway? The courts would need magic to divine that. The future was no-fault divorce, that's what the future was, and judges liked bringing a taste of the future even into the present. It would be *need* that would matter in a divorce, said Mr. Schuldig, not that old-fashioned notion of fault, like children saying he-did-this-she-did-that; and if it was to be need, then Kazmer would get the worst of it whether he had been cruel or not, because he had the house and the business and all Petrona had were the children and the expense of bringing them up.

"Expense?" asked Kazmer. "I take children. Then no expense."

"Why, is your wife an unfit mother?"

"Petrona, she fit mother," said Kazmer. "Me, I fit father. Not so good to watch TV like she, but better to cook."

Well, maybe so, said Mr. Schuldig, now Kazmer was saying something progressive for a change, but perhaps it was a bit *too* progressive for the law. For the time being, mothers still had the inside track when it came to who was going to get the children. Unless they drank, which Mrs. Harcsa did not. Or did she? Because if she did they might get somewhere, al-though Mr. Schuldig would not suggest for the world that Kazmer should say that she did, unless it was true.

But if she didn't drink and she had the children, then the greater need was Petrona's, continued Mr. Schuldig. Petrona had no skill to earn as much money as Kazmer. What was she working at, a switchboard? Well, the courts might feel that Kazmer should support her until she could upgrade her skills, never mind whether she had a good reason to leave him or not. For instance, she might want to go to university.

Kazmer got red in the face at this.

"Sure, Petrona she want to go to university, make more money," he said. "I want to learn to fly big jet, make more money too. Why she no pay me to learn?"

"It's hardly the same thing, Kazmer. Be fair. She couldn't very well go to school while she was looking after your house. Or your children."

Kazmer took a big breath. "Now is *your* children?" he asked. "Law says is *her* children before, when she take them. Is *your* house? I offer her half in cash money. Mr. Loeblich, he says not good enough. *Your* house? Petrona wife, like any other. She no go to school to look after *her* house, *her* children, same as me."

Mr. Schuldig sighed at this, looked at his watch, and said that Kazmer wasn't paying him to argue with him but to have him argue with his wife's lawyer, which was true enough. Anyway, said Mr. Schuldig, a) right now he was late for another court, and b) he couldn't change the law for Kazmer, whether he thought the law was right or wrong. "Here's the bottom line, Kazmer," Mr. Schuldig said from the doorway, "you're gonna pay. Maybe your wife won't get her divorce if the judge decides you were not cruel, but he'll make you pay her anyway. She's a woman with children, she wants money, she'll get some. The only question is how much, and that's what we're trying to settle because it may be cheaper for you that way. Do you understand?"

And even if Mr. Schuldig had waited for an answer, which he did not, what could Kazmer have said in reply? He understood that Petrona wanted money—well, at least Mr. Loeblich did, that was for sure, for what would Petrona have used to pay him with if she didn't get any from Kazmer? But if she wanted it for herself—and for all that was wrong with her,

Petrona had never been like that, grasping or money-hungry—but if she wanted it now, could Mr. Schuldig understand that he wasn't upset over the money? For all he cared, she could have it all, she and the children; and it wasn't what Kazmer understood, but did Mr. Schuldig and Judge Winkler understand *that*? His lawyer and the kind old judge looking out for his wallet, maybe thinking that it was all that mattered to him, who knows, or maybe thinking that it was all that ought to matter. For didn't they say "mature adult" every time the talk was about how much for the house, how much for the children? Maybe in America "mature" meant only dollars and cents, that's what grown men talked about, all the other words had pimples on their faces.

It was then that Kazmer had a very good thought, because he knew a Mr. Marosvári who used to be a lawyer himself. True, that was back in Cluj between the two wars, and now he was mostly looking after a parking lot to help with his old-age pension. But that didn't matter, for over the years Kazmer had fixed up enough rickety armoires and escritoires for him to know that Mr. Marosvári would not refuse his help now that Kazmer needed a letter in perfect English. A letter, as he explained to Mr. Marosvári, that another lawyer could understand. It was a fine idea because Mr. Marosvári said, gladly, and that he'd do Kazmer proud.

> Highly respected Mr. Schuldig! [Mr. Marosvári's letter ran] knowing that you are much preoccupied, I seek your pardon for availing myself of opportunity to write you thus. Also, my lack of English mother-tongue forces me to turn to trusted friend for help in claiming your kind attention with this short epistle. He used to be Transylvanian lawyer.
>
> *Primo*, I have natural paternal affection toward my minor issues, Johnny and Borbala Harcsa, and bear no malice to my wedded spouse Mrs. Petrona Harcsa who ambulated

from my residence in March last. Contrariwise, I wish them safe and untrammeled existence.

Secundo, I am only insistent on cleaning my name from these unnatural and heinous accusations of spousal crueltion which have been laid on it.

Tertio, and most importantly, upon which I attach all respectful emphasis, I wish to prevent deprivation of Johnny and Borbala aforesaid from due patrimony, to wit, my house and work-shop, by forced squandering to satisfy illegitimate claims. I am man of few means. It took much labor for me to acquire one property, for my children to inherit, so they should not enter life like orphans. If spouse's claim too substantial to borrow, I have to sell house and my children grow up to nothing. It cannot be the honorable Court's desire to deprive children, for it repeatedly explicated that I should think of children like mature adult. I am thinking of children. If I could not explicate my position before, due to poor English, be pleased, much esteemed and learned Mr. Schuldig, to be instructed by it at this time.

Very respectfully yours, Kazmer Harcsa.

Composed at Mr. Harcsa's request by
Dr. Szilárd Marosvári
Doctor Juris, magna cum laude,
Universitatum Clujii, etc.

Kazmer felt much better after he mailed off his letter, because at least people might understand what was bothering him, apart from the pain in his heart, which was nobody's business. And yes, perhaps he was talking about dollars and cents after all, just like the judge and the lawyers, but was he talking about dollars and cents he wanted to save for himself? True, at forty-seven he was not ready to be buried yet. True, he liked living in his own house and let people who didn't, cast the first stone. Hell, he might even marry again and have another family of his own, back home it wasn't so rare for men to start families in their forties. But the house would still go to Johnny and Borbala because he *was* thinking of them, just as Judge Winkler wanted him to.

And soon it was April again, the second April since the one that saw Kazmer hiding at the crossing in front of the Catholic school, and this April was no less slushy or slick. But it was hard to tell if Mr. Schuldig received his letter or not, because he did not reply and he did not return the phone call Kazmer made to him either. By the end of the month, though, he called on his own, or least his secretary did, saying that Kazmer was to meet Mr. Schuldig in the courthouse Wednesday next, he could talk to him there.

And true enough, Mr. Schuldig was in the courthouse, but in no mood to talk with Kazmer about the letter. He only wanted to know if Kazmer had brought his checkbook, which his girl should have told him on the phone but forgot, and it was lucky that Kazmer had been to the bank that very morning so that he had the checkbook on him, and lucky, too, that he was wearing his Sunday suit. For it seemed that they were going into court right then and there to defend Kazmer against his wife's charges of cruelty—though first Mr. Schuldig wanted him to make out a check for $1,500, to cover the rest of his legal fees and *disbursements*, which Mr. Schuldig said his office should have asked Kazmer for a long time ago. All right, Kazmer made out the check in front of the courtroom door. It was not as if Mr. Schuldig hadn't warned him before that the first thousand dollars would only be a down payment. Even Mr. Perkins had said, your divorce will be three, four thousand dollars, Kazmer, and not a penny less, I'm telling you now. But Kazmer still felt a little ashamed for Mr. Schuldig, an educated man like this holding out his hand for money in the hallway, and he felt ashamed for himself, too. Yet was it any wonder? Why shouldn't he seem to Mr. Schuldig the kind of man who might not pay for the wine after he had emptied the cup, when his own wife, who ought to know him best, was taking him to strangers for judgment?

This time it was a real courtroom, with blond teak benches and teakwood paneling, and they used teak even for the plinth in front of the judge's dais. It made sense to Kazmer, walnut would have cost the earth for such a big place. There were strangers sitting there, maybe a dozen men and women and a whole row of lawyers, but Kazmer knew it was a public court and, hell, he would not have to lay eyes on any of these people ever again. If in a big city like Toronto a man had no neighbors to lend him a helping hand, at least there were no neighbors before whom he would have to hang his head in shame. Another good surprise was that the judge was a lady, Madame Justice Abigail Fitzsimons, and she looked every bit as gracious and dignified as the old Count's sister back in Bugyi, though perhaps a little younger. Kazmer was happy to see her, it was another thing they were smart about in America. Back home, people said that a man saw no deeper into a woman than her skin, but another woman could see right through her, but they still wouldn't be smart enough to make a woman a judge.

But even though Kazmer liked Judge Fitzsimons, they started out on the wrong foot. It came about, and it was just a stupid thing, when it was his turn to take the witness stand, and Mr. Schuldig asked him to tell the court where he was born and Kazmer answered: "Bugyi, Transylvania."

"Transylvania, and where is that?" asked Mr. Schuldig absentmindedly, his eyes scanning a piece of paper in his hand for more important questions.

"Transylvania?" said Kazmer, surprised. "Is in Transylvania."

"Yes, and which country?" said Mr. Schuldig, still looking at his piece of paper.

"Is now belong to Rumania," replied Kazmer, truthfully.

"All right, Mr. Harcsa, so you are a Rumanian-Canadian, and now can you tell the Court when . . . "

"I'm Transylvanian-Canadian," said Kazmer.

Mr. Schuldig looked up from his paper.

"Sorry, what?"

"Not Rumanian," explained Kazmer. "Me, I'm Canadian citizen from Hungarian-language Transylvania."

"Well, just for the record," said Judge Fitzsimons, "since your country is called Rumania, I'm sure you don't mind if we call you a Rumanian-Canadian, do you?"

A titter ran through the courtroom and Kazmer got red in the face.

"Supreme Court call me Rumanian now," he replied, turning to Judge Fitzsimons, "is same as Supreme Court call me cruel husband before. I don't mind, only is not true. For record."

The laughter in the courtroom was now on Kazmer's side, but it may not have been worth it, for Madame Justice Fitzsimons sniffed, and tossed her head a little, and even arched her eyebrows. "Well, just proceed, whatever you are," she said. And hadn't Uncle Harcsa cautioned Kazmer when he was still wearing short pants that a good word spoken was silver, but unspoken it was gold? A big pinch of salt it mattered what they called him here, a million miles from home!

It was a pity, too, because up till then things hadn't been too bad, that young lawyer Mr. Loeblich never got very far with Petrona, trying as he might to make her tell all kinds of lies about Kazmer. But she didn't, not really; everybody in the courtroom could see that she was on the side of her wedded husband and loath to throw dirt at him even now, no matter how hard her lawyer pushed her. She even admitted, when it was Mr. Schuldig's turn to question her, that Kazmer was a steady man, no drinker and a good provider, too. She never had any complaints against him on that score, and if he had his set ways about men being men and women, women, he probably didn't mean it to be cruel, he wasn't doing what he did to drive Petrona to an early grave, even if she had one foot in it by the time she decided to take the children and walk out of the door.

Kazmer couldn't understand why Mr. Schuldig was sucking his teeth so unhappily during the break, which they called a *recess*, after which it would be his turn to take the Bible in his hand. It wasn't as if Petrona hadn't done him credit, as much as any wife could in a divorce court, even by the nice way she dressed up, just like earlier in Judge Winkler's office, none of that tight sweater stuff and no blue paint over her eyes. But Mr. Schuldig said, that's just it, Garry Loeblich was very clever about the *image* he got her to project, right down to making her admit Kazmer's good points and that he didn't mean to be cruel to her. Garry took a *calculated risk*, Mr. Schuldig said, he made Petrona *credible*, a shy, devoted wife and mother, with not a bad thing to say about her brutal husband, not even when Garry was begging her in court. Let Kazmer prove *himself* to be a monster on the witness stand, that was Garry's plan, and Mr. Schuldig said he hoped at least that Kazmer wouldn't fall into that trap.

And wasn't he off to a good start with this stupid business about not being a Rumanian, when there was no call for it, and why should these people at the far end of the world know any better? So Kazmer pulled himself together, and he got through the rest of Mr. Schuldig's questions with no trouble, just answering "yes" and "no" to most of them. All Mr. Schuldig took was about half an hour anyway, maybe even less, and when he said, I have no more questions, Kazmer was so relieved he started getting out of the witness box right away, and stopped only when he heard Mr. Loeblich say, "Well, I have a few questions now, Mr. Harcsa, if you don't mind."

And what came after that was an ordeal lasting the rest of the afternoon and part of the following morning, too; an ordeal such as Kazmer would never forget, not if he lived to be a hundred, even though when he tried to recall it afterward, it would come back to him only in pitiful little snatches. One long sleepless night would bring back one part of it, and another, another. For example, when Mr. Loeblich asked him:

"And did you have a normal, affectionate relationship, as between man and wife?"

Kazmer shrugged, "Was normal, yes," he said.

"Did you make love to her?"

Kazmer looked at Judge Fitzsimons first, then at Mr. Schuldig, but he seemed to be on his own. "Two children born to her, Mr. Lawyer," he replied finally, "and Petrona, she not like St. Mary."

"Oh, you made love to her twice, then, is that it? In ten years?"

"Many more than twice," said Kazmer, turning red.

"How many, three times, four times? Once every year?"

"You make love your wife in this country, you count? We no count."

"Oh, I don't want to tax your memory, Mr. Harcsa," said Mr. Loeblich, "or your ability to count. Just tell the court roughly, once a week, once a month, once every six months?"

"You her lawyer, you ask my wife."

"Answer the question, please," said Judge Fitzsimons.

"We did ask your wife, Mr. Harcsa," said Mr. Loeblich, "and she answered. Right in this courtroom, or don't you remember that either? Would you like the court reporter to read her reply back to you? She said you refused conjugal relationship with her. Is that true?"

"I no understand 'conjugal.'"

"Try sex. How often did you have sex with your wife?"

Kazmer had had enough. "Enough of this dirty talk for me," he said, feeling his own voice drop and tighten. "You like dirty talk, you go watch Johnny Carson on TV."

At this Mr. Schuldig rose, asking, "Is this really relevant?" but Mr. Loeblich said that if, in his friend's view, sex wasn't relevant to marriage, his friend might have the same problem as his client, and even Judge Fitzsimons smiled before telling Kazmer again to answer the question.

"I withdraw the question," said Mr. Loeblich. "If talking

about sex makes you feel uncomfortable, I'll ask you something you may feel more comfortable about. Did you ever hit your wife?"

"Once I hit her, yes," said Kazmer.

"I see. Where? In the body, in the face?"

"I hit her in face."

"You hit your wife in the face, I see. How hard? Did she faint?"

"She faint a little, not much," said Kazmer.

"You hit your wife in the face so that she fainted. Okay. Now what was she doing to you when you hit her? Was she . . . oh, I don't know, was she demanding money from you?"

"No."

"Was she asking for new clothes, jewelry, holidays?"

"She no ask for nothing."

"Well, she must have done something for you to hit her in the face hard enough to make her faint. Did she want to go out with another man?"

"No, and please don't say no such thing," said Kazmer angrily.

"All right, Mr. Harcsa, you tell the Court, then. Why did you hit her?"

Kazmer was silent for a while. "Petrona, she wanted. . ." he said finally, "she told me . . . she . . . Oh, to hell what she said, I'm not saying."

"She wanted you to make love to her," said Mr. Loeblich. "I put it to you that that was what she wanted, before you hit her in the face. Well, isn't that the truth, Mr. Harcsa?"

This was bad, and even if Kazmer might have made it better for himself by telling the *whole* truth, he just couldn't. What kind of a man would it take to talk about such things? Tell a bunch of gaping women in court how his wife wanted to have her cunt licked, was that what the law was asking a husband to do? And the way things got twisted around it might not have helped even if he had told, for he did tell about the children, but it sounded bad even to himself by the time Mr. Loeblich got through with him.

"You took the children to your house and wouldn't give them back to her, isn't that true?"

"No true. I take children to her rooming house, but man says she out shopping."

"Well, was it part of your agreement that she had to be there in person, every time you brought the children back?"

"No agreement, but what I do, let children stay with strange man, when she shop on Sunday?"

"Well, how long was she away, a month, a week?"

"No, she come back same evening, she come for children."

"I see," said Mr. Loeblich. "She was late, then, isn't that the fact, she was a little late, maybe the subway broke down, you didn't know, but you decided to take the children away from her. Isn't that the truth?"

"I give little girl back to her, when she come next day."

"Well, that's generous. What about the little boy? Did you give him back to your wife, too?"

"No. He say he stay with me."

"I'm suggesting that you held the boy forcibly, held him by the hand, so that your wife couldn't take him. Isn't that a fact?"

"No force," said Kazmer. "Petrona, she pull, I hold. No force."

"I see, first you snatch him, then hold him, but no force. Very well, Mr. Harcsa, and what happened next?"

"What you mean, what happen?" Kazmer asked. "Johnny, he stay with me. Borbala, she go with Petrona. Nothing happen."

"You mean your wife gave up, she never tried to get the boy back?"

"Well, once, maybe twice, she try," said Kazmer. "She hang around school, like, where Johnny is, try to talk to him. I tell teacher, you no let her, she come, you call me."

"In fact, you had her barred from the school grounds, isn't that true? You *threatened* the principal, didn't you?"

"I say to Mr. Teacher, you call me, no trouble; you no call me, trouble. I never make no threat. Petrona, she come once, twice, she go, nothing never happen."

"Nothing ever happened?" asked Mr. Loeblich. "You mean your son is still living with you?"

Kazmer got angry at this again, though he should have known better.

"Why you ask when you know is not true. Johnny, he no live with me."

"Oh, then something did happen. Isn't it a fact that your son had to get his mother's phone number from a teacher?"

"Yes."

"And when he did get it, isn't it a fact that he called his mother to come and take him from your shop?"

"Yes, Johnny phone her."

"And did she in fact come and take him back to live with her, at your son's request?"

"She come."

"Why would your son ask her to do that, Mr. Harcsa?"

"Johnny, he little boy, he no like violin lessons."

"Go on."

"Well, he make faces, you know, he talk back to me."

"Yes, and?"

"And I lose temper a little, I go to him like this, next day he pack suitcase, he call mother."

"Go to him like *this*?" asked Mr. Loeblich. "You mean you threatened to hit your son? Is that what you mean, Mr. Harcsa?"

"Slap him like bad boy, yes."

"Thank you, Mr. Harcsa," said Mr. Loeblich. "I wonder if this is a convenient time for a brief recess?"

And so it went, for a whole afternoon and the next morning, Mr. Loeblich cutting him up about the things he did while he was living with Petrona and the things he did after she left him, always calling for a break just when Kazmer said something bad, to let it sink in with the judge, as Mr. Schuldig explained. And mostly he threw his knives at Kazmer in a polite tone of voice so that Kazmer could not even hear them coming, though to the end he tried to catch a few and throw them back at Mr. Loeblich, not that it was much use. If only the knives had been made of steel, not words, maybe it wouldn't have gone so well for Petrona's lawyer, never mind if he had an exercycle in his basement or that he was ten years younger. Nor was Mr. Loeblich always polite, sometimes he'd yell, he'd throw a hammer at Kazmer instead of a knife, just to keep him off balance. "You snooped. You snooped and you threatened! Didn't you stand behind the curtain to see who'd be driving your wife home from her seminar? Behind the *curtain*! Didn't you make a scene when she got a lift with her instructor? Just answer, yes or no!"

And the question had to be answered yes or no, that's what Judge Fitzsimons said, even if Mr. Schuldig told Mr. Loeblich to stop *badgering* the witness, and Mr. Loeblich said, all right, I'm sorry. But did he make a scene or did he not? Because if he did, he humiliated his wife, and that's cruel, and that's what we are here to find out.

But what was a husband to do in this new country if it was cruel to remind his wife that she was a married woman? If it was cruel to ask her not to sit in other men's cars? A husband would have to die right after the nuptials and the first payment for the life insurance, or else he might turn off the light in the bedroom, buy a blue truck, demand blood pudding for his supper or even beget his wife a son to suckle. Petrona didn't like his ways, fine, Kazmer wasn't asking the law to force them on her, but could he have called her cruel for not liking her ways any better? Because he never did, not the color TV, not the blue paint, not the tight sweaters, but would the law let him walk out of the door for that with the children? And if he walked out anyway, would the law let him sue Petrona for money?

Kazmer made up his mind to say as much of this as he could, because it needed saying, and he grasped the rail of the witness box tightly when Mr. Loeblich finally told Judge Fitzsimons that he had no more questions. "All right, you may step down," the judge nodded at Kazmer, but Kazmer didn't move. "Please Miss Judge," he said, "I tell the truth to lawyers, but not *whole* truth, because they never ask. I took Bible oath to tell whole truth. Now you let me tell with no more questions from lawyers, please." But Judge Fitzsimons refused, saying he couldn't talk, unless his own lawyer wanted to *re-examine* him, but Mr. Schuldig shook his head, no. It was in Kazmer's best interest, the lawyer explained to him afterward, because he may be a good man, no one said he wasn't, but he was a *terrible* witness.

And that was all, there was nothing more to do but walk down the three small marble steps of the Supreme Court and go home, whether it was worth $2,500 or not, because Judge Fitzsimons said at the end she'd *reserve* her judgment. Mr. Schuldig said, well, it was a good sign, he didn't mind; but Mr. Loeblich only shook his head and smiled, then Kazmer heard him say to Mr. Schuldig that this was good old Abigail for you, she could never make up her mind about anything. He wasn't far wrong, either, for Kazmer heard not a word from the Supreme Court of Ontario for nearly one more year.

It was all right, though, if they weren't anxious to talk to him, he wasn't anxious to talk to them, and that was the truth. It was no pain, spending his spare time and his spare money on Johnny and Borbala instead of the lawyers. It wasn't a bad year, in many ways it was perhaps the best since Petrona left, even if the customers weren't breaking down his door at the shop, because picking up the children on Sundays was no trouble, she even let him have them for two whole weeks that summer, that was when he took them to Disneyland. Besides, the hurt itself was passing. The only thing that would keep him awake at night would be the thought of Mr. Loeblich going at him in that courtroom, not the black eyes of Petrona. She would come into his mind—well, Kazmer couldn't say never, because her picture still stood on the mantelpiece, he couldn't just put it face down in a drawer, even though he tried—but she'd come into his mind less and less. Days could pass without his thinking of her once, unless his glance fell on the picture, it even worried him at first. Was that all there was to it, and she the person he had promised to cherish! If that was all, maybe Petrona was right to walk out of the door with so little fuss. A marriage was for fun, like anything else men and women did together in America, and when it was no more fun, it was no more worth the bother. The world was full of other men and women.

But other women, Kazmer wasn't ready for them, not yet, whatever Petrona might be doing with other men, which was a thought Kazmer took care to put out of his mind. Not that he'd never feel the urge in his body, it was natural, but all he ever did about it was to pay thirty dollars to a fat lady downtown, who was nice enough, and then thirty more to a black girl, six months later, who had a condom taped to the back of her head under her hair. Well, that put no stars in Kazmer's eyes. All the same, he lay beside her on the top of the bedspread for a while, who could say why, maybe not to hurt her feelings or not to let the thirty dollars go to waste. Maybe he just wanted to hold somebody, whore or no whore, it was nothing to be ashamed of. Except he *was* ashamed, and when the mail happened to bring Madame Justice Fitzsimons's judgment on him a couple of mornings later, it crossed Kazmer's mind that he was getting back his just due from Petrona for the black girl.

And he was getting it back with interest, Kazmer could see that right off, if only from the way the lady judge was sticking to her guns, calling him "a former national of Rumania" in the very first line. As for the rest of her judgment, well, Kazmer understood enough of it by the third reading to know that she had found for Petrona. Or maybe only for Mr. Loeblich, because (as Mr. Schuldig explained to him a week later) Petrona didn't come off so well in the judgment either, but Mr. Loeblich got everything he asked for. The saying back home about a woman seeing through another woman seemed halfway right;

the lady judge wrote that some of Petrona's complaints about her husband were "close to being frivolous," but that there was still "sufficient evidence" to call Kazmer a cruel man, officially this time, under the great seal of Her Majesty the Queen. And that he would have to pay her money, $400 every month for herself and the children, which Mr. Schuldig said was pretty reasonable, and then pay the costs for the Court and for Mr. Loeblich. (Well, maybe another three, four thousand, Mr. Schuldig said, Kazmer was not to worry, he'd talk to Garry about that.) As for his house, that was *matrimonial property*, and Madame Justice Fitzsimons was ordering it to be sold. Kazmer was to get rid of it for whatever it would fetch, the house he was saving for Johnny and Borbala, then give half of the money to Petrona. He could go on seeing the children though, Judge Fitzsimons was not denying him *access*; Mr. Schuldig said that she at least wasn't buying Garry's argument about that *incident* with Johnny's violin lessons. And this was good news, to be sure, except Kazmer hadn't realized until this moment that Mr. Loeblich had even asked the Court to stop him from seeing his children.

And that was a moment Kazmer could still remember, because he happened to be looking out of the window in Mr. Schuldig's twenty-ninth-floor office, the whole of Yonge Street stretching north, a beautiful snowy, sunny day. Mr. Schuldig's voice seemed to come at him from a great distance, though he could hear what he was saying, that Kazmer might appeal the judgment but perhaps it wasn't so smart to fight Petrona through the courts, she'd probably qualify for *legal aid* and fight him for nothing, while as an independent businessman Kazmer would have to pay for every step of the way. His advice, Mr. Schuldig said, was to think of this judgment as a victory, hell, it wasn't the end of the world. Kazmer could settle with the Court and Mr. Loeblich for his share of the house, even have money left over, have peace in his time, it wasn't such a high price for peace.

But hearing Mr. Schuldig was one thing, taking him in was another. Suddenly it seemed to Kazmer that he was fighting with a bunch of shadows saying "decree nisi" and "final decree," playing some kind of crazy, wicked game with letters and long words, like television, except that he was playing with his real life. He paid them real money for the game, gave them up his real wife, and now they were threatening his real house and real children. He must have been crazy himself to do it, but thank God he was coming to his senses. To give up his children's house, real brick, wood and mortar, paid for by the real work of his own hands, for what, a black-robed lady's crazy piece of paper? They were all people from the color TV come to life, these lawyers, judges, this young man from the women's lecture, and he, stupid, stupid, taking them seriously, oh Petrona! Instead of just reaching out with his hand and switching them off.

Then the moment passed, and he knew again that his enemies were real, as real as he himself, as real as Mr. Schuldig waiting for his reply, but the resolution stayed. Kazmer got up, shook his head, and said, "Thank you, but no house. I still owe you money, you send me bill, I pay. Goodbye." Then he walked along the hard-twist broadloom, past the typing secretaries with wires coming out of their ears, and pressed the button for the elevator.

After that everything was quiet for a time. Kazmer was picking up the children as before, saying nothing to Petrona and she nothing to him, with just a nod passing between them every Sunday, and the money, whatever he could afford. Court orders, never mind, it was still a man's family, a father knew who needed what, who deserved what, better than those color TV people. In the shop the bell was still ringing above the door, pine chairs and cabinets, wood shavings sizzling under his hand, and on Saturdays a bottle of red wine to go with his bacon and bread. To hell with lawyers and judges, he was still running his own life. Perhaps the shadows saw that he was not joking, they could get nothing more from him, they crawled back into the TV picture, the bald, blinking men and silver-earring women who took his wife and came after his children. But wasn't Johnny still standing in the driveway, washing and polishing the blue truck until only a single drop of water would sit on the hood, fat and sparkling? Just like his father, for however hard you shake a tree, the apple never falls too far from it.

And maybe it shouldn't have been, but it was a surprise when the letter came, just when Kazmer thought the shadows had given up on him, only this time it came from a shadow called the *Master*. He turned out to be some kind of a judge, too, the Master, only he was older and as deaf as a bellringer's ass. He couldn't understand a word of what Kazmer was saying the day he went to see him in the Supreme Court Master's office, whatever that place was supposed to be. Kazmer went alone, foolish or not, he needed no more $1,000 bills from Mr. Schuldig. Nor did he care by then if the Master could hear him or not, though Mr. Loeblich cared: the Master couldn't hear him much better than he could hear Kazmer, and he seemed to think that Mr. Loeblich was Kazmer's lawyer. The Master kept yelling at Mr. Loeblich not to start speaking until the other party's lawyer showed up, while Mr. Loeblich yelled back that *he* was the other party. Then the old judge, and he was an ill-tempered bastard, vented his anger on Kazmer, as though it was Kazmer's fault that the frosts of time had hardened the wax in his ears.

"You'd better pay your wife, Mister! You'd better sell your house or we'll sell it for you! You think a court order is some kind of a joke? You think you can just ignore it?"

But ignoring was easy, even a stone could do it, and if the Supreme Court had always been too deaf to hear Kazmer's voice, why should his ears be any better? Shouting at a man was not the best way to get his attention, not around the river Olt and Murder Lake, anyway, and Kazmer just looked out of the window when Mr. Loeblich decided to do a bit of yelling of his own. But the Master didn't like that, he turned on Mr. Loeblich, saying there was no need to yell, nobody was hard-of-hearing in that office. And Mr. Loeblich shouted his apologies at the top of his lungs, which the old judge couldn't understand, and the two were still hollering at each other when Kazmer stood up and walked out of the door.

But if the law had been asleep until then, slamming that door woke it up in a hurry, and Kazmer didn't have to wait another year for its next letter. In less than three weeks' time, as he was coming home from the shop one night, there it was, a note on the front door of his house. It was as fine a note as Kazmer had ever seen, straight from the Sheriff's office, and it was an *order*, that's what the big black letters said it was, for Kazmer not to go inside. He didn't know what to make of it at first, if it was some kind of a joke, an order not to go inside his own house, only it didn't look too funny. Then it sent the blood pounding from his heart, and not because of fear. Sheriffs, hell, you couldn't keep a groundhog from its hole, not without a big bucket of water, and maybe a whole truckload of sheriffs might keep him from crossing his own threshold or using the furniture he had made with his own hands. Kazmer didn't mind keeping a carpenter's awl next to his bed for a while, and let the sheriffs come if they needed a third hole in their noses.

But even the sheriffs were smarter than that, they must have been watching him coming and going, ignoring the order they pasted on his door, because about two weeks later as Kazmer was putting his key in the lock late at night it wouldn't go in, whichever way he tried. He ran for the flashlight in the truck, he never knew he could run so fast, made it from the porch to the driveway and back in less than two seconds. Sure enough, the lock had been changed on his door. Kazmer could even see how they had scratched the panels changing it. And robbing him of his property was one thing, but that they were clumsy and had no respect. Scratching his children's house like that, the law! Judge Winkler giving him a sermon about how to put his children first, as if Kazmer had ever damaged anything that belonged to Johnny and Borbala!

And it would have been easy to put his shoulder to the door, and it would have suited his temper, too, but it was still his house, and why break a doorpost when in a few seconds he could take it gently off the hinges. And inside there was another order from the Sheriff's office, which Kazmer shouldn't have been reading at all if he wanted to obey it, saying as it did that Kazmer shouldn't be inside the house. But he was, all the same, and it was the Sheriff's order that went outside into the garbage can. He had to fish it out again, though, for the address, because this time he was sending the Sheriff a note, by registered letter.

> Dear Mr. Sheriff!
> The judge, she no let me talk, my lawyer, he no read my letter just take my money, you now terror me and my children, if this law to call me cruel is not better than bandit.
>
> Kazmer Harcsa

Kazmer couldn't have said exactly what he thought his letter would do, had anyone asked him. Not that anybody did, for he wasn't talking to people about his troubles. But maybe it would make them think a little, a note like this, it would show that he wasn't just disobeying the law out of meanness. The note would tell them that Kazmer had some right on his side, at least he thought he did, and he was fighting back, not just running away. Nor was he wrong, because in about a week a politely worded letter came back, asking Kazmer to come to court again. Come to court, the letter said, so that they might talk this matter of the house over with him. No threats in this letter, nothing like get out or else, and perhaps they were going to listen to Kazmer after all.

Judge Winkler, Kazmer thought, perhaps he'd ask for Judge Winkler again, the first you see is often the best, that's how the saying had it. Judge Winkler might see that Kazmer couldn't squander away his children's real estate, it wasn't what a mature adult would do. As for explaining it in perfect English, that was no problem, because Mr. Marosvári would do that for him. Mr. Marosvári couldn't *act* for Kazmer, not in this country, but he said he could translate for him, there was nothing wrong with that, nor would he charge any money for it. And on Wednesday at nine, just as the letter said, Kazmer and Mr. Marosvári walked up the steps of the Supreme Court.

But at one p.m., four hours later, the judge was still too busy to see them, and when he was ready it was Mr. Loeblich who had to make a quick appearance in another court, only there was nothing quick about it. At two-thirty Mr. Marosvári said, "Sorry Harcsa, but I've got to go, I'm all alone in the parking lot today." Maybe it was just a little thing, waiting there in court, and even losing Mr. Marosvári wasn't much compared to all the rest, but it's often a little thing that makes a man brim over, and that's what happened when Kazmer slapped the letter on a secretary's desk and walked out of the courthouse.

He had already reached the street when Mr. Loeblich caught up with him, perhaps somebody sent word to him that Kazmer was walking out. Mr. Loeblich was furious, he said in a loud voice that Kazmer had better come back to court, and he even put his hand on Kazmer's arm. Kazmer just stood there looking into his eyes for a second before Mr. Loeblich remembered himself and slowly removed his hand. It was bad, but in the end all Kazmer said was: "First judge busy, then you busy, now I'm busy." It was true, because at three o'clock there were two customers coming to the shop, and as for Mr. Marosvári, by that time he had got onto a streetcar anyway.

The next day, just as Kazmer opened the shop in the morning, two policemen walked in to ask him if his name was Harcsa.

"Is my name, yeah."

"Don't you know you're supposed to be in court?"

"Who pay me for yesterday court when I lose time?"

The policemen looked at each other, then one of them said, "Well, is it going to be the easy way or the hard way? Because it makes no difference to us."

Kazmer went with them, what else could he do, he didn't even have the awl handy. They put him in the back of a police car, and when they walked into the courtroom one of the policemen said, "Here's the prisoner Harcsa," which was another lie, the police didn't have to capture him, he went with them willingly enough. But one more lie or less, what did it matter?

It was the lady judge sitting on the bench, and in a minute Mr. Loeblich came in with Mr. Schuldig, maybe the both of them were working against him now, Kazmer would not have been surprised. But what Mr. Schuldig said was, and he came over to say it to Kazmer in a low voice, that Mr. Loeblich had just telephoned him, because Mr. Loeblich wanted to put Kazmer in jail but he did not want him to be *unrepresented*. In jail, in jail for what, for sleeping in his own house? It sounded like lawyer talk to scare him out of some more money, and Kazmer said, "I'm not paying you nothing," but Mr. Schuldig replied that there was no charge for this. "Just promise you'll sell the house, the way the judge ordered it," Mr. Schuldig whispered, "and you'll walk out of here a free man."

Kazmer almost said yes. He'd sell his children's house, perhaps he could get a good price, pay off everyone, why spend a lifetime fighting? It wasn't as if he were an old man, he could work, if it took ten years to buy this house, another ten years wasn't the world either. He almost said yes, but it was Mr. Loeblich's turn to speak first.

"Is he going to vacate immediately, right this minute?" asked Petrona's lawyer. "Is he going to move out of that house this afternoon?"

And where would he move, and put his furniture, and where would he get more money for an apartment, what with the bank loan, the rent for the shop, the insurance? And would Mr. Loeblich get the house, maybe, for what they were supposed to owe him? So Kazmer shook his head, no, and said, "I no move nowhere, never," even though Mr. Schuldig was still whispering in his ear.

"Well, I'll give you five days to think it over," said Madame Justice Fitzsimons. It was only when she added, in the direction of Mr. Schuldig, "Since he's not giving me any choice," that Kazmer understood that she meant five days in jail. And that was that, except for the long ride down the elevator between the two policemen.

"What are you, rape, murder?" asked the sergeant in the courthouse jail where the policemen took him down into the basement. And Kazmer remembered something Mr. Schuldig had said, and replied, "No-fault divorce," but he must have remembered it wrong because all three policemen laughed.

NEVER TAKE MORE
THAN FIFTY PERCENT
FROM THE HUSBAND

NOT THAT ANYONE could tell by looking at him, but Kazmer
was worried because of the stories he had heard about jail from
the men who'd been there, back home, or from Uncle Harcsa
about the French stockades in Algiers, enough to curdle your
blood. Well, jail in Toronto was nothing like that, the wardens
shoved you around a little but used no boots or sticks, not unless you shoved them back, which Kazmer didn't. There were
plastic trays of warm food three times a day, as good as the cafe-
teria in the furniture factory, and Kazmer couldn't eat much of
that muck, either. The five days wasn't even five the way they
figured it; only three and a half. By Saturday night they said,
"Off you go, Charlie," and Kazmer was back in the street.

The surprise of it was that he would have been just as happy if
they had kept him in until Monday, maybe even happier. Perhaps

then a thought might have come to him about what to do with his life. Because where was he to go from here? Saturday night, a man of forty-eight, closer to forty-nine, with twenty dollars and a subway token in his pocket. It was not as if he still had a house to go to. His house, the house he had built for his family, well, Kazmer didn't even know who his house belonged to now. Perhaps it belonged to the Supreme Court of Ontario.

And what about his clothes, his furniture, his shaving things, who had the ownership of those? If they were still his—the lawyers had said nothing about them—how was he to get them out of the house? A padlock, that's what the Sheriff put on it this time, Kazmer could see it plainly after he took a bus to the shop and picked up his truck. He drove the truck past the house, as he dared not turn into his own driveway. He knew the padlock would come off in a minute, he had the tools right there in the truck, but the furniture wouldn't fit into the shop anyway, not even half of it, and he'd only ruin it if he tried. Besides, the lawyers would send him back to jail. True, he would just as soon have stayed there another night or two, it was as good a place as any to catch his breath, but being sent back to jail could break a man's heart. Unless he was born to it, and Kazmer wasn't.

People who were born to jail—well, they were *freer*. They were, and never mind that they spent half their lives behind bars, most of them. They didn't suffer, the three or four such souls Kazmer had seen there, even if they bitched louder than all the others. They bitched, but it didn't break *their* hearts. For what is wrong with jail, unless they beat or starve you? Four walls and a window—hell, half of life is four walls and a window. A factory is, and so is an office, maybe even a home. And what is wrong with four walls and a window if you belong there, if you share it with your own kind?

And if it is jail that you belong to, if it is no shame, if that is where your friends are, you are free. You care about nothing, and they can take nothing from you, that's the deal. There was a one-eyed Hungarian in the other cell they called Hollo, he showed Kazmer what was what in jail, and all the while Kazmer was thinking, what could a lady judge threaten this Hollo with, unless it was to put out his other eye, which even the Supreme Court couldn't order. Well, in some places maybe, but not in Toronto.

But no one could help being what he was, himself no more than a one-eyed jailbird, if the Reverend Vegvari had been right about the way God worked things with predestination. Maybe even Mr. Loeblich couldn't help being a lawyer if it was ordained. Nor was there any profit in wondering what he'd do if he were somebody he wasn't. Kazmer knew anyway what he'd do if he were a jailbird. Burn his own house to the ground with all the sheriffs in it. That's what.

But since Kazmer was not born to jail he burned down nothing, and spent Sunday building himself a sleeping nook in the back of his shop instead. He knew there'd be enough space if he used part of the washroom, it was even cozy. He built a few shelves, too, that was no trouble, and as for cooking, there had always been a hotplate for warming up his lunch. It would just have to do for now, he had no pots or pans or cutlery anyway, they were all back at the house. Fixing up that small table and a couple of rickety old chairs he had in the shed was easy, then just a few pegs in the beam for his clothes, and Monday he could buy a curtain to close his nook off from the main shop. There, there was nothing wrong with that.

He had hardly finished putting up the blue curtain the next day when the phone rang. It was Mr. Loeblich himself on the telephone, and Kazmer could hardly believe his ears when he heard the lawyer's voice.

"Yes, this is Mr. Loeblich speaking," he said. "I want you to know, in case you're thinking of breaking into that house again, you can save yourself the trouble."

"Me, I never . . ." Kazmer started, but the other interrupted him.

"Come on, Mr. Harcsa, who are you kidding? You think the neighbors didn't see you snooping around in that blue truck Saturday night? But never mind that," the lawyer continued, "I'm just trying to do you a favor. You don't want to go back to jail for nothing, do you, because your furniture isn't there anymore. Do you understand me?"

"Where you put my things?"

"Your things are in storage, Mr. Harcsa. In storage. My office will send you the bill. You can keep them there, or pick them up, I don't care. Just stay away from that house, that's all. Goodbye."

After the bill came—and it was for $165—Kazmer drove to the address, just to look at his belongings, because by that time he had no $165 to pay to anybody, what from, nor could he pay the $80 the bill said they'd charge him every month until he picked his furniture up. But he had to look at his things all the same, even if that place was in the north end, Kazmer didn't even know Toronto went that far north. And the man in the office said he was welcome to look all he wanted, there was no charge for looking.

But there was no thanks in it either, because all the beautiful things he and Petrona had called their own in ten years of married life were just a pile of junk now, one heaped on top of the other. End tables, cushions, chairs, the rug, whether store-bought or made by his own hands, crammed into that little space like garbage. And it was not so much the damage, because things could be mended, but the brutal disrespect; the law calling him cruel when it was throwing his entire life onto the dung-heap like that. When would Kazmer have done that to anybody? When a thing belonged to another person, a customer or just a neighbor, he'd handle it with such care as if it were an Easter egg.

Because who could tell what anything meant to someone else, even if it was an old thing, hardly worth the fixing? Would the Supreme Court know that Petrona had clapped her hands and kissed Kazmer on the mouth, right in front of everybody in the store, when he had bought that bedroom mirror for her? She thought it was so *elegant*; well, it didn't look so elegant now, turned against the brick wall in the corner. And did Petrona know what her lawyer was doing with the things she had left behind, ten years of her own life, too, these things she cleaned and dusted? Or wouldn't she have cried to look at them now? But who could tell what would make Petrona cry, not Kazmer, not anymore.

Still, everything was there, Kazmer could see that, except that hobbyhorse he had carved for Johnny. The jet black Hortobagy stallion, for the boy's third birthday. True, it was too big for Johnny at the time, but he grew up to it soon enough, and now he'd still ride it once in a while at the house on Sundays. Only a year ago he did, when he was nine; and could the movers have left that hobbyhorse behind?

They must have, because the man at the office knew nothing about it, he said he was too busy to look for wooden horses. And Kazmer didn't press him, he got into the truck and left. But when he could not get it out of his mind through that long drive back to the shop, he knew that it was the last straw, that horse. Somebody would have to pay for that.

But just for now, if there was paying to be done, it was Kazmer who was doing all of it. Except Mr. Schuldig was wrong again, you couldn't buy peace for a price. For even though he had abandoned his house and kept handing Petrona the $100 every Sunday as the lady judge ordered, it was still no good, the threatening letters were coming through the mail slot much as before. They came from Mr. Loeblich now, saying that he owed Petrona for the three years he wasn't giving her any $400 a month, because it was *retroactive*, and he owed him for his lawyer's fees, and there was a new fee every time Mr. Loeblich had to write Kazmer a letter. He owed for taxes and insurance and utility on the house that wasn't his, and he owed on the furniture piled up in the warehouse, because Kazmer had never signed for the storage and they were billing Mr. Loeblich for it. If he didn't pay for storage, Mr. Loeblich wrote, he'd have Kazmer's furniture dumped right in the laneway behind the shop, he didn't care. And he didn't, and he did, only two months later.

Kazmer happened to be out when the men came with the truck, but some of the furniture was still piled up in the slush when he got home that evening. Only some of it, because much was missing altogether, including Petrona's elegant mirror, whether it was the deliverymen who stole it or the passersby took their pick, who could tell? It was hard enough to cram the remainder inside the shop anyway; Kazmer left one or two pieces lying in the snow himself, and let the vultures come. There was even a wave of savage pleasure as he looked at the last things from his marriage spread out in the dirt. It was the right place for them.

But it was no use saying that the furniture was the least of it, after all the things that had happened to him, because it was still from that day on that Kazmer couldn't sleep, couldn't eat, some mornings he could not even shave himself or clip his mustache. It wasn't half as bad as when Petrona left or after the Supreme Court's letter, and if it made no sense for it to be worse, it was worse all the same. The customers started noticing it, asking him what was wrong, or why the pine chest he had promised for Monday was still not finished. For it was going on to four years that Kazmer had been apart from Petrona, time enough to heal any wound, yet some customers or neighbors were only hearing about it for the first time, he had shown no sign of it until then. True, he had been living in his own house, not in a nook behind his shop, and how could people not notice?

And if before all this nothing would have mortified Kazmer more than people noticing, now he didn't mind anymore. He even started telling one or two about his troubles. For if a wound was not allowed to heal, it festered, it got bigger and more painful, and hurt came even before pride if it was bad enough. Except who could have helped him? Well, perhaps Uncle Harcsa would have had a good answer for Kazmer, another *ruse de guerre*. But nobody else did, though people were generous enough with free advice.

People liked talking about his troubles, once they understood what was ailing him, he didn't even have to ask. They'd tell him what to do with his life at the drop of a hat, or what they'd do if they were in Kazmer's shoes. Only it seemed that they wouldn't do anything very smart. And sometimes Kazmer would see it right away, but sometimes it sounded good enough, the advice, and he'd find out only later that it wasn't.

One man, for instance, an Irish paint salesman Kazmer had known for years, he said: "Kazmer, you're crazy. This time next week you could be in Calgary, you think they don't need any carpenters there?"

And there was Kazmer, thinking the Irish were full of tricks! Well, a person would not have to travel far from home for Mr. Sampson's advice, Kazmer could have come up with that spoonful of wisdom all by himself. Not that it wasn't true, as far as it went, the sheriffs couldn't find him in Calgary, maybe not even in the next street if he took to calling himself Zerge or Vajda, there were plenty of good Hungarian names to choose from. But what good would that do? He wanted to get closer to justice, not run away from it. Maybe running looks smart to a young man who has a whole lifetime in which to run, or thinks he does. But in his late forties a man's breath is much shorter, he gets tired of running. He'd rather turn around and fight.

Besides, would he cut off his nose to spite his face, and not see Johnny and Borbala anymore? For all the talk in court about the children, it was only Kazmer's breath that caught at the thought of that little boy and girl becoming orphans. And that included Petrona with her great big mother's heart, of which Mr. Schuldig said the law took such care not to deprive the children. The law might trust the children to her, but should Kazmer, when long words and hard mouths and being her own person have mattered more to her than Johnny and Borbala growing up without a father? A father, about whom even she could say nothing worse in court than that he stopped kissing her the way she liked it? Not that it wasn't enough, because times have changed, Petrona was right about that; Mr. Loeblich would get her mother's rights for her, and never mind whether or not she'd paid her mother's dues.

But she was welcome to her mother's rights. If there was one thing over which Kazmer had no quarrel with the law, it was sharing the children with Petrona. He never really wanted to take them from her, well, not after that first time, anyway. Even a poor mother was better than none, it was nature, and if only the law had glimpsed the rights of nature in all other things! If it had only seen that it was nature, not cruelty, for a man to want his wife inside the house and not outside, sitting in young men's cars. And maybe it was all over now, but he still couldn't help brooding about it, or thinking little of Mr. Sampson's advice. Running off to Calgary! That would be the day, leaving Johnny and Borbala in Petrona's care, hers and the color television's!

"Your kids wouldn't have to starve," Mr. Sampson had said, "just send them what you've been giving them anyway." But if, on his own, he would have given Petrona less money, it wouldn't have been to keep more for himself. He would have covered the porch, fixed up the basement, maybe even built a two-room attic. He might have enlarged the shop, bought a new lathe, hired an apprentice. He could pair up his pennies to breed dollars, unlike Petrona, that's why he didn't want to hand the money to her. Even if he had lost the knack of making his mouth real hard when he kissed, he still knew what was best for his family, he never lost his knack for knowing that. But the Supreme Court said, if you're not good at kissing, you're no good at looking after your children's money, you just better hand it over to your wife. And wouldn't he prove the Supreme Court right if he skipped to Calgary, if he took Mr. Sampson's advice?

That young man Willard had a better idea. He was Mr. Perkins's friend, came in with him to see Kazmer one day because, he said, "I'm into Canadiana, too," and he was, he couldn't restore those old pine benches either, just like Mr. Perkins. He dressed like Mr. Perkins, too, in blue denims, except he was very tall and lanky and didn't look like such a mother's hero. Kazmer never understood what he did for a living, he said he worked in some kind of *storefront* for protecting *consumers*. But he liked what Willard said, because he said that all lawyers were crooks—he ought to know, he went to law school himself, until he realized it was too *materialistic*.

This Willard took it into his head that Kazmer should see the government about his troubles. Willard said it was a little *activism* that was needed to help Kazmer, and that was right in Willard's pasture, seeing that Kazmer was a kind of consumer, too, a consumer of justice. Well, if that's what he was, that's what he was; better a consumer than a cruel husband, if people had to call him names. Besides, Willard offered to go with him to the government at no charge, which showed a kind heart, there being no shared blood or bread between them.

As Willard had it, it was the *Ombudsman* they had to see first, which was fine with Kazmer. What harm could an *Ombudsman* do, nothing worse than a judge or a master. And it was true, the Ombudsman did no harm, except he didn't do much good either, because it was the courts that Kazmer was complaining about, and that was a pity, the Ombudsman had no say over what the courts did. But while the telling of this didn't take a minute, the finding out of it took much longer, because Willard started out by yelling at everybody in the Ombudsman's office, right from the girl at the reception desk; you had to do that if you were an *activist*, as he later explained it to Kazmer. Maybe Willard knew what he was doing, Kazmer

didn't doubt it, he only wished that Willard had explained it
to him beforehand. Because he might not have gone with him
if he knew that Willard was going to yell at people who had
done him no harm, and even force Kazmer to sit on the floor
with him, saying to the girl, "Never mind your power trip
about an appointment, we're going nowhere until the Ombudsman comes."

Kazmer wished the floor had opened and swallowed him up,
he was so embarrassed, and he also thought if it was five days'
jail for sleeping in his own house, this time he'd be locked up
for a month. And maybe on his own he would have been, but
with Willard there, the people in the office must have seen
that this was activism, they never called the police, just
laughed and walked around them until lunchtime. Then the
Ombudsman came—and from the name Kazmer expected a
giant, but he was tiny with a squeaky gay voice like a skylark,
maybe he was only a vice-ombudsman —and he screeched at
Willard, "Look, buddy, I have no *jurisdiction*, you want me to
show you the *Act?*" And there it was, another day's work lost.

Kazmer was ready to give up on the government after that,
but Willard said no, the government had many other *branches*,
and what could Kazmer lose? It was true enough, what could he
lose, expect maybe time, for nobody was charging him cash
money; but Willard was still wrong in a way that Kazmer could
not have explained, he didn't even try. Maybe there were people for whom being laughed at by switchboard girls or
screeched at by Ombudsmen was all in a day's work, people
who didn't mind sitting on the floor, like Willard, in a place
where they were not wanted. It was all right if you had a beg-
gar's heart, for nobody kicked you and someone might even
throw you a crumb. But it was still begging, what difference did
it make whether for food or love or justice? Back home people
liked to earn a thing, or take it unearned sometimes, but they
wouldn't importune others for it, crawling and spitting; and if
that was activism it wouldn't get you too far in the mountains.

But the mountains were seven seas away; this was Willard's country, and tough mutton if Kazmer had no stomach for it.

Anyway, as Willard explained it, the Ombudsman was just a long shot. He knew, Willard said, before they set foot in there that the Ombudsman's bit of government was mainly to look out for people who were being kicked around by the rest of the government, which Kazmer wasn't; he was being kicked around by the *judicial system*, so they'd have to see the judicial system's own watchdogs about it. Well, Kazmer supposed, maybe this new land was still better than the old countries where people were being kicked around just as much, only the authorities that did the kicking, they would never post any dogs to keep a watch over themselves. And maybe he should be grateful for small mercies, go with Willard who only wished him well, and stop feeling outraged and ashamed as though he had been the first man in the world to find pigeon droppings on his Sunday hat.

But in the Attorney General's office, where they went next—and Kazmer was much happier there because Willard didn't mortify him by shouting or sitting on the floor; he said later it was the wrong branch of government for that sort of activism—anyway, the Assistant Deputy Attorney General said his office wasn't the right place for Kazmer's kind of trouble. No office was the right place, if you asked the Assistant Deputy, not until Kazmer *exhausted all legal avenues*, and hell, he had hardly taken the first step. What about the Ontario Court of Appeal or the Supreme Court of Canada? Those were the really good courts, the Assistant Deputy said, he used to have a roaring good time in them himself when he was younger, and the courts that Kazmer had been to were just *Mickey Mouse* in comparison. Nothing of any real importance was decided in those lower courts—well, maybe things were decided about people and such, but no *legal precedents*. Unless, of course, the parties were lazy or stingy or *unimaginative* and took them no further.

"With due respect, sir," Willard said, "this man is not lazy or stingy, only poor. He has lots of imagination but no money."

It was a good reply, but the Assistant Deputy had an even better one. He said that if Kazmer wanted a cake he'd need money for it, and after he ate it he'd need money for the doctor to have his stomach pumped, and why should justice be free if his belly wasn't? Kazmer chuckled at that, though with a bad conscience, for Willard was only trying to push his wagon out of the ditch, but what could he do, he agreed more with the Assistant Deputy than with Willard. Most people would have, back home in the mountains, for they wouldn't expect justice for nothing either. True, they might try to take it with a pitch-fork if they couldn't afford to buy it.

But the Assistant Deputy, who was a big man with a boom-ing voice, they should have made *him* the Ombudsman, maybe, he just got up and said, "Don't give me this bullshit about this guy having no money. Then why doesn't he qualify for legal aid?"

And that was true, too, Kazmer had heard about legal aid before; a pretty good deal for people who had nothing to begin with. But for him, well, he'd have to pay the law every penny he saved before it would give him a free lawyer to get back some of it, and he said to the Assistant Deputy, "Is law like mugger in newspaper, takes old lady's purse and gives her back streetcar ticket for legal aid?" at which the Assistant Deputy laughed, and he even shook Kazmer's hand before he ushered them out of his office.

After that there was one more place Willard wanted Kazmer to go to, and that was in Queen's Park where the gov-ernment looked after people who were *multicultural*, which Willard said Kazmer was, too, even if he didn't know it. It cost nothing, this branch of government, for it was set up to help people who ran into trouble because they didn't know their way around this new country, like Kazmer. They even adver-tised in the *ethnic media*, Willard said, which meant the radio, and Kazmer could listen to what they said himself. And he did, the following Thursday he listened, and sure enough they said in some funny kind of Hungarian, if you are in trouble, come to us, we'll help, that's what we're here for. Well, he was in trouble all right, there was no doubt about that.

Willard said that Kazmer could go to this government office without him, they'd have someone there to speak his language, he could explain everything to them, besides which Willard wasn't going to have the time for the next two weeks. He had to go to protest for the *environment* in British Columbia, it had even bigger troubles than Kazmer. It was a relief, not that he wasn't grateful to Willard, but he wasn't sure he could take much more yelling and sitting on the floor. In truth, he wasn't sure he could take any more begging even if he did it in his own way, but he went to Queen's Park all the same, first thing Monday morning.

Well, he must have owed one trip to the devil, because he went for nothing, unless it was for aggravation. That girl in the Queen's Park office had no idea what Kazmer wanted, maybe even less than other girls in other offices. Not that she didn't speak to him politely, because she did, though only in English; and she even offered him a cup of coffee. While he was sipping it—just to be friendly, because it had a vile taste—she put her head together with some other girls and they came up very pleased with themselves, saying that Kazmer should go and see the Attorney General, and if not him, then the Ombudsman. He didn't even have the heart to tell them what was what, they seemed so happy with their idea, young girls, all smelling good and dressed up pretty. And before he left, the girl who gave him the coffee handed him a little picture book, which said LIVING TOGETHER on the cover in white letters, and the photograph behind it, Kazmer could hardly believe his eyes, was of a bunch of Rumanians dancing merrily in their shaggy boots.

Kazmer stayed in his nook after that for almost a week. He didn't feel like talking to anyone, what was the use? But he couldn't stay there brooding forever, nor should the children see their father on Sunday unshaven and without a clean shirt, so by Friday he took the BACK IN 5 MINUTES sign off his window and replaced it with the one that read OPEN. And it so happened that the first customer to walk into the shop after lunch was Mr. Perkins.

"I've been thinking, Kazmer," Mr. Perkins offered without even saying how-do-you-do, "and I'll tell you what, I'm gonna give you the name of my doctor."

Well, Mr. Perkins had given him the name of his lawyer before, not that there were many thanks in it. But that wasn't his fault, it was Kazmer who had asked him. A doctor, though, what would he want with a doctor? "I no need one," he said to Mr. Perkins darkly. "Maybe other people, they need a doctor when I through with them."

Mr. Perkins shook his head and laughed unhappily, which was pretty much the only way Kazmer had ever seen him laugh. "Looking at you," he said to Kazmer, "is like seeing myself only a short time ago. Yes, I was despondent, Kazmer, after my wife left me. Even *suicidal*. Yes, yes. And when the bills started coming, I thought the whole world was *conspiring* against me."

Mr. Perkins sat down on a stool next to the bench, and started ticking off on his fingers the bills he had had to pay, for his children and his wife, for his lawyer and her lawyer and her doctor, and the real estate agents and the Court, and it was true, they came to more than Kazmer's bills. "Boy, you're not the only one to pay out," Mr. Perkins said, "and you're not the only one who thinks it's wrong. Let me tell you, I used to run from lawyer to lawyer.

"But a year ago," Mr. Perkins continued, "when I thought I couldn't take it anymore, I went to see this doctor. A psychiatrist, you understand. Well, he put me right. It took a little time, but he explained to me that I wasn't getting a rough deal at all."

He swept a small jar of glue off the bench, as he was waving his hands, and Kazmer picked it up from the floor. The thick glass didn't even crack.

"Sorry," said Mr. Perkins. "Do you know who was getting a rough deal all along? I'll tell you, even if you won't believe it. It was my *wife*."

Then Mr. Perkins went on explaining how it all took a long time, because at first he didn't see what his doctor was getting at, he was always good to his wife, never cheated on her, even brought her breakfast in bed, he said. But then slowly, *gradually*, he started getting the point. The point, Mr. Perkins said, was that all wives were wronged, and all women, even the ones who never married, because that was the way society had been set up for a long time, it was *male-dominated*, and women had no equality in it. All wives were wronged, Petrona, too, maybe some more *blatantly* than others, but they were all hurt very badly, and what Mr. Perkins and Kazmer had to do now was to make up for all that hurt. And if Kazmer could do that happily, instead of brooding or running to lawyers, he wouldn't feel picked upon or injured anymore. He'd feel *adjusted* and content.

"Look at me," Mr. Perkins said, spreading his arms, "I'm a new man."

Kazmer had never heard Mr. Perkins talk like that, not in all the years he had been coming to the shop, and he wondered if he should bring him a glass of water. And who would have thought that Mr. Perkins had done all those things! True, people had no windows in their souls, but even so, to think of Mr. Perkins dominating women all these years, when to look at him no person would think he'd dominate a dish of cabbage. Well, maybe it wasn't true anyway; Mr. Perkins had been through a lot, enough to confuse the head of any man.

"Believe me, Kazmer," said Mr. Perkins, trying to stab Kazmer with his eyes and pointing a finger, too, in case his eyes were not up to the job, "I was a monster, and so were you. Here, take this card."

And Kazmer took the card that had the doctor's name on it, not that he meant to use it, but why hurt Mr. Perkins's feelings when he was only trying to help? Besides, who could tell, maybe he *was* a monster to his wife. But even if he only liked being taken for one, who could blame him? Kazmer himself might feel a lot better about being branded for a cruel husband if he had drunk up the household money or let his hand stray under other women's skirts; except he hadn't, and no doctor could talk him into believing that he had.

Besides, whatever he had to put right with Petrona, he had nothing to put right with the Supreme Court or with Mr. Loeblich. Yet it was they who were taking his house and life away, for his wife was only reaching into his pockets for hundreds but the lawyers were reaching into it for thousands. And he was glad that Mr. Perkins came, he went and fetched the tools that he wanted to borrow—to put up some bookshelves, Mr. Perkins explained for his ex-wife and her boyfriend—because his visit had helped Kazmer anyway, and never mind the doctor and his card.

Kazmer still had three $100 bills in his tobacco tin, and if it was feeding live mice to a dead cat, he didn't care. Mr. Marosvári had told him about another lawyer, a young man whose father came from *Hódmezővásárhely*. Kazmer was not interested at the time, even though Mr. Marosvári had said, "He's a son of a bitch, Kazmer, like his father used to be, may he rest in peace. But he'd be a son of a bitch for you, at least."

And now, after Mr. Perkins had left, Kazmer picked up the telephone.

"Please Mr. Marosvári, that son-of-a-bitch lawyer, would he talk to me for $300?"

"He would, Harcsa, if I called and asked him."

"Well, I said before don't call him, Mr. Marosvári," Kazmer sighed, "but now, God bless you, call him anyway."

But when he held out the envelope with the $100 bills in it the following Wednesday, the young lawyer brushed his hand aside. "Later, Uncle," he said to Kazmer, speaking in Hungarian. "Let me see those papers first."

While the lawyer was leafing through the court papers—and they filled a paper bag by now, counting Mr. Loeblich's letters—Kazmer looked around the office. It was only on the eighth floor, not the twenty-ninth like Mr. Schuldig's, but what about that fireplace and the big desk, made of real mahogany? Tell them to wrap that up, and they wouldn't give you back much change from a penny!

The young lawyer looked up from the papers.

"What do you want, Uncle," he asked Kazmer, "the bird-song or the bird?"

Well, at least *his* father had taught him how to speak, even if he was a crook, and could Kazmer ever do as much for Johnny and Borbala?

"Only the bird."

"Go home, then," the lawyer said, "and save your money."

Kazmer just held his breath.

"Excuse me, sir, but am I in the wrong?"

The lawyer shrugged. "Where are you from, Uncle?" he asked.

"Bugyi by the Olt, why?"

The young man laughed and, true enough, the name of his village could mean "panties" in Hungarian, and Kazmer had heard other plainspeople laugh at him for that. "Well, I tell you," said the lawyer when he finished laughing, "because you come from Bugyi. It's not whether you're right or wrong, but that as dogs go, you aren't very big."

Kazmer understood the saying well enough. Where there's one bitch in the pack, the biggest dog gets to do the fucking. Yes, well, that's $300 to find out that the law is a bitch. But when Kazmer got up and held out the envelope again to the lawyer, he just shook his head and wouldn't take it. Maybe he wasn't such a bad crook after all.

Maybe he was no crook, this young lawyer, only he liked to show people the bird that made the song, and people blamed him if the song was big, but the bird, puny. The truth was free; and it was the lie that had cost him thousands, when Mr. Schuldig had said, "Sit down, Kazmer, you've come to the right place." Yet, hell, Kazmer caught himself wishing in the elevator going down that he had paid out his last $300 for a good lie, rather than have it still sitting in his pocket next to a bad truth. For a lie would have taken him home from the young lawyer's office, but where was the truth going to take him now?

It took him straight to Mr. Loeblich's office, that's where, he didn't even know how it happened, because he was just driving the truck. But there it was, he knew the address, there were enough letters in his paper bag to teach it to him by heart. And where he stopped the truck was right next to the sign that said No Stopping Any Time which he had never done before. It was wrong, even if a lot of people did it; besides, who'd wager ten dollars to save a dime? But now Kazmer did it himself, and let the Green Hornet police lady worry about writing up a ticket. Because if he drove around the block he'd never come back, not that Kazmer knew what it was that he wanted to come back for. Well, it was to speak to Mr. Loeblich; but what was it that he wanted to say to him?

And what he said to Mr. Loeblich, outside in the waiting room where he came out to meet Kazmer, was: "Why do you do this to me, please? What I done to you that you do this to me?"

"What the *hell* are you talking about?"

The way Mr. Loeblich asked this, it was with such surprise, there was no way a person could pretend to be surprised like this. True, he had only seen Kazmer two, three times, maybe he didn't remember him by face, a lot of stamp-licking people were shortsighted anyway. So Kazmer took a step closer to Mr. Loeblich and said:

"This is Kazmer Harcsa."

"I know who you are. I just don't know what the hell you're talking about."

And could this be true, this young man taking his life away and not knowing it; looking startled as if the grass he cut would cry out, or a termite underfoot? Some people could be that blind, Kazmer supposed, no matter how many books they read. But perhaps all they needed was a little patience.

"You write letters, you think you hoe potatoes? A man speak to you, you think is weed?"

"You're crazy," Mr. Loeblich said, stepping back.

"Please no say crazy when I talk nice. I no come for trouble," Kazmer replied, taking a step back himself to make his meaning clear. "Petrona she gone, is okay, is not you. My house gone is you, I go to jail is you, people steal furniture is you, but I say okay, I no come for that."

"What do you want, Mr. Harcsa? I haven't got much time."

"I want you not take my skin," said Kazmer.

"I think you need professional help."

Kazmer didn't understand what Mr. Loeblich was saying, but it was all right, he could see that the young man did not understand him either. "Don't send no more letters, please," he said. "I live behind shop, is enough. I give hundred dollars every Sunday, I work, who knows, maybe ten years I buy house again, is enough. You leave me peace now, okay?"

Mr. Loeblich cocked his head and scrunched up his face at that, as if he still couldn't understand Kazmer, though Kazmer saw that this time he understood him well enough. "I beg your pardon?" Mr. Loeblich said. "Maybe we have a language problem here. Did you come to my office to tell me that you don't want to fulfill your obligations?"

"Is gone, all I have, what more you want?"

"I want what you owe me," Mr. Loeblich said. "What do you think this is, some kind of kindergarten? I've got a court order. You don't come here to bargain with me."

"Please Mr. Loeblich, I no come to bargain. I tell you," and here Kazmer pulled out his wallet, "I no got *nothing*. Is empty."

And it was, except for a $5 bill, but even as he was holding out his wallet Kazmer remembered with a pang of conscience the envelope with the $300 in his coat pocket. And Mr. Loeblich, he must have read his mind, because he started laughing, though not in a friendly way.

"Mr. Harcsa," he said, and this time it was he who stepped closer to Kazmer, "you're trying to fuck me around, and I don't like that. I never take more than fifty percent from the husband, and I didn't from you, and I even waited for you to start playing ball. There isn't anyone in this town who would listen to your crap, they'd just tell you to buzz off and talk to your own lawyer."

"I no got . . ." Kazmer started, but the other interrupted him.

"That's your problem. You no got no money, you no got no lawyer, I don't care what you no got. You've got a shop, haven't you? Well, smarten up, get off your ass and work, you owe us a few thousand dollars. Pay me, pay your wife, and that's all. Because if you don't . . . ."

Mr. Loeblich paused for a second, because a girl was coming out of the office to hand him a piece of paper, and he stopped in the middle of his own speech to start reading it, it was more important than what he was going to do to Kazmer.

"What more you do to me, if I no pay?"

"What?" asked Mr. Loeblich, looking up from the paper. "Oh, well, how would you like to lose your visitation rights? You know, kiss your children goodbye?"

At first Kazmer couldn't believe it; but what would he have believed if anyone had told him four years ago: Petrona's note, the Supreme Court's letter, or himself eating prison bread? Yet there they were in his shopping bag, the note, the letter, and he could still taste the jail mush in his mouth. Why not the children, too, if all the rest could happen?

And it was worse, for a man might rob an eagle's nest if he's bold enough; but would he climb up to it ringing a bell? Would he shout at ten feet of wings and beak and claws, circling right overhead, "Hey, I've come for your young"? *Shoo*, he'd shoo a hen from the nest maybe, not an eagle.

It was then that the fury came, for there was this young man, waving his arms at him as if he were a chicken, shoo, shoo, I want your eggs! It was still one thing that he'd *do* it, but that he'd say it right into Kazmer's face. True, it might come to that one day, who could help getting weak and old and crippled, and a bandit might say anything to him. But hell, not yet. Not yet.

And Kazmer turned around, for this was past words, but in the doorway he remembered something else and he turned back: "Now you make second mistake," he said to the lawyer. "You make first mistake you steal Johnny's horse."

"What?" said Mr. Loeblich as Kazmer was walking out again. "Did he say I stole a *horse?*" he asked the girl who was still standing next to him. "Jesus, this guy's out to lunch!"

Kazmer could hear but he made no reply; he went to the elevator, and from the elevator to the truck in the street. He tore up the meter maid's yellow tag, climbed into the cab and fired up the engine. Then he took a deep breath, because a man did not have to hurry if he knew where he was going, and he drove slowly and carefully to his old house at the Beaches.

It was still broad daylight as he parked, right in his own driveway; and let the neighbors watch him if they cared. He even took his time getting the toolbox, and if he had his pipe with him, he would have lit it before wrenching the padlock off the door. The empty house smelled differently from the way it used to: Kazmer expected it to look different, but not the smell. It was funny, the bare walls didn't bother him at all, it was the smell that gripped his heart, and not even with sadness. Was it anger, or was it more like fear?

But let a strange smell stop a dog, for it won't stop a man, and Kazmer walked through the empty rooms and down into the basement. There were some odds and ends, a half roll of linoleum, a bicycle wheel with a few spokes broken, and Johnny's horse, behind the water heater. The black Hortobagy stallion, and no wonder the moving people missed it. A good thing too, for who could tell what would have happened to it in the slush behind the laneway? Now at least the wooden horse was safe.

Kazmer didn't even bother shutting the front door behind him as he carried the hobbyhorse out of the house, let the wind blow through it as it pleased. This was the last time he would set foot in that house, and good for Mr. Loeblich! Maybe he should phone and thank him, for if the lawyer hadn't threatened to take his children Kazmer wouldn't have come at all, and even Johnny's black horse would be lost. Well, let them keep up the threats, they'll make him a free man yet. As free as Hollo the one-eyed jailbird.

And if Kazmer's thoughts stayed dark, he couldn't help it, for they stayed dark even the following Sunday when he took the children fishing to the mouth of the Moon River. It was then that he thought he had glimpsed Petrona's face peering out from behind the curtain as he was picking them up. It was then that he asked the little girl who had her cheekbones, "Were you good, Borbala, honey?" and she replied that her name was Barbara, because Mommy said so.

It was then, too, looking at Johnny and Borbala casting their small shadows across the rippling waves of the Moon River, that the thought came to him: suppose something happened and somebody asked, could he tell his story straight? Could he tell it from the beginning, and where was the beginning, if there was one at all? Or would people take him for a crazy, demented person, out to lunch, as Mr. Loeblich had it, a man fit only for Mr. Perkins's doctor? Was he going around and around like a sheep? And for what, for nothing, just something that happened all the time, that's what the police said on the phone. Your wife left a note, well, there was no law against that. Maybe one day she'll write you another that she's coming back, there's no law against that either.

And that night as Kazmer brought the children home, pulling up a little ways from the house, Petrona was there waiting for them on the porch. Not that this was much, lots of divorced mothers waited for their children on the porch on Sundays, except Petrona never did, she'd wait inside the house for them. But this Sunday she was there on the porch, and not only that but she spoke to Kazmer as he handed sleepy Borbala over to her. It was strange, Kazmer hadn't heard the sound of her voice for almost two years. He might have had some trouble recognizing it if he hadn't been looking at her face.

"Well, did you have a good time?" Petrona said, and she could have been asking the children, except she had her eyes on Kazmer and she was speaking in Hungarian.

"It wasn't warm enough," he replied, and he had to clear his throat right after he said the words because there was a little hoarseness in it.

She nodded, and when the children had kissed Kazmer she herded them inside, but instead of closing the door she just stood there, looking at him. "You have a little gray in your hair now," she said, "but it suits you fine."

"Well . . ." he replied, because he couldn't think of anything else, but then he added, "You're looking all right, too."

And it was true, no one could tell from glancing at Petrona that she was almost thirty-seven now, although she was. Mother of Jesus, and she had been twenty-three when they got married! But then Kazmer himself wasn't much more than thirty-five back in those days, and even younger when they had first met in that dance hall on Eighty-second Street. She looked heartbreaking, she was so beautiful, with her black hair piled up high, and her black eyes and her cheekbones, which she inherited from her Polish father, not that Kazmer knew anything about that then. He didn't even know that she could speak some Hungarian, for most of the girls couldn't, even though it was supposed to be a Hungarian dance hall.

He would have asked her to dance anyway, what the hell, he had asked other girls, though it bothered him a lot that he couldn't talk to them. But what could he do, some people were quick with languages, some weren't, and four years in New York had done little to turn the pebbles of English into words in Kazmer's mouth. Not that he needed much English in Mr. Aggteleki's factory, everybody spoke Hungarian there; and all the boss wanted to know, when he had come out to meet the refugees in Idlewild, was if there was anybody on that plane who knew how to work with wood? Because, as he explained to Kazmer and the other young men who put up their hands, there were plenty of people in America who knew how to speak English, but few who could plane a piece of white birch to pass muster, and even fewer who'd do it day in and day out, without having to sleep it off every other Monday. Or joining that *union*, Mr. Aggteleki added, as if they weren't getting better money than they deserved, anyway.

And it was no lie, at least as Kazmer looked at it back then, for there wasn't a soul in Bugyi who had ever laid eyes on wages the like of which Mr. Aggteleki was handing out in those little brown envelopes, maybe not even Comrade Lei. And the machines they gave them to work on, and the tools, Kazmer wished that he could have sent pictures of them back to Mr. Görény, and wouldn't they have made his mouth water! But if New York was paradise, with nothing to tell a Sunday meal from any other—for he could have put red meat on his fork every day, and chicken, too, if he had wanted it—still New York was a faraway place even after four years. Almost as far away, and who would ever have guessed that, as if Kazmer had never left Bugyi, because only his hands and eyes were in New York, and his heart never got on that turboprop that carried the rest of him to Idlewild. Not that his heart would never make it, as one old-timer at the factory explained to Kazmer, only it was taking a much later plane. But that's how it was when people changed one country for another, and there was nothing anybody could do about that.

No, but to hold a girl in his arms would be a step in the right direction, and talking to her would be better still, for nothing entices the heart to catch up more quickly than the sound of a woman's voice. Kazmer saw Petrona's glance come back to him for the second time as she was whirling by with some young boy, while he stood with the rest of the men at the edge of the dance floor. Well, it didn't matter if she would laugh at his bad English, let her laugh if she had the teeth for it. He walked up to her boldly when the music stopped, even though her partner was still jabbering away at her.

"You dance?"

She raised her eyebrows, and it was then that Kazmer had seen that bold look of challenge for the first time in her black eyes. Except it was all right then, for how else should a girl look at someone who accosts her? She wouldn't blush or giggle, not if she had a spark of spirit.

"I dance, and what about you?"

"I dance you now," Kazmer replied, steering her away from the boy, and she let him pull her without too much trouble. Her hand felt soft, soft and dry, but strong, too, and Kazmer was hoping to hold it in his hand longer, but the musicians wouldn't strike up again, they were going on a break. So he had to let her go after a second or two, nor was there anything he could say to her. She guessed what was what, too, because she looked at him and laughed.

"Well, is 'I dance you' the only English you know?"

"I no speak good," said Kazmer truthfully.

"Lucky you don't have to," Petrona replied, speaking in Hungarian.

He could have picked her up in his arms, right then and there, this beautiful raven-haired creature who spoke some of his language, nor would she have minded it perhaps, for she danced with no one else the rest of that night, and it wasn't as if no one else had asked her. It was that first night, too, that she started calling him "Mr. Harcsa," out of respect, as she put it, because he was so much older. Kazmer liked that, but there wasn't much he didn't like about Petrona that first night.

"Mind that you go on respecting me a little longer," he said to her.

"It's hot in here," she replied. "Come out the back door, unless the chill's too much for your old bones."

And when he kissed her in the backyard, with the buses thundering down Second Avenue on the other side of the plywood fence, what she said was this:

"Well, younger men are quicker on their feet, Mr. Harcsa, but you're quicker with your lips. And I don't mean when you're talking, either."

Her father had died when she was a little girl, Petrona told Kazmer on their second date, and it was her mother who had brought her up. She was still living with her at home, not that they were getting on all that well. That was why she never learned much Hungarian, Petrona said, it was her mother's language, and she would sooner have learned her father's, except he never gave her a chance, dying when he did.

"And aren't you happy now," asked Kazmer, "that your mother taught you how to speak a little?"

Petrona looked at him and laughed. "Oh, don't you think you're such a big fish, Mr. Harcsa," she said. "I've caught bigger and thrown them back, too."

But she slipped her hand into his as she said it, while all Kazmer could think about was how to keep the treasure he had found. Because—and this happened only a month before he met Petrona—Mr. Aggteleki had said to him, well, Harcsa, I'm opening a new factory in Toronto, that is in Canada, not far from here, and would you like to be a foreman there? Because I can get your papers for you if you do. And he had said yes, and how could he go back on his word now? But how could he leave this black-eyed girl behind?

And Kazmer could still remember the deafening clatter of the E train through that endless tunnel under the East River as he was seeing Petrona home, wondering what to do. For girls who could make a man's heart stand still, as this girl could, whenever he looked at her, did not grow along the ditches like clover; he had not laid eyes on another one even at home after Katika died, nor in New York, for all its wonders, not once in four years. And why should that Toronto be different, wherever it was?

"Well, it's like this," he said to Petrona, just as the train was slowing down for Roosevelt Avenue, where they were supposed to get out, "in a month's time I'll be off to another place, because I'm getting a new job there. So I thought, why don't you and I get married?"

But whatever he expected Petrona to say to this, he did not expect her to reply as she did. Because what she did say was: "Uh-oh. I think we're in trouble." And she not only said it, but moved closer to Kazmer and held on to his arm.

He followed her glance along the subway car, empty, for it was nearly midnight, except for a couple of kids, maybe nineteen or so, who were now getting up and making their way toward them. Kazmer had noticed them sitting there, though he paid no attention, because in four years he had seen thousands of black people before. It was not like when he first came to New York, for then his eyes nearly popped out with curiosity at the sight of all those Saracens, which was what black people were called back home, not that anyone had ever seen any in the whole of Transylvania. But these two seemed no different from all the others, and what was Petrona being upset about? If it pleased God to make people all kinds of color, He must have known why; He had created cats and dogs, too, to be black or white or amber.

"Well, never mind those two, my treasure," he said to Petrona, "but did you hear this question that I asked you?" And when she'd still not look at him, only stare at those Saracens, he added, "I'll be making good money, and hell, I'd carry you in the palm of my hand like a pearl."

"Mr. Harcsa, we're going to be mugged," said Petrona, in Hungarian of course, because those two were now coming to stand right over them, there was no good reason for anyone to stand so close to other people in an empty train. Well, and let them come, for Kazmer had more important things on his mind.

"Not today, we won't," he replied to Petrona, pulling her up by the hand and steering her to the door, for the subway train was coming into the station now, screeching like a banshee as it was braking to a stop. But there were no people on the platform, either, only the two Saracen boys getting off the subway and following right behind Kazmer and Petrona.

"They're coming after us," Petrona whispered, as if he didn't know it, everyone has a third eye in the back of his head when he's being followed. "Oh, Mr. Harcsa, what are you going to do?"

"Well, what are you going to do, Petrona?" he asked, stopping. "A church wedding, it has to be booked three weeks ahead of time."

"Oh, book it, are you crazy, I don't care," she screamed at him. "This is New York, or don't you read the papers?"

But New York or not, there was never such a clap of thunder echoing down the empty platform at Roosevelt Avenue as Kazmer smacking his two palms together, nor such a shout for joy as when he picked Petrona up and twirled her around. Only the rocks in the clouds above Murder Lake would hear such echoes, and not even the rocks, unless a man wanted to let them know that he was happy. For in the mountains there were no papers to put the news in, but the world heard all the same when a girl in a village allowed herself to be spoken for.

And the two Saracens, whoever they were and whatever they wanted, heard it with no trouble and they saw it, too, when Kazmer put his hands on his hips and danced a slow csárdás around Petrona, tara-tara-tara-tara-tararom, humming the melody himself for the music. And she, well, she didn't much know which foot to stand on, or whether to laugh or to cry, while Kazmer smiled at her, proud as a morning rooster, and then he smiled at the two black youngsters as he started dancing around *them*, only there was no thanks in his smile. "Hey, you're crazy, man," one of them said uneasily, while Kazmer said, only he said it in Hungarian, "Come on, little bandits, smile, little Saracen muggers, because I am a happy man!" And they just backed off and walked away, and true, Kazmer didn't look like the best person to be mugged just then, not when there were plenty of old ladies around from the Bronx to Jamaica.

Where was that night now anyway, merciful Father in Heaven, the past was the past, yesterday or a million years distant, it made no difference. And where was *that* Petrona now, or *that* Kazmer, because the shivering woman on the porch who wore her skin was not the same person, nor the bent man, shuffling his feet, maybe to avoid stepping on his glance. For they were both casting their eyes on the ground, who would want to look at the dead when they could look away and remember the living? But resurrection, now there was a thought; even if it had never happened since the Lord Jesus.

And Kazmer said, though still without looking at Petrona, "How are you feeling, then, these days?"

"Miserable, if you want to know," she replied.

"You . . . are you seeing someone, or what?" he asked after a long silence.

"Nobody," she said. 'Well, I was seeing that guy for a while, you know the one in the car, but. . . ." She broke off with a little laugh, and shook her head.

Well, he could guess that, it was no surprise, but hearing it hurt all the same. She sensed it, too, because she added quickly, "That had nothing to do with, you know, my leaving, nothing at all." He just nodded, what did it matter whether it did or not. But he could see then that it was broken too badly, whatever it

was that held a man and wife together, it was just foolishness to
try and mend it now.

"How are you managing?" Petrona asked him.

He looked at her, then shrugged and looked away.

"I want you to know," she said, "and I guess it makes no difference now, but I'm truly sorry . . . I don't mean just the
house and that, but us, and everything. It's not the way they
said it was going to be, the lawyers and everybody, but . . . I
just wanted you to know that, Mr. Harcsa."

Well, he knew it then, for all the good it did him, and he
said, "Goodbye, Petrona," then turned and started walking
back to his truck. And that damn fool woman, she leaned
over the railing of the porch, yelling for all the world to hear:
"I know it's too late now, but I loved you. *I loved you, Mr.
Harcsa!*" and Kazmer started running because he hadn't cried
since he was a child, or anything close to it, but now he could
feel the tears coming to his eyes. His life, his children's lives,
for nothing, nothing, oh Petrona, Petrona!

And that same night, whatever another person might have
done, Kazmer pulled out a scrap of paper with that number he
got from Hollo the one-eyed jailbird. It was a number Hollo
had said, if you're in trouble, brother, or you need something,
you call it. Kazmer had put it away, it was kindly offered,
though he never thought that he'd use it; but here he was, using it all the same. Maybe they should have let him sleep in
his own house, that lady judge and Mr. Loeblich. A father
watching over his children's home deserved some respect, and
if they had shown him some, maybe he wouldn't have a number now to telephone that Hollo.

And that was the word Hollo used himself, respect, it'll get
you some respect, when Kazmer told him that he wanted to
buy a gun. Well, and it showed what Hollo had in his head for
brains, thinking that a gun would buy respect, which only a
fool would believe. But a gun could buy protection for a man
and his children and, if not that, at least justice.

And it was only a week or not even a week after that phone call that the stranger who was going to help Kazmer bring justice into the world parked his Chevrolet in front of the workshop and dropped a dime into the parking meter. From where Kazmer was sitting behind his bench in the basement, all he could see was the stranger's feet and the frayed edges of his dark overcoat. But it would have made no difference if he could see his face, for Kazmer had never laid eyes on the stranger before.

PART THREE

PRINCE CSABA'S ARMIES

WELL, HE HAD the gun now; the visitor left him even the patterned handkerchief in which it came, made of fine cotton and almost new. The gun looked like a good weapon, smelling of fresh oil, somebody had taken good care of it. The clip slid out easily when Kazmer pressed the button. He counted the bullets through the little holes, there were four, just as the stranger said; and he also pulled back the top carriage that cocked the hammer to make sure the breech was empty. It was, but never mind, he still thumbed down the safety catch before putting his finger on the trigger and sighting along the barrel. One could never tell about guns and it was smarter to be cautious.

He toyed with the Mauser for a while, just because it was nicely made, who could resist such a snug machine? Those Germans certainly knew what they were about, even the neat way they metal-stamped those words *Mauser-Werke* A. G.

Oberndorf a N along the top carriage, or those numbers *Kal. 7.65 mm* showing through the little window on the other side. He aimed it this way and that, it was steady in his hand, and Kazmer was aching to try it out; the noise would have been nothing, no worse than the sound of hammering coming from his shop and the neighbors were all used to that. But why waste one bullet out of four?

Four bullets might not be enough for what he wanted, but God alone knew how many bullets would have been enough for that. For what was it that he wanted when he had called Hollo for that gun? Did he want it for the next time the Sheriff might come knocking on his door? Or maybe the two policemen, saying it made no difference whether he'd come along with them the easy or the hard way? But if he had that gun it would; it would make a hell of a difference to any two mortal policemen.

Because when God created people, He made them short and tall or kindly and wicked; and also men and women He made them; but of all the different kinds, He never created one to stand against bullets. And if God didn't, He must have had a reason, it would have been no harder to do that than making some men strong enough to twist a bull's head sideways. Or smart like the miller's son Peter, who could play the flute at weddings before he turned seven, and it wasn't as though the boy had had a teacher, because he had none.

Nor was God's mind so hard to read, not about this one thing, because a person who could withstand bullets would have no end to his wickedness if the devil got into him. Such a person, if God had created one, could have trampled over any other person with no more thought than trampling over an ant. And maybe this was God's way of saying, I have given men dominion over beasts, but not over other men. No matter how great and powerful I created one man, I gave him no dominion over even the weakest of his own kind. Even the mightiest may not feed off the weakest the way I let men feed off birds and fishes.

But was this really true, Kazmer asked himself. Did God really say that, when men have always been lording it over other men, in Bugyi no less than in New York or Toronto? But no, that was no proof against God's word. Or else why would the mighty have needed great locks on their doors? No person needed protection against the chicken in the barnyard and the carp in the lake, even after he slaughtered all their brothers. Nor was it just power, for a brown bear could crush a man's spine, yet brown bears knew nothing about revenge. God gave them no sense of being wronged, and if a man shot a she-bear, her yearling would still follow him on a chain like a dog or wrestle him gently at the fair.

But when a man took the law in his own hands, it must have been ordained, or else the thought could not even enter his mind, no more than a beast's mind, against the will of God. And man-made laws could be evil, or evil men could pervert good laws, but who could pervert God's will? If God didn't want it, it didn't happen, and if it happened, God wanted it: it was as simple as that.

Kazmer was toying with the gun, thinking these thoughts, when he turned red in the face, even though he was all alone. What was he doing, for shame, getting religion like some old woman, or angling for the Reverend Vegvari's job when he hadn't even been near a church for twenty years, except the one time when he got married? Why mix God up with whatever dark thoughts were crossing his mind? Maybe his thoughts came from the devil!

But if they did, they were not any the less powerful for that, because Kazmer couldn't get rid of them even after he had wrapped the gun up in the cotton handkerchief and put it under his workshirts on the shelf. Wherever his thoughts came from, wouldn't it have been a joy to have that snug piece of metal in his palm the next time a sheriff came knocking on the door? To watch the smug, righteous faces of those policemen go soft with surprise as they glimpsed their own death in his hand. Maybe they would curl up their mouths and cry, if he gave them enough time, babble like children if he waited for the thought to sink in that they weren't going home to *their* wives tonight, walking into their own houses as though nothing had happened, after turning another man out of his. But why the policemen, Kazmer thought, why would he worry about policemen?

They knew nothing, those twenty-year-old boys, stuck in a blue uniform. Somebody handed them a piece of paper and said, bring this man to court, whether he wants to come or not. And that man could be a thief, for all a policeman would know about him, he might have robbed his own mother or drank up his children's milk. There were such men, fit only for jail or fit only for the gallows; and somebody had to go out and bring such men to justice. The arm of the law, that's what policemen were called even back home, and the arm only does what the mind tells it to do. And who would quarrel with an arm or a hand? Well, a dog would, it would even sink its teeth in a stick held by a hand, but a human being would look for the person behind the stick. But that stick of the Supreme Court's, who were the persons behind that?

Petrona, for one; and there was no way of escaping that thought, whichever way Kazmer tried to twist his mind, for who had done greater injury to him and the children than Petrona? There would have been no letters in his mailbox, no sheriffs on his doorstep, without Petrona calling them down on his head first, for the Supreme Court did not pick his name out of a telephone book. And not only that, but who else betrayed a sacred duty, a wife's and a mother's? Those lawyers, Mr. Schuldig and Mr. Loeblich, they were no kin to Kazmer, they were out for what they could get; and as for the young man in the car or the lady judge, they owed him nothing. No other person but Petrona had stood up in church to say, I'll love my husband and cherish him. Yet when another man came along and opened the door of his car (and why shouldn't he), she got right in and maybe even said thank you into the bargain. Then she called the law to turn Kazmer out of his house for being cruel.

So it was Petrona, and it would take a stupid man not to see that; but what good did it do that Kazmer was not stupid and he could see it clearly? He could still not harm a hair on her head when he'd be breaking his own marriage vows if he did. For it *was* a·church, that low squat building in New Jersey, even if it looked more like a skating rink from the outside; and maybe it would have been smarter to make only a little promise to God, like "I do, Lord, as long as she does," or "I won't be the first to abandon her, Lord," but that was just looking for a hat after the rain, for in that church Kazmer had made a much bigger promise. And God was holding him to it, there was no doubt about that, for his own heart would nearly stop whenever he thought of pointing that gun at her heart.

Because it would have been a lie to say that he never thought about it; he did and not only once, and long before he even had a gun to point. The thought would come and go, not so much after he had found her note, but when she walked Johnny out of his shop with the suitcase, and the worst just after the Supreme Court's letter. Sometimes the thought came during the day while Kazmer was doing his chores, sitting at his bench picking up a piece of wood, or talking to a customer maybe, but mostly it came at night just as he was getting ready to sleep. Often he thought only of the moment when he'd twist Petrona's head sideways like a trout's, crushing her windpipe between his thumbs, or holding her head back with his left hand while the awl in his right poked in her coal black eyes. But some nights it was the whole story of how he'd do it, how he'd wait for her where she worked, or put on a dark coat on a moonless night and sneak into that rented house where she lived, through the back porch. Maybe he'd even catch her in bed with someone, well, he could kill them both, though the other man could be stronger, Petrona liked big men, and maybe it would be safer to take a gun. Except he had no gun to take, not then, and what was wrong with a carving knife? A knife would fit his hand better than a gun, anyway, and he wouldn't even have to carry one, there would be plenty of good knives in Petrona's kitchen. And who could ever prove that it was he who did it, when they'd find them the next day under the bloody sheets, if he did it with Petrona's knife and burned his clothes when he got back home?

But no sooner would he think of his hand drawing the knife out from under Petrona's breast—for the knife was always in the same place, the spot he used to like kissing, her skin was so sweet and tender there—than Kazmer's own chest would twist in agony, and once he even had to press his hand against it to quell the pain. And wasn't this God holding him to his promise? It must have been, for there was no pain in Kazmer's chest at the thought of sticking the knife in the man in her bed. No, that was a good thought, and it only helped to bring him peaceful sleep. Yet the men in Petrona's bed were innocent.

The men in Petrona's bed had never betrayed him, that was plain enough, maybe they didn't even know that Kazmer existed, except one, that one young man in the car. For all the other men knew, Petrona might have been a widow or a deserted woman. Why shouldn't they lie in her bed if she called on them to share it? But it would have been a joy to stab any of those men, even if he had no quarrel with them, and the reason for this had to be that God was jealous, just as the Reverend Vegvari had always said He was, except He would not go along with Kazmer spilling Petrona's blood. Nor was God wrong, for what if the children woke up to see the source of one half of their lives taking away the other half? There could be nothing worse than that.

But her lovers, what would be the point of harming them, even if God had put no commandment against harming them in his heart? It would make no sense, killing a stranger; nor would it be justice, not with the innocent dying in the same bed in which the guilty escaped all punishment. It would satisfy nothing except his thirst for vengeance—and maybe not even that in the end.

For it was a powerful thirst, vengeance, and it could not be quenched willy-nilly by any man's blood who happened to walk by Kazmer's house for ill luck just when the devil got into his wife. Might as well kick a stone or smash a plate, at least that wasn't against the law, and if it didn't satisfy him he could always kick or smash another. But what if killing that young man in the car, the first one, didn't remove the thorn from his soul? What would he do, go on killing Petrona's lovers one by one till the end of time?

But then what did he want with that gun, now that he had it lying on the shelf under his shirts? It had cost him the last of his money; and if that gun wasn't for the sheriffs or the men in Petrona's bed, who was it for? Was it for Petrona herself, after all?

Except that couldn't have been true, either, because when Petrona telephoned a week later—for she did telephone, and a thrush could have knocked Kazmer down with a wing when he heard the sound of her voice—he didn't hang up on her, or anything close to it. Instead Kazmer listened, with his heart pounding in his mouth.

"It's only me," Petrona said. "I just thought I'd phone."

She went on when he didn't answer: "To ask you, like, if you were picking up the children on Sunday."

Well, and she didn't call him for that, whatever she did call him for, because there hadn't been a Sunday that Kazmer would not have picked the children up, ever since they parted, nor had she ever phoned him about it before. But all he answered was, "Yes."

"I've been thinking," Petrona continued, when it was clear that Kazmer was not going to say anything more, "the other day, you know, when you just walked away after what I said, and I was really hurt. So I've been thinking, do you hate me?"

And it would take that woman to ask him that question, oh Petrona, with their children's house gone and their furniture dumped in the snow! To ask him four years after she had left with a note, then dragged him through court and jail, then put him to live behind a blue curtain in his shop. But why blame her, when all Kazmer could hear himself reply, instead of the truth, was: "I don't hate you, Petrona."

And, hell, what was the truth anyway, was it the gun under his shirts? Was it his bedtime thoughts of a knife in her breast and an awl stuck into her eye? Or was the truth his heart standing still at the sound of her voice and then his own voice replying, "I don't hate you, my treasure," for he said it again, as if once hadn't been enough. But what could he do, he even said "my treasure," the words just came out of his mouth without bothering to pass through his mind.

And Petrona was surprised herself, because she said, "Well, I couldn't blame you if you did." Then she added, "Because it was my fault, I'll never deny that. Well, mostly my fault, anyway. But it's not as if I didn't suffer for it, you know. For it hasn't been a bed of roses for me, Mr. Harcsa, and don't you think it has."

"Yes, well," he said, because he couldn't think of anything else to say, "what's done is done, Petrona."

"Oh, I know. Don't think I don't know that," she said. "I mean, that's not why I called you or anything. What we had is over, it's finished whether I like it or not. . . . Except I don't like it, do you?"

He said nothing.

"Well, maybe you do," Petrona continued, and from the sound of her voice Kazmer could almost see how she'd be shrugging her shoulder, she always had a funny way of doing that. "Maybe you have somebody younger now to look after you."

And the way she said it, well, it was almost like an accusation, something for which Kazmer should feel guilty. And the funny part of it was that he did; he even denied it quickly, saying, "No,

I've got nobody younger," as if it were any of her business after what she did to him. He cursed himself for saying that, but what could he do, the words were out, he couldn't take them back. And the shameless woman, she even went on, replying, "Oh Mr. Harcsa, as if I couldn't hear what people are saying, but never mind." Well, that was Petrona, running off with a young man, then forgiving Kazmer for something he didn't even do to put herself in the right, but she always had a knack for doing that. She could do that with no trouble even if nobody ever showed her how, but nobody had to teach a frog to jump or a woman to twist things around.

And maybe that wasn't Petrona's reason anyway, maybe she just wanted to know if Kazmer *had* found anybody else. For the next thing she said was: "Well, what if I let you take me for a cup of coffee? Next week, you know, I could come by the shop one evening after work."

"Well, you can come Thursday, if you care to," he said, adding, "Come after seven," as if it mattered at what time she came. And he was angry, angry and ashamed at himself for saying it, for rising to her bait again like some hungry fish, but what could he do when his heart was thumping in his chest for joy. Maybe, maybe this time. Though if someone had asked him, "This time what?" he couldn't answer.

Still, there was never a week in Kazmer's whole life that passed more slowly, not even the week before Christmas when he was a child. Not that he just waited for Petrona, because there was wood to be carved; and not that he had only kind thoughts about her coming, because the truth was that his thoughts were like the April sky, smiling one minute, weeping the next. Or if he thought kindly of it during the day, he'd dream about it the other way around. Because he did dream about it every night that week.

He'd see her coming to the shop with other men in his dreams, or surrounded by black-robed lawyers, except they had Mr. Perkins's face or the Ombudsman's, and he'd always end up going at her with a hammer. Then, waking up in a sweat, he'd lie in bed shivering and thinking why, why, if he had come to hate that woman so much, why would his soul ache to see her again? But it cut both ways, for why would she want him to take her for coffee? After what she had done to get away from him.

On the morning following his second night of dreams, Kazmer walked across the street to the shop where they sold television sets. He knew the people who owned the store, they had been on the street almost as long as he had, a whole family of slender dark people, who came from mountains even taller, and more oceans away than Kazmer. Kazmer got on with them, particularly the old man, who'd sit in front of the store on a stool whenever the sun was shining, and even told Kazmer the name of their mountains once, it was called the Himalayas. Well, and they must have had some foul weather there, because the old man was always talking about the weather, but very politely, saying to Kazmer, "It's somewhat beautiful today, isn't it?" or "Oh, today it is a little bit grisly." But he meant it to be friendly.

Kazmer could see that, even though back home people would never say such things. Any fool could tell what kind of weather it was just by looking at it.

He walked into the shop and said to the old man, who was standing behind the cash register, "You give me color TV for a week, maybe?"

"Oh sir, we have very nice television set for you to buy, very cheap," the old man replied, grinning.

"No buy. You have for me to take for maybe a week?"

"Do you want to rent? We have a most excellent television set, only for you."

Kazmer didn't care if it was a foolish thought, though it probably was, nor about the twelve dollars the old Himalayan wanted for the week. He took the color TV back across the street and set it at the foot of his camp bed behind the blue curtain.

He'd turn it on and watch it, like it or not, he'd even watch Johnny Carson; for maybe the color TV could tell him the answer if he gave it a chance, if he looked at it carefully enough. Maybe it was all there, why Petrona would do what she did, why she would leave and why she'd want to come back, if that was what she wanted. Or why she'd ask to be taken for coffee if she did not.

Besides, after they went for that coffee, he and Petrona, she might sit with him for a while in the shop; and she might sit a little longer if he had a color TV there for her to watch. For what else could they do? He couldn't hold her in his arms, not just like that, even if she wanted to be held; and without that TV she would have to leave when they ran out of words. But maybe with the TV she'd see that he was trying, whatever it was he was supposed to try. And he could try it right away, for practice.

Well, those people on the TV hadn't changed much in four years; they just sneered and snarled and smashed up their beautiful new cars, or laughed when there was nothing for them to laugh at. There was only one man Kazmer liked, he always came on at the same time, a fat man with a kind, serious face. What this man did was to show people how to repaint old furniture, and he did it the right way, stripping and sanding, then putting on the fresh paint with an even stroke. Kazmer liked watching him, he even enjoyed the sound of his voice. They should have had more of his kind on TV, except they didn't. But, Kazmer thought, maybe there was one TV man he could talk about with Petrona; who could tell, maybe she liked him, too. It was better than nothing.

But he was restless and worried; and as he was leaving for the supermarket the next day—only to buy milk and sugar— he turned back from the doorway, got the Mauser from under the shirts and tucked it into his belt. He carried the gun with him for the rest of the day, he didn't know why. It calmed him, even if the feel of that lump of metal against his body wasn't comfortable. But if anybody tried to take anything that belonged to him now, he wouldn't have to scrape and bow and say "yes, sir" to them. Whatever they said, the lawyers, the judges, the policemen, he wouldn't even have to reply, just come up with the Mauser in his hand and watch them melt away like spring ice on the river. Instead of sitting before a color TV like a child, to get on their good side.

But if this was a bright thought, this gun, he should have come up with it a long time ago, because now it was just throwing a stone after the dog that tore off his pants. Even the writing on the old Count's sword, the one Uncle Harcsa told tales about when he was a child, the curved Turkish blade with the ivory handle, it warned: "Know *how* well, but know *when* better," because their fathers' fathers didn't need to run next door for a cup of wisdom. It was only their children who did, like Kazmer himself, except nowadays they had no wisdom to spare at the neighbors' either.

And how they would have all turned away from him in disgust, the ancients, the ancestors, Prince Csaba's soldiers, if they could see him wandering the streets, fuming, thinking dark thoughts, with cartons of milk and bags of sugar in his hands. Yes, and an old gun tucked into his belt, the kind his aunt Rosie used to scare the crows with. Spitting, cursing, sitting on office floors, running from pillar to post, begging government ladies to give him back his house! Dreaming about strangling his wife, stabbing her lovers, then scurrying to the color television to please her. Squatting on his camp bed, behind a blue curtain!

Because forgiveness is one thing, true forgiveness, even if it takes a saint; and love, too, whether it's Christian love or the love of a man for a woman. Back home people wouldn't laugh at him for loving, if he could love truly. Kazmer remembered the songs and legends about good men and women, persons who would turn the other cheek. There was nothing shameful about them, they were heroes. Except they didn't dream of

knives while saying "my treasure." Saints didn't dream of
knives, and brave men used them; but it was cowards who
only used them in their dreams.

So it has come to that: a hateful, contemptible fool, thirsting for bitter justice, but no taste for it, and no strength to
raise the cup to his lips. Waiting to welcome back his wife, but
with a gun hidden on a shelf under his shirts. Thinking mur-
derous thoughts about policemen and lawyers, but taking the
gun where, to the Supreme Court? No, to the supermarket for
sugar and milk.

The next morning Mr. Perkins walked into the shop and
said, "Well, have you seen the doctor yet, Kazmer, the one I
told you about?"

"No."

"You really should. You're looking awful. Tell you what,"
Mr. Perkins continued, taking out a little book from his pocket. "I have to cancel my appointment tonight, because something came up at the office. Why don't you take my place?"

Kazmer just shook his head, but Mr. Perkins went on and
on, saying how it would make him feel better and it was just
foolish to be stubborn; and in the end Kazmer thought, what
the hell. Once he had got that color television, a doctor
couldn't be worse.

The truth was, though, the doctor didn't seem any more anxious to see Kazmer than he to see the doctor, and Mr. Perkins
had to spend a good ten minutes on the phone to convince
him. "He doesn't like giving new appointments without a *refer-
ral*," Mr. Perkins said to Kazmer when it was all settled, "but he
said he'd do it for me. I told him you were looking pretty bad."

Well, and didn't Petrona say that she went to a doctor, and
if she did why shouldn't he, if that's what husbands and wives
did in this new country. It even made sense, for doctors were
there to cure sick people; and wasn't it a sickness, first for
Petrona to do what she did, and then for him to do nothing
about it? Except fret and mope, while lawyers and judges were

robbing him of his whole life. And in spite of everything, Kazmer had to laugh, for suddenly he thought of Uncle Harcsa, and what *he* would have done if Aunt Rosie had walked into the bushes with some young man, and then sent a policeman back to turn Uncle Harcsa out of his house. Kazmer couldn't help laughing at the thought, it was so funny.

The doctor's office was on the sixteenth floor, a long ride in the elevator, and who could tell why lawyers and doctors liked to nest in the clouds like great birds of prey? But from the inside, Dr. Aurel Witstein's office didn't look like a bird's nest at all, for no bird Kazmer had ever seen would feather its nest with leather and bakelite and plastic flowers, birds had more sense than that. There was not a piece of wood to be seen in the waiting room, for even the legs of the chairs were made of chromed metal, unless you counted the pulp on which the glossy magazines were printed, like Petrona's at home.

But the doctor himself was different, not somebody tall and hard and dressed up in a white gown, as Kazmer would have expected him to be, but just a chubby little man with flecks of cigarette ash on his tie and great yellow stains on his index finger. And he looked, well, Kazmer thought that he looked *worried* somehow, and very, very tired. But seeing such an untidy, worried man made all the tension go away from Kazmer's own body, and he almost felt like asking Dr. Witstein if *he* was feeling all right, except it would have been a stupid question to ask a doctor.

And what happened next was even more surprising, and Kazmer wouldn't have believed anyone who said that he could do it, but he told Dr. Witstein all about his life with Petrona. And not only that, but his words just burst from him, like an artesian well from a garden, and never mind that he had to talk in English. Nor was it as if the doctor had been prodding him with questions, because he hardly said a word, just nodded now and again or cleared his throat, and he even had his eyes closed half the time. Yet Kazmer felt his heart ease, just talking at this sleepy little man, as though nothing had weighed on it except his own unspoken words. It was a miracle, and for once Mr. Perkins may have been right.

And because talking to this doctor was just like talking to himself, so that for the first time Kazmer could hope for some understanding, he had no trouble putting even the big question into words, perhaps the only question that mattered.

"What is it wrong?" Kazmer asked Dr. Witstein. "What is it sick in my head that I say okay, okay, I do nothing?"

The doctor opened his eyes, then closed them again.

"How do you mean that?" he asked.

"Look, my hand, it is all right," explained Kazmer. "My legs, I no sit in wheelchair. At home, old man, grandfather, walk with cane, but when soldiers come with gun—not just gun, it goes ra-tatata-ra-tatata, you know—old man says, you no come in here, stabs him with pitchfork. Me? Children, house, young man in car, I say take, take, please, thank you. You want money too, I give you. Am I man?"

"Hmm," said the doctor. "What do you think?"

"I no understand," said Kazmer, shaking his head. "I sick maybe, no? Petrona, she phone the other day, she say go for coffee. She make my children orphan, spit on my house like whore, put me in jail with lawyer, but I say yes, you come Thursday, I buy you coffee. No sick?"

"Go on," said the doctor.

"Why I not take . . ." and Kazmer stopped for a second because he didn't want to say "gun," not even to the doctor, "why I not take *ax*, go to judge lady who call me cruel husband, who call me Rumanian, and I cut her? Why I not go to lawyer who rob me with ax? Law say, you bad husband, you no lick your wife, you go to jail; and I have big ax, why I not cut policeman's head?"

"Well, why don't you?" asked Dr. Witstein.

"Why? I come here you tell me why," said Kazmer. "Maybe I scared like rabbit, no?"

"Maybe," said the doctor, "or maybe it's something else. What is it?"

Well, it was true, it could have been all the other things he thought about: his own promise in church, or that the sheriffs or the men in Petrona's bed didn't know any better. And hell, even Petrona herself, whatever that crazy feeling was that got hold of her, it must have been strong, it must have been something she couldn't resist. Because it couldn't have been easy for her, taking two small children and a few sticks of furniture into a rooming house; and what was that $600 cash money she took with her, nothing. That woman must have been desperate to walk out of her own home like that, for never mind black eyes and high breasts, she was even then a woman of thirty-three, without an acre of land coming to her, nor a family, except a father long dead and an old-age-security mother somewhere in New Jersey. And not only desperate, but that woman had spirit. She would not be broken to the harness for a bale of hay.

Because it wasn't as if Petrona had nine lives like a cat; and if the one at her husband's side was breaking her heart, she didn't have another coming to her. And whatever she needed, she *needed* it; hard mouths or Johnny Carson. Who could set himself up to judge another being's needs?

Who could tell the number of Petrona's sleepless nights before that note came to be left on the kitchen table? Certainly not Kazmer, for he had been snoring at her side, smug and content. And would it have made any difference if he had been awake? He would have paid no more mind to what was going on around him than a pig, happy at the trough, while tubs of hot water are carried into the courtyard and the knives are being sharpened!

And even this was only half true, because for Petrona it wasn't like killing a pig: she could not plunge a knife into his heart without piercing her own, any more than he could hurt her without hurting himself; and the only difference was that she did it anyway. But did this make her a worse person? Perhaps not: only braver.

"You fall off horse, not your fault?" Kazmer asked Dr. Witstein. "You beat horse for it if you bad rider?"

"Right," said the doctor. "Well, that's as far as we can take it today, Mr. Harcsa. Have this prescription filled at any drugstore, and I'll see you here same time next week."

But the drugstore in the doctor's building was closed, and Kazmer was already starting up the blue truck to find another, when the thought came to him. The thought that came to him was that Dr. Witstein never told *him* any of those things he was supposed to have explained to Mr. Perkins, about how all wives were being badly treated and how husbands had to make it up to them. Because in that office Kazmer did the explaining and all Dr. Witstein did was listen.

And maybe they weren't so foolish, these glass-and-metal people! That doctor could see what was wrong with him: he was a mother's hero, just like Mr. Perkins. What use was it, talking to such a person, who looked like a man only because he shaved in the morning? Such people would explain it away all by themselves, why they did nothing; this reason, that reason, like a fish tugging on the line and setting the hook deeper in its jaw. No wonder Dr. Witstein could make Mr. Perkins happy. He just listened, that's what he did, while Mr. Perkins came up with that excuse about women being badly treated. Then maybe he prescribed some little pills for him, too. As for the fifty dollars it cost—well, wasn't a week's happiness worth fifty dollars to a person in pain? Even for an aching tooth, and never mind a soul in torment.

But hell, Dr. Witstein had earned his fifty dollars, even if he could ease Kazmer's torment only for an hour. Because it wasn't the doctor's fault if he was nobody's fool. Nor was it such a blessing, being nobody's fool. For Mr. Perkins had become a new man, as he himself had put it; but what could Kazmer do in all his wisdom? Nothing, only roll the prescription into a little ball and throw it down the gutter.

But that was all right, too, for even a fool's paradise didn't last forever. The sheep were happy enough on the hillside, but they still ended up on the butcher's slab. Only foxes were unhappy, smelling danger day and night; yet who, having the choice, would not rather be a fox than a sheep? Except a sheep, Kazmer supposed, a sheep would not wish to be a fox or even a man. But that was only another way of saying that no one had a choice; and hadn't the Reverend Vegvari explained *that* a long time ago? And if it was God's hand, who was Kazmer to stay it; and what with, Dr. Witstein's prescription?

And since there was no way of knowing God's plan, not until He made it manifest, there was little reason for Kazmer not to follow his own heart in the meantime, and by Thursday afternoon the shop was cleaned and dusted. Petrona could never stand a mess, not when it had to do with things anyway, and if only the insides of people's heads were as easy to scour clean as old cooking pots. Nor was a little place a small matter to make tidy, not when it was workshop, kitchen and bedroom all in one; and anybody would have thought that the smaller a room the easier to make it sparkle, but it wasn't. By the time Kazmer finished it was nearly six o'clock, and Petrona would be knocking on the door in an hour.

He didn't keep the water running while he was shaving himself, for it made an awful noise in the big tin sink and he might not hear her knocking if she got there earlier. Not that it was likely she would, because she'd get there later if anything; but a person could never tell, not with Petrona. She might get there anytime and she might even not come at all.

She might change her mind, and maybe phone him later that night or in the morning to say that she just couldn't do it. She might say it, who could tell why, maybe to make Kazmer ask her to come, beg her even, except he wouldn't. He worked out in his mind, while he was drying his face, what he'd say to her if she did that. He'd say, "Well, I guess it's just as well you didn't come, Petrona," that's what.

Except it wouldn't be true and she'd know it, and why should grown people play at such things so late in the day? A man of fifty and a woman two summers from forty, when these were games for courting girls and boys, well, even young animals played them, trying out their strength. But you sow in the spring and reap in the fall, and only a fool would try to do it the other way around. Except they were all fools in this new country, trying to cheat time with games and blue paint around their eyes, as if sowing in autumn was all you needed to stop winter from setting in.

But time could pass in little ways, not only big, and there was no point wasting too much of it thinking. By the time he put on his good suit, it was just a minute or two before seven; and it was ten after when he finished tying the knot in his tie because the collar was too stiff. Well, Petrona wouldn't be on time anyway, and even wrestling with a starched collar was better than just waiting for her all dressed up. Not that in the end it didn't come to that, because it did: the clock showed 7:25 and there was still nobody at the door. Kazmer even sauntered to the front of the store to check it, but then he just walked up and down between the head of the bed and the blue curtain. That suit wasn't so comfortable to sit down in, nor was there any sense in wrinkling the trousers. She'd come in her own good time if she was coming; whether he stood or sat, it made no difference.

But there was no sound at the door, even though it was twenty to eight, and the telephone was also silent, and not because the line was out of order, for Kazmer checked to see that it was not. He even switched on the color television. It couldn't hurt, and at least it brought some other people in the room to keep him company. It was even a pleasure to see how Petrona kept all those TV people waiting, too, only a pity that none of them was Johnny Carson. But he kept the volume low, for fear that it might drown out her knock at the door.

He needn't have bothered because when the knock came— and it was nearly eight o'clock when it did—it was loud enough for him to hear over any television. And not only that, but the knocking came again before he could even get to the door. Well, all that noise was just to show how much she had hurried, because now she'd be all out of breath and full of apologies and tell him how it wasn't her fault that she had been an hour late. But what did it matter? That was Petrona and that's what she was like; and if it bothered him, well, he didn't have to wait for her at all. It wasn't as if anybody had ever forced him to put up with her ways at the point of a gun.

And never mind a gun, the truth was he was so glad that she had come at all that he even said "Petrona!" as he was pulling back the latch. Except it wasn't Petrona. It was a tall man standing right at the door, and a shorter man just a couple of steps behind him.

Kazmer didn't know who the two men were because he had never seen them before, and for a second he thought, God alone knew why, that they might be bringing him some word from Petrona. And in a way they were, because the taller man said, "Well, I guess you're Kazmer Harcsa."

"Yeah."

"We have a warrant here for your arrest on a charge of breaking and entering."

"What you say?"

The two men looked at each other, and then the shorter one said, "Come on, Kazmer, you broke off that padlock and took out something from your house. Whatever the hell it was. People saw you, they said it looked like a kid's horse. What the hell, you shouldn't have done it, but what the hell."

"Yeah, Kazmer," the taller man added uneasily, "it's not the end of the world. We go downtown, and you'll be out on bail in the morning."

Kazmer walked to the car with them, not even bothering to lock the door or switch the television off, though the men said he could go back inside for his coat, they didn't mind waiting. But he just shook his head, knowing that if he went inside he would come out not with his coat but the gun, and it would take a fool to do that. A fool, who didn't know that that gun was ordained for other things.

He did look at the sky, though, as they were walking to the policemen's car, because it would have been a comfort to catch a glimpse of Prince Csaba's army thundering down the Avenue of the Hosts. If Prince Csaba's soldiers ever came riding to his rescue they'd be up there now, in the chilly, dark blue November dusk, but Kazmer couldn't see them. The Avenue was there all right, the great clouds of stars people here called the Milky Way, but only a faint orange dot was moving along it slowly. Kazmer knew what it was, too, because it was one of those *satellites*. He had even shown one like it to the children on a clear night up at the Moon River. An orange dot, and if only it were the dust stirred up in the sky by the hooves of Prince Csaba's horses, but it wasn't. Just a satellite, Russian or American, who could tell?

SMOKING GUN

THIS TIME IT was the truth, what the two policemen had said to Kazmer, because the next morning the judge only told him, "Come back after Christmas and bring a lawyer," and then something about Kazmer being on his own *recognizance*. But that was all right, a man in court explained that this only meant that nobody had to put up any money for him to make sure he'd be coming back. Nor was the judge wrong, for Kazmer knew that he'd be back. He'd be in that court, maybe even before the Lord Jesus would have another birthday.

But that was for him to know and no one else, not even Petrona when she phoned to say, that same afternoon, that it was none of her doing, Kazmer being dragged to court again. "I want you to know that, Mr. Harcsa," she said, "because I even gave my lawyer a real piece of my mind about it, when I heard."

"When did you hear?" he asked her.

"Only this morning," she said. "Only this morning, I swear. And I said to Mr. Loeblich, I said . . ."

But he interrupted her, for what difference did it make what she said to him, and he asked her instead, "Why didn't you come when you said you would, last night?"

Petrona was silent for a second.

"That had nothing to do with it," she answered, and he could almost see her face, pouting like a little girl, as he heard her voice. "I just couldn't. I had my coat on and everything, but I just couldn't. You understand?"

He said nothing, and she said after a while, "Anyway, it would only have been trouble, like, the way it turned out. I mean, I want to see you again, it's not as if I don't, but I'm so confused. Maybe I need a little more time."

And when he said nothing to that either, for what could he say, she continued, "I don't care if you think I'm making it up, because I don't. My doctor, he says that I'm in a very delicate state, you know, psychologically. And my lawyer, well, he says it's none of his business, but he doesn't know if it's such a good idea, me having coffee with you until everything is settled. . . . Because, and you don't know about that, but I had a really bad case of feeling guilty, because of the children and everything, and of course being programmed in this double standard like every woman. . . . I'm just getting over it now, and sure I want to have coffee with you, I mean I asked you myself, but what if I said the wrong thing or you said the wrong thing, and I . . ."

He didn't hang up the phone, only put it quietly on the workbench, then sat on the stool with his head between his hands. Her voice rose thinly from the receiver for another minute, maybe even longer, although Kazmer couldn't make out the words anymore. He just listened to the voice of the woman who used to be his wife, the mother of his children, oh, her high cheekbones, the proud line of her neck, her coal black eyes, and what kind of creature did these people turn her into, oh Petrona, Petrona. The same people who painted the poster of the harvester-combine back home, then cut off Katika's hands with its shiny new blades. The same people followed him to New York and Toronto to take his second woman from him, poster people, color TV people, what was the difference? Except it was worse this time, for the mangled dead couldn't come back to haunt him, but the woman who used to be Petrona, she was still talking at him in her glass-and-metal voice through the wires. And it was worse, too, because of Johnny and Borbala.

He couldn't tell when Petrona stopped speaking, but after a while there were these quick, sharp whistles coming from the phone, so he just put the receiver back on the hook. No one could see into the future, but he knew that he would not hear the sound of her voice again, well, maybe in another life, but not in this one. And not that it didn't break his heart and not that he didn't wish he could cry. But once a well went dry, it took more than wishes to draw water from it.

It was time to do what had to be done, nor was it any good pretending that it was still too early. They were breaking great laws, the poster people, the color TV people, greater laws than the Supreme Court's; and they were passing the word that they wouldn't stop, either, not until somebody stopped them. Nor was it too late. A man would do nothing, unless it was to make life easier for himself, if it were ever too late for justice.

But seven rabbits, for he had said seven to the stranger Hollo had sent to him with the gun—well, that was just a number he must have liked the sound of, because it made no sense to him now. Maybe the lady judge and the two lawyers would make the first three; and it would be five if he added the young man in the car and Petrona herself. But then why not old Judge Winkler, too, and the deaf Master yelling at him, and maybe the Ombudsman for good measure?

But if he could only get to one person, why make it any of these? Why when there were all the TV people, the bald, blinking men and silver-earring women, maybe even Johnny Carson himself? New York, for that's where Petrona said Johnny Carson was, unless she was wrong about that, too. Well, if he could get

to New York from Bugyi he could get to it from Toronto; and if
the money the Supreme Court had left him wasn't enough for a
plane ticket, he could always drive the blue truck. Go for Johnny Carson in the blue truck, the one *she* hated so, that would be
a thought!

Yes, but it was a child's thought, because Kazmer wasn't
putting that Mauser in his belt just to get his picture in the
papers, only crazy people did that. Those four bullets were
there to say something to the world, but who would understand what it was he wanted to say if he drove to New York
and fired them into Johnny Carson? Petrona would, but no
one else. And killing a man just so that he could say something to Petrona, no, he wouldn't have that burden on his
conscience.

But it was a tempting thought, and if he only had a way
with words like Mr. Marosvári, to make his reasons clear to
people afterward, Kazmer would have started up the blue truck
right then and there and headed it down the Queen Elizabeth
Way to the border at Fort Erie. Just like when he was driving
to Disneyland, yes, and New York wasn't even half the distance. But as it was, Kazmer only picked up the telephone and
dialed Mr. Loeblich's number.

"Sorry, Mr. Loeblich is not coming back today," the secretary said after he told her his name, but not right away because first she kept him waiting on the line, and Kazmer knew
that she must be lying. That young lawyer wouldn't talk to
him, and no wonder. He would never get to see him, not after
everything that happened. At least, not without a good *ruse de
guerre*, and hell, Uncle Harcsa could think up a dozen, but
could he think of one? Only one, now that he needed it, if he
was flesh of his flesh!

"You tell him please," Kazmer said, "you tell him I got money
for him to pay. He got number, he phone me before."

Then he sat by the telephone and waited, without taking
his eyes off the black machine he waited, willing it to ring.

The words he said, "money," perhaps it wouldn't be enough for Mr. Loeblich to see him, but it must be enough for him to phone him back. This young man putting him in jail, trying to take away his children, twisting his words around in court, well, this young man had no hatred for him. And if he didn't, why else would he do what he did but for money? There were such people all over the world, black, white, brown, it made no difference. And sure, when they got their hands on the law books, they would quickly write "no-fault divorce" into them, just as Mr. Schuldig explained it. Because then they would always have a person to owe them money, whether he did anything wrong or not.

But the phone didn't ring, not until it was nearly five o'clock, and Kazmer needed all his strength not to snatch it up after the first ring. But he didn't, he even let it ring three times before putting the receiver to his ear.

"I've got Mr. Loeblich on the line for you now," the girl's voice said.

And she did, because the next thing Kazmer heard was Mr. Loeblich saying, "Hello, yes?"

"Mr. Loeblich?" he asked, just to make sure.

"This is Mr. Loeblich."

"Here is Kazmer Harcsa speaking," Kazmer said. "When I can come and see you for appointment, please?"

"I don't think you've got any reason to see me," the young man said, and Kazmer's heart nearly stopped. He almost said something right then, just to push the bait a little closer to the lawyer's mouth. But it was a good thing he didn't, for Mr. Loeblich continued, "What is this money you told my secretary about?"

"Is money I got. For you."

"Oh yeah? And where did you get money from all of a sudden? You were always telling us you were broke."

Well, and let God decide, because he was going to answer him now, and if the lawyer only laughed or told Kazmer to go to hell because he didn't believe him, well, that was how God wanted it. "My number, she come in lottery," Kazmer said, lowering his voice. "You know, Wintario, big prize. So now I want you get my money, no bother me no more."

And it was clear what God wanted, because Mr. Loeblich said nothing for a couple of seconds, and then he said:

"Fancy that. How much?"

A good strike, not only a nibble, Kazmer could feel it, just as if he had been holding a fishing rod in his hand. "I no say, not on phone," he said. "People, they envy too much. They say, put in paper; I say I no want bandits come to my shop."

"All right, all right," said Mr. Loeblich. "Let's see, I'm in court tomorrow until one. In the afternoon I'm back in the office but I've got appointments. Best thing you come and see me in the courthouse. Be there at one o'clock."

"Supreme Court house?" Kazmer asked.

"Yes, same place we had your divorce hearing. Same floor. Remember?"

Well, and this was one thing Mr. Loeblich did not have to worry about, for if they had put out his eyes with a burning piece of coal he would still have remembered how to find the Supreme Court of Ontario. Even so it was good, the young lawyer asking him this question. It was always little things, like a small knot in the wood that could break a tooth off a brand-new saw, and it was important to be careful.

If a thing had to be done at all, as this thing did, it had to be done right; and to do it right a lot had to be taken care of. For instance a hasty person, Kazmer thought, as he was putting the receiver back on its cradle, well, a hasty person might just get into his blue truck and drive it down to the courthouse at noon. But what if that truck got a flat tire on the way? It could happen, for a nail lying in the roadway wouldn't know that that truck was on an errand of justice, and neither would a sharp piece of glass. Or another driver, window-shopping, could bump into Kazmer from behind; that happened every day, too. What if he couldn't find a parking spot, and a policeman chased him away as he was pulling up to the curb? Why take the risk, when the streetcar stopped only a block away?

As for that gun, that was a puzzle, because what would a smart person do about that gun? An old gun, bought off a stranger just like that; who could tell if it would fire? And those bullets, even if the gun was all right, those bullets might have been lying at the bottom of somebody's toolbox since the last war; and sure he could take them out of the clip and look at them, but no one would find out much about those bullets just by looking. They looked all right, anyway; maybe turning a little black around the copper casing.

The thing to do, then, was to try one out, and Kazmer nearly did. He even filled up an old box with sawdust, which ought to stop a bullet from going into the floor. But then he didn't fire because he heard a voice—at least he could have sworn he did, and not only that, but it sounded like Uncle Harcsa's voice—calling him a fool. What if the first bullet was the only good one? There he'd go, wasting his chance for nothing! Or worse, what if the first bullet was a dud but the rest were fine? If that gun didn't fire now, he wouldn't even show up at the courthouse because he'd lose heart; and then what would he do for the rest of his life, pay fifty dollars to the doctor every week, like Mr. Perkins?

Let glass-and-metal people worry about whether a gun would fire or not. It would or it wouldn't, as God willed it, and all Kazmer had to worry about was to put a fish knife in his boot. If that fish knife was sharp enough, it could clear a path for justice as wide as a bullet.

The gun, the knife, the tokens for the subway, and what else was there to do? Well, laying out clean underwear, because wherever he'd end up, in hospital or jail, there'd be strangers looking at him as he undressed, and that was one lesson the Supreme Court had taught him. What Kazmer couldn't do—although his hand was on the phone, he wanted to do it so badly—was to speak to Johnny and Borbala. It would be a long time before he heard their voices unless he spoke to them now. Or never, because children's voices change and their faces change, too, and all parents have is maybe a year for enjoying a child because after that, what comes along is a different child again. But he couldn't just call them out of the blue, he had never done that before, and Petrona might suspect something. There was no point in risking that. Nor was there any need, because what could he say to a boy of eleven and a girl of nine, just that he loved them? Well, a lot of parents might; in this new country they might even spend their money and their children's money on long-distance telephone calls to say it. Hell, if they did, they knew best; maybe *their* children needed to be told. But Johnny and Borbala would know it anyway. And maybe when they grew up they'd understand that whatever their father did, he did it for them. Though it made no difference, whether they understood it or not.

As for the rent, it was settled for the month, nor did he owe customers any work because no one had paid him in advance. That left only the old Himalayan's color television, which he had forgotten about. Well, he could take it across the street in the morning and pay him something for the extra day. And since it was in the room, he even turned it on before going to bed, just to see if that man would come on, the one he liked, the fat man who showed people how to repaint old furniture. But he didn't, not that night; and it crossed Kazmer's mind that he had meant to ask Petrona about this furniture man. He meant to ask her if she liked watching him, too, but he forgot. Well, that was one thing now that he'd never know.

He slept when it was time to sleep; and he slept soundly, as he did most of the time, except when he had been dreaming about Petrona or that other dream he used to have, about the border guards catching him as he was sneaking across a strip of plowed land with a lantern. But not this night, for this night he dreamed about nothing. The only thing was that when he woke up in the morning, he felt a great, powerful hunger, just as if he had been starving for days. He couldn't understand it, he was never much of a man for breakfast; but hell, there was no sense in being hungry, not when there was enough bread and dry sausage on the shelf under the windowsill. So Kazmer ate, taking his time, cutting the bread and sausage into bite-size chunks with his knife.

When he finished, he unplugged the color TV and carried it across the street into the old Himalayan's store. He wasn't there, though, only his wife was standing behind the cash register, a really fat woman, such as Kazmer could not remember seeing the like of, with folds of brown flesh bulging out from that funny silk wrap she wore that left her naked at the waist. But she seemed like a kind person, with black eyes even bigger and more beautiful than Petrona's, and a friendly smile.

"Are you going to work now?" she asked after Kazmer had paid her, and he replied politely:

"I go work."

But he didn't, because he only walked back to the shop and sat in front of the workbench, resting his hands on a plank of white birch and looking through the basement window from which he could see the feet of people passing by. There they were, going about their business, boots and high-heeled shoes, pants and skirts. Kazmer sat there, he didn't know for how long, maybe it was for ten minutes, maybe an hour. The telephone rang once, but he didn't answer it. Then he looked at the clock on the wall, and it was a quarter to twelve, time to tuck the gun in his belt and the fish knife in his boot-top, which he did; and before locking the door he turned the sign over in the window so that it said BACK IN 5 MINUTES.

The streetcar took him to the Supreme Court house with time to spare, for it was not even twelve-thirty; except there was hardly any room to stand up because the hallway on the third floor was so crowded with people waiting to get their divorces.

Well, and that policeman on the phone wasn't lying when he said it happened all the time. There wasn't an empty bench along the corridor, not that Kazmer minded pacing for a while; nor did anybody care in that place whether he sat or walked up and down. There was only a guard in uniform, an old man who sat behind a little table, telling people which way to go if they asked him; and he didn't seem to care either, but Kazmer's eyes kept coming back to him for a different reason. That old guard looked familiar, and where could he have seen his face before? Maybe it was from the time when he was here with Mr. Schuldig, getting his own divorce.

Anyway, pacing was better than sitting down when a man had to think, nor was it easy thinking up the right words that he would have to say when Mr. Loeblich came. Kazmer would have had trouble with those words in his own language, never mind in English. True, it was hard to believe that anybody could do the things that Mr. Loeblich had done and not understand, but maybe he didn't. And if he didn't, it wasn't right for such a thing to happen to a man without him knowing why.

Or maybe it was for Kazmer's own sake, who could tell, for if he did something like that and couldn't even explain it, would it not put him in the wrong? But what should he say?

Should he say: "You ruin everything for children"? Or: "You young man still, you ruin much other children if you no stopped"? Or maybe: "Is no good, what you do to this country, make bad law"? Perhaps "You no put father in jail for saving children's house" or "You no make fun of husband for chasing young man from wife" would be the best. But better still: "If bandit come, take everything, you no shoot?"

And better or not, it was too late to think up other words, because there was Mr. Loeblich coming out of the courtroom at the far end of the hallway. There were people walking right behind him, two men and a young woman, and it was more important to watch out for them than to think of good words anyway. Because a person ought to be flogged for a fool if he hurt these innocent people by mistake. Kazmer's glance fell on the guard, and there he was, only God knew why, this old man nodding his head at him, telling Kazmer to go ahead, do what he had to do. Where had he seen that guard's face before? Nor was there time to worry about that either, because Mr. Loeblich had already walked by, still not seeing him even though he seemed to be looking, and it was good that he did walk past Kazmer because now there were no other people behind him. The words now, what were the best words?

And since Kazmer couldn't remember them, all he said was, "Hi, Mr. Loeblich!" He must have taken the gun from his belt, though, because by the time the young lawyer turned he could feel his thumb pulling back the safety catch. And Mr. Loeblich, he could not have seen the gun in Kazmer's hand, he must have been too close, because there was nothing in his face, no fear and no surprise, only the eyes of a person recognizing someone he was waiting to meet.

And if that's how it was, that's how it was, and perhaps it was for the best. Because Mr. Loeblich's eyes did not even flinch at the sound, perhaps he never even heard it, as the gun went off with a bang when Kazmer pulled the trigger. But he did look down at his blue vest, then raised his left hand as if to touch the hole where the bullet went into his chest, before his legs gave out and he fell down in the hallway, saying only "Oh!" as he fell.

There was silence after the shot rang out, such silence as Kazmer had never heard before. Suddenly every person in that hallway stopped speaking or moving, and for a second perhaps they didn't even breathe. Not that this silence lasted long, because first a knocking sound came, like a breeze rattling an unlatched door, except it came from Mr. Loeblich's right shoe twitching up and down against the tiled floor. Then a woman screamed, and people began running, some dashing away from where Kazmer stood but one or two almost brushing up against him as they ran past him to the other end of the hall.

One man threw himself flat on the floor, pulling a woman down with him, and they both lay there covering their heads with their hands. When Kazmer looked around, the only man standing on his feet in that corridor was the old guard. And he not only stood but started walking toward where Kazmer himself was standing, gun in hand, over the body of Mr. Loeblich.

Kazmer looked at the old man as he kept coming, slowly, with a little stiff limp, maybe because he had rheumatism, it often happened to people when they got old. An old man with a stiff leg; yet he was the only one to stand up to him, for the younger men were all scattered or lying on the floor covering their heads. Never mind the three bullets left in the gun, there was no way Kazmer would hurt such an old man. No, not even if this old man hadn't been someone he knew; except he was, Kazmer now recognized him clearly, and how could he have been so blind before? No wonder he kept nodding his head from behind that little table, approving, encouraging Kazmer to do what had to be done. Just like the last time, when they had said goodbye at the fork in the road, except it wasn't "goodbye" because Kazmer could still remember the words. *Well, I won't take too much shit, either,* he had said, and *Hell, boy,* the reply came, followed by a little pipe juice aimed at the ground, *no Harcsa ever has.* It was Uncle Harcsa, this old man, and what was wrong with his eyes that he did not know him at a glance?

Well then, God be praised, Uncle Harcsa had come to see Kazmer stand up for his family! And if he could no longer defend them, to see at least that justice would be done. Or to take word to Prince Csaba, maybe: was it time to send that army thundering down the Avenue of the Hosts? But it was all right for all those dead spirits to rest a little longer. Because their grandchildren could still look out for themselves, hell, they were in no trouble yet!

"Just drop that gun," Uncle Harcsa said, speaking in English; and who could tell why he spoke in English or why he pretended to be wearing that guard's uniform? But he must have had his reasons, whatever they were, so Kazmer nodded and put the Mauser on the floor. Then Uncle Harcsa pointed to a door and said, "Sit down in that room and wait," and Kazmer, well, he walked into the room and pulled up a chair, doing as he was told. Because now it was done, the thing that he had to do; and the rest wasn't up to him anymore.

From where he was sitting he could still see Mr. Loeblich lying in the hall, except he couldn't see his face because his head was turned the other way. Mr. Loeblich's right shoe made no sound now, though his foot was twitching as before, only it wasn't touching the floor. Now it was moving just a little but much more quickly, as if the chilly tiles made Mr. Loeblich shiver from the cold. And on his upturned palm the fingers were quivering the same way, all of them together, but more slowly than his foot. It was almost like a man trying to get hold of something but not being able to close his fingers over it; and then trying again and again. Once he even said something, it was more like a sigh, it went "Eh-eh-eh-eh," as if he were exasperated over not being able to grasp whatever it was he wanted to hold in his hand. And maybe Kazmer should have felt pity, but the truth was he felt pride: a young man so clever with words that maybe five minutes ago he had still been explaining in court how some husband was being cruel to his wife, and now all he could say was "Oh!" and "Eh-eh-eh!" People were complaining that God created the world all wrong, that there would be more justice in it if they changed it this way or that, but maybe God wasn't so wrong after all. If a man was ready to pay what it cost, he could still see his enemy lying at his feet.

And not only that, but what was it the old people had been saying back home? They always said, slay an enemy and he will be your servant in the other world! Not the Reverend Vegvari, because if you listened to him it was just a superstition and unchristian to boot; but the Reverend Vegvari didn't know everything. And if it was the old people who had the truth, well, it wouldn't be so bad, having Mr. Loeblich around to wash his shirts and cook his supper, for a man who had no wife anymore to do it for him.

And Kazmer glanced at Mr. Loeblich again, perhaps just to see what kind of a servant he would make, but there were people standing around him now and all Kazmer could see, coming from between their feet, was a long trickle of dark blood. It stopped, as he was watching it, and collected in a small pool like a fist, and then a thinner trickle started flowing from it and pointed like a finger to where Kazmer was sitting in the room. Well, it was all right, if Mr. Loeblich wanted to point at him for everyone to see. He wasn't running anywhere. And a man did come, he looked like another young lawyer, but when Kazmer raised his head and looked him in the eye he just backed away, smearing Mr. Loeblich's blood all over the tiles.

Then nobody came for a long time, except more and more people to stand around the body. Once when Kazmer looked again, he saw somebody putting a briefcase under Mr. Loeblich's head, as if a briefcase made any difference. Though it might to a lawyer, Kazmer thought, even to a dead one. But then, when he glanced up a minute or two later, there were four policemen standing right in front of him; and they weren't backing away either when Kazmer looked them in the eye. They weren't backing away, but neither were they cocky and smug, like the two who came to his house, nor did they say anything about how it would make no difference whether Kazmer went along with them the easy or the hard way.

"Just relax, eh?" one of them said. "You just take it easy. Everything's gonna be all right."

"You wanna get up now?" the other policeman asked. "If you wanna get up, it's okay. We'll all go together, and no trouble."

Kazmer nodded. "Is okay," he said, getting to his feet. In the doorway he craned his neck to see if he could catch another glimpse of Uncle Harcsa, but he couldn't. Wherever he came from, and wherever he went, Uncle Harcsa wasn't in that hallway anymore. Then, with a policeman in front and one behind and two more on either side of him, Kazmer marched into the elevator, out into the lobby, and down the three small marble steps of the Supreme Court.

The police station looked the same as the one where they took him for no-fault divorce, except this time it was different. For one thing, they were calling him a different name now, and Kazmer soon found out what that name was, because while he was waiting in a little room that had nothing but a table and two chairs in it, a new policeman stuck his head in the door, then asked the other policeman who was standing outside:

"Who have you got in there?"

"Oh, that's that smoking gun."

Well, and names were only names, one was no worse than the other, whether it was a cruel husband or a no-fault divorce. Or a consumer of justice, as that young Willard had called him, and now a smoking gun. And perhaps being a smoking gun was the best, for it wasn't like the last time, nobody laughed in Kazmer's face or snickered behind his back, and it wasn't "Off you go, Charlie" but only "please" and "thank you" and being polite. And the two older policemen who came after the rest, the ones in civilian clothes, they even had a typewriter brought into the room where he was waiting, to make sure they would miss nothing that Kazmer was going to say. Cigarettes, light, whatever he wanted, and no paper cups but coffee served in a mug.

It was then that Kazmer asked, "You no want me give you this?" taking the fish knife out of his boot. That was when the older of the two policemen said "thank you" for the first time, when he took the knife, though he went very pale in the face. And the younger one, his name was Staff Sergeant Gorshaw, he picked the knife up and carried it into the hallway and Kazmer could hear him shouting, "Which asshole didn't search this guy when you brought him in?" which was kind of funny, and Kazmer half expected the whole lot of them to reply "Me!" because none of them had.

But there was nothing funny about when Staff Sergeant Gorshaw came back and told Kazmer that he had been arrested on a charge of first-degree murder, and that he didn't have to say anything in answer to that charge now, but if he did, they'd take it all down in writing. And it was true, because the older policeman was already clattering away on the typewriter, taking down Kazmer's full name and address.

"You understand that charge, Kazmer?" Staff Sergeant Gorshaw asked.

Well, he understood murder, whatever that first-degree meant, and Kazmer nodded his head, yes. Then, remembering that young lawyer's fingers opening and closing on the tiled floor, maybe still trying to grab at his house, his wife, his children, he added, "Yeah, he got it coming for him," and the typewriter started clattering again.

Sergeant Gorshaw waited until the typing machine stopped. Then he looked at a piece of paper in front of him, took a deep breath, and said: "Shortly after 1 p.m. police officers were called to attend at 145 Queen Street West in Toronto; and while there they had occasion to investigate a shooting occurrence involving a victim by the name of Garry Loeblich who was later pronounced dead at St. Michael's Hospital; and what if anything can you tell us about this incident?"

Well, Kazmer just sighed, because he knew that it would come to that. Something would happen, and somebody would ask him to tell about everything that led up to it; and when that time came, as it did now, could he tell his story straight? Could he tell it from the beginning, and where was the beginning, if there was one at all? Was it when he came to this country? Was it when he first met Petrona? He knew it would be foolish when that thing happened and they asked him, if he couldn't tell them why. Because what would they take him for?

They'd take him for a demented crazy person, that's what. They would shut him up in some place where they kept people who did things for no reason, and rightly, because even a sheep isn't worth the shearing once it begins to go around and around. A man is no better. He's best forgotten. Feed him water and bread.

And because that wasn't to happen, whatever else did, Kazmer began to tell his story, slowly, carefully, oh Petrona, Petrona! He told Sergeant Gorshaw about the note on the kitchen table, about Johnny and Borbala crossing the slushy April street, about Petrona's funny Sunday shopping and the next morning's tug-of-war. He told him about Johnny's violin lesson and the Supreme Court's letter and the $1,000 check to Mr. Schuldig. He told about the jail and the furniture and Johnny's wooden horse and the deaf Master yelling. And Mr. Loeblich, he told everything about Mr. Loeblich, too, from the first time he laid eyes on him in Judge Winkler's office to that last telephone call about the big lottery prize, and Mr. Loeblich replying, fancy that! But still Kazmer didn't tell Sergeant Gorshaw everything, because he said nothing about one-eyed Hollo and the stranger who had brought him the gun, nor about the thing Petrona wanted him to do with his mouth in their marriage bed. And he said nothing about the color TV, or Prince Csaba's soldiers, or about Uncle Harcsa watching him, pretending to be a guard. Kazmer said nothing about any of this. They were nobody's business.

Even so it was almost morning, by the time it was all finished and typed, because they got him to read over every page; and not only that, but he had to put his *initials* on all of them, next to the mistakes they said they made in typing, perhaps just to show that he had read everything they wrote, who could tell? And when it was all over, and the coffee cold and slimy in the mug, Sergeant Gorshaw was still asking:

"Is that everything, Kazmer? Nothing more you want to say? Nothing, you know, to explain in that statement?"

Kazmer just shrugged, and it wasn't as if he had been tired because he wasn't, but what else could he say? Did he tell about the lady judge calling him a Rumanian national, well, maybe he told them about that, too. "Yeah, I think is all," he said, closing his eyes. "The rest, maybe little troubles, all the things that happen, but who can remember?"

SECTION 16

THE MOST CURIOUS thing happened the very first night they took Kazmer to the real jail. Because he could not go to that jail, Sergeant Gorshaw had said, till after he had been remanded, and he'd just have to stay in the holding cell at the police station until then. But not to worry, he added, they'd see that he was comfortable enough; and they did, because there were plenty of warm blankets and they even brought him a pillow. For food, well, they sent out to the restaurant at the corner, and when Kazmer told the policeman who brought it to take the money for it from his wallet, which the sergeant at the desk had put in an envelope, the policeman just said, never mind. There it was, his third time in a police cell, and it would have been the best never to have seen the inside of one for sure. But if it had to be, it was better for first-degree murder than for no-fault divorce, there was no doubt about that either. Well, Kazmer supposed, the police were only men like the rest, and who wouldn't take better care of a horse than of a horsefly?

Nor was what happened curious just because it was terrible, for Kazmer had expected something terrible to happen sooner or later. But he expected it to come from the jailers, or from the other prisoners maybe; some of the ones he had seen who were like animals, and just by looking at one or two Kazmer could believe all the stories he had ever heard about jail. But what he did not expect was for that thing to come out of the night, when he was all alone. Out of nothing.

It started out like any other night, because he fell sound asleep as soon as he closed his eyes, which was the way it had always been except for maybe a handful of times in his life. But he couldn't have been asleep more than a minute when he woke up, and no wonder because there was Mr. Loeblich, sitting on his chest.

Kazmer cried out, for who wouldn't have, and tried to push Mr. Loeblich away. But it was no use, there wasn't a limb he could move, not even a finger of his hand. And Mr. Loeblich, he looked at Kazmer with such hatred that his lips curled back, but he wouldn't say anything except "Eh-eh-eh-eh!" and let a trickle of dark blood drip onto Kazmer's face from the corner of his mouth. And then, just as suddenly as he came, he was gone.

Well, Kazmer was shaking like a leaf when he got up from his bunk; and it was a good thing they had put nobody else with him in that cell, he would not have wanted anybody to see him frightened like that. And it wasn't as if he didn't know that it was just a nightmare, because he knew it as soon as he stood on his feet, even though he couldn't help looking at his palm after he wiped his face; but it was his own sweat, not Mr. Loeblich's blood, and what else did he expect? The dead didn't walk, except maybe on the color TV. But that young lawyer who took his house, who was getting set to take his children or, hell, even his skin if he had let him, why would that young lawyer be giving him any nightmares? It wasn't as if he had killed an innocent man!

And if Kazmer's fright passed in a minute, his indignation at this undeserved scare stayed with him, and it wouldn't let him go back to sleep for another hour or two. Some servant, that Mr. Loeblich, saying "Eh-eh-eh-eh!" and dripping blood, but maybe the old people back home didn't know much about the other world either. And for this to happen now, being worried by ghosts in his sleep like some bandit who strangled an old woman for her purse, just when he was feeling like a man again, for the first time since the Supreme Court's letter. Because what was he until he plucked up enough courage to put that gun in his belt? Nothing, a shadow, a Big Mac Daddy, a pill-eating mother's hero, just like the rest.

But the minute Kazmer fell asleep again, there was Mr. Loeblich crawling up at him from the foot of the bunk, dear Lord Jesus! His hand opening and closing, Kazmer could see it clearly, as he was trying to get hold of the blanket to pull himself up, and it was a good thing he didn't have the strength. It was a good thing, too, that Kazmer's limbs obeyed him with no trouble this time, and he could kick Mr. Loeblich off the bunk, and then jump on him and hold him until neither his foot nor his hand was twitching anymore. But it was smarter to be safe, and Kazmer fired the other three bullets into his chest and cut his throat with the fish knife for good measure. And then there was no way Mr. Loeblich could be anything but dead. Except what if he wasn't; and how many times would he have to kill this damn lawyer over again?

After that only a fool would have gone to sleep, and Kazmer just gathered the blankets around him and sat on his bunk, propping his back against the wall. But maybe he did fall asleep, he must have, for suddenly there was the Reverend Vegvari sitting next to him on the bunk, and not only that, but he was looking at Kazmer and shaking his head. Kazmer was in for it now, because the Reverend would pull his ear mercilessly and smack his hand with his walnut stick, and it would sting for days the way he'd do it. But maybe he didn't

know what Kazmer had done. The Reverend wasn't reading
the Toronto papers and he didn't even understand English;
though he didn't need to if he had seen the *Sun*, because that
paper even had Kazmer's picture in it. And he must have seen
it, he had it in his hand, though it was folded the other way.

"Kazmer, Kazmer," said the Reverend Vegvari, his voice
filled with reproach. "And you an orphan, too! Is this your
gratitude to strangers when they take you in, bringing such
disgrace on the parish?"

"I wasn't after anybody's bacon in the chimney," Kazmer
mumbled, "only looking out for my own."

"Then why don't you hold out your hand for me to see?"

Well, Kazmer couldn't do that because there was blood on
it, but wasn't that lawyer a bandit who deserved to die? Except
the Reverend Vegvari, he only laughed at that.

"We all know that, you fool," he said, "you think the good
Lord would let him die if he didn't deserve it? But it was still
you who killed him, Kazmer, for it wasn't the pestilence. Or
can you show me a passage in the Bible that says 'Thou shalt
not kill, unless a person deserves it'?"

And it was true that he couldn't, for all the Bible said was
"Thou shalt not kill," with no ifs and buts about it. Only it
wasn't fair. There was God, sending a man out to do justice, and
then turning around and punishing him for it. But it was no
good, saying this to the Reverend Vegvari, because he didn't
even laugh anymore and only looked at Kazmer with great pity.

"And whoever told you that God the Lord was *fair*," he
asked, "because you never heard such blasphemy in my
church. God the Lord is *terrible*, and if you only looked up His
word in the book you'd know it. For He never made any bones
about it, and neither did I."

And sitting up on the bunk was no better than lying down
that night, because if it wasn't Mr. Loeblich it was the Reverend Vegvari; nor was it all over when he woke up Kazmer by
smacking him with the walnut stick. Because the next person

to come along was Johnny Carson, sitting right there in the color TV with Petrona and Judge Winkler, only the judge had Comrade Lei's face. They were speaking in Hungarian, too, not that it made what they were saying any better. "He wasn't a mature adult," Judge Lei was saying, "and he didn't know the first damn thing about progress." And Petrona, she looked up at Johnny Carson, who was holding her hand, and she said, "Well, I loved him, I really did, but he just wouldn't let me be my own person. I couldn't fulfill my potential with him, and Johnny, did you know I named my son after you? I bet you can make your mouth real hard when you kiss."

And Kazmer, he just smashed the nightmare television, for all the good that did him, when he ought to have smashed the real one many years before. Even Mr. Loeblich might be alive today if he had done it then: a young man like that, who might have had children of his own. Because it was a terrible thing that was done to him, to be shot in the chest on an ordinary day at work, and for what, perhaps nothing but an itch between the legs of a strange woman who was neither kin nor cattle to him. And how could Kazmer have done such a thing and think of it with pride? That young lawyer being his servant in the other world, well, maybe if Mr. Loeblich had had a gun, too, and had come looking for Kazmer with it. But all he had was a briefcase for someone to put under his head when he lay there dying, and maybe it was Kazmer who ought to be Mr. Loeblich's servant if they ever met up in that world beyond.

The next day the jailers said Kazmer had a visitor, and his heart jumped because who else could it be but Petrona; and he said to the guard who came to fetch him, "You tell her I no see her." But it was still good, good to know that she had come.

"What do you mean, you don't want to see her?" said the guard. "It's a him. It's your lawyer."

And it was, or at least it was the young crooked lawyer, the one Mr. Marosvári had sent Kazmer to; the one of whom they said that his father had also been a son of a bitch from way back. The young lawyer who showed Kazmer the little bird that made the big song, and wouldn't take the $300 for it. Well, he was here now, in that visitors' room with the green walls, sitting behind a plain big table; and Kazmer didn't know if he was glad to see that young lawyer or not. He almost asked him if he came because he had changed his mind about the $300.

But that young man, he was nobody's fool, and he must have guessed what Kazmer had on his mind. "Well, Uncle," he said in Hungarian, extending his hand to Kazmer, "and I was smart not to take your bit of money when you came to see me."

And when Kazmer said nothing, though he accepted the lawyer's hand, the young man said, "Aren't you going to ask me why?"

"Well, then, why?" asked Kazmer politely.

"Because now you're a big dog, Uncle," the lawyer said, "not like the last time when you were only a little one. Now the two of us can bark up a storm, if you still want to."

Well, the young man was joking, Kazmer could see that, though perhaps it wasn't only a joke. And what else could he do but reply in kind, even if his heart wasn't in it.

"But it would still have been better for you then, sir," he said, sitting down at the table.

"How's that?"

"Well, then I was a little dog with a scrap of bone," Kazmer said, "and now I'm a big dog with none."

The young lawyer laughed.

"Yes, but now you don't need any, Uncle," he said. "The way it works, all the little dogs will bring me their scraps if they see that I'm friends with the big one."

Then he continued, "Anyway, now you qualify for legal aid so don't worry about the money. The question is, do you have a lawyer? Because I shouldn't even be talking to you if you do."

"I have no lawyer," Kazmer said.

"Okay, I didn't think you had. Now, do you want me to defend you?"

And didn't Mr. Marosvári say, he's a son of a bitch, but at least he'd be a son of a bitch for you, Kazmer. Except, big dog or not, why would any lawyer be so eager to come knocking on *his* door? "Excuse me, sir," Kazmer said, "but why would you want to stand up for me? It's not as if I didn't kill one of your kind."

The lawyer just looked at him.

"One of my kind?" he asked. "Why, you're a carpenter; and is every carpenter your kind, then?"

It was a good reply, but the young man didn't stop at that, because he went on to say, "Anyway, I didn't see you kill anybody; all I know is what the police say. And what do you think, Uncle, if people took the police's word for everything, what would they pay all those judges for? Because they don't sit on the bench for nothing."

Yes, but what was the point of playing with words, because that's all it was, even if they were good words. "I killed him all right," Kazmer said, "and you don't have to take it from me, sir, because there were lots of people there to see it."

But if he thought that this would stop the lawyer, it didn't.

"Well, if you say so, Uncle," he replied, offering Kazmer a smoke. "Maybe you did shoot poor Garry Loeblich. The paper pretty much says you did, and maybe this once the paper has it right. But do you know what the *law* says it is, when you hold a gun in your hand and it goes off and kills a man?"

Well, Kazmer knew that, because Staff Sergeant Gorshaw had told him. "First-degree murder," he said, and he said it in English. And such is vanity that he was proud he could remember it so well.

"Maybe," the lawyer replied. "And maybe it's second-degree murder. Or manslaughter. Or maybe negligence or accident or self-defence, which you don't go to jail for at all. Or maybe it's some other thing, and *you* couldn't tell which one it is just from holding the gun. And that's why we have courts and juries, or else we could save us the time, lock you up in a dungeon right now and throw away the key."

And it was true, Kazmer couldn't tell, not when he didn't even understand some of those words. But it still wasn't as the young lawyer had it, what name they'd put to what he did, manslaughter or murder. What it was, was for people to hear why he had to fire that gun. Once people heard that, it would make no difference even if they put him in jail for life.

He tried to explain this to the young lawyer, saying, "It's not so much what they do to me, sir, because I killed a man and God will punish me for it. He'll punish me even if He meant it for me to kill this man, because that is His way.

"But what I want, I want to tell people why, so that everybody can hear it in court. Because a lot of people don't know the law about husbands and wives; or how bad it is, like color TV. Or how they let some lawyers twist things, or send letters with lies in them, Supreme Court letters that you can't do anything about, not even for two, three thousand dollars. And how they can take a man's property that belongs to his children, or send him to jail for sleeping in his own house. Or make out that he is cruel for keeping together his family; but the one who wants to break up the family, the judges help that person. Like crazy people, to make it easy for bad husbands and bad wives.

"And if people hear that in court they'll understand, and who knows, maybe they'll change things for later. You know, to make them better for the children. It's something for me to leave for Johnny and Borbala, just a little thing, now that I have no house to leave them anymore."

And who could tell if that young lawyer understood him, but maybe he did, because he said to Kazmer, "Uncle, I think we're getting somewhere. Did I hear you say that God had meant for you to shoot Garry Loeblich?"

Kazmer nodded, for it was one of the things that he had said. Although he only said it in passing, and who could read God's mind? For his money it wasn't the most important thing anyway, nor was it anybody's business, but that young lawyer, he seemed to remember it the best. And he liked it, too, because he went on saying, "Beautiful. And was there, you know, a *voice*, or did God send a person to you, maybe?"

Well, that was a hard question to answer. Because if God had nothing to do with Uncle Harcsa being in that hallway, speaking English and wearing a guard's uniform, who did? But Kazmer wasn't saying anything about this to anybody, no matter what, because no person would believe it anyway. And maybe it was only his mind, playing tricks on him, though Kazmer didn't think so. That guard *was* Uncle Harcsa, however he got there, one way or another.

And when the young lawyer saw Kazmer hesitate, he said, "Never mind, Uncle, you don't have to tell me about it now. But I think I have a defence for you. I don't like promising things, you never know which way a jury'll jump, but if you stick with me I think it'll be an acquittal. Now, what do you say?"

And what did this young lawyer mean by that word "acquittal," did he mean no jail? And he replied, yes, that's what he meant, when Kazmer asked him.

Well, and wouldn't that be something, not going to jail for shooting a man, when it was jail for sleeping in his own house, even if only for three days and a bit; and who could tell how much jail it would be for going back again to fetch Johnny's horse? Either the law was crazy or this young lawyer was really crooked, just as some people said he was. And Kazmer couldn't resist the question, just because he was curious, and he said, "Well, what is this excuse that you have for me, sir, if you don't mind me asking?"

And the lawyer replied, "Uncle, have you ever heard of Section 16? Well, that's what I think *you* are."

So now he was a Section 16, too, and not only a smoking gun. Or a cruel husband, oh Petrona! And what Section 16 was, it was a page in some dark red book the lawyer pulled out of his briefcase that had MARTIN'S ANNUAL CRIMINAL CODE printed on its spine in gold letters. And that page was a *law*, as the lawyer explained it, saying that no person should go to jail, no matter what he did, unless he understood what he was doing and knew that it was wrong.

That's what the law said; and Kazmer—well, it was true enough, he didn't think that it was wrong to go after a bandit with a gun, not when the bandit was robbing his children. For he wouldn't have done it if he had thought that it was wrong.

"A pity that you weren't my lawyer earlier," Kazmer said, "because I never thought that it was wrong to sleep in my house either. But they took me to jail for it all the same, and maybe I should have told that lady judge that I was a Section 16."

The lawyer laughed at this, not that Kazmer saw anything funny about it, and then he said, "Well, make up your mind. You're in big trouble and I can get you out of it, and it's not even going to cost you any money."

For some reason Kazmer hesitated like a cat before jumping on the hot stove. But then he thought, hell, when this crooked lawyer couldn't help, he never beat around the bush, he just said so. He wasn't like Mr. Schuldig, and why shouldn't a person believe him now? It would be foolish for a man to be no smarter than a cat. Once a cat had burned itself on a hot stove, it would not jump on the cold stove either, not even to get away from the dogs; but wasn't a man a man to know the difference?

And he had to have a lawyer anyway, Staff Sergeant Gorshaw had explained that to him; he even said the court would force a lawyer on him if he didn't bring one. Kazmer could just see it, some lady judge telling him to take on Mr. Schuldig for another thousand dollars, well, that'd be the day! Mr. Schuldig who even said "no more questions" when he was trying to tell the court his side of what it was like, being married to Petrona. Because, he said, you may be a good man, Kazmer, but you are a terrible witness.

"And will you let me explain it in court, sir?" he asked, just to be sure. "Will you let me tell people why?"

"I *want* you to tell people," the crooked lawyer replied. "And I want you to tell it in English, no interpreter, right to the jury's face. I don't care if you stay on the witness stand all day telling it; that's the beauty of being a Section 16."

"All right, then," Kazmer said, "because it doesn't matter to me now, jail is just a place like any other. But I want the people to know."

So they shook hands on that, the two of them, and then the lawyer said, "Now when I leave here, pretty soon the police will come to you. Maybe Sergeant Gorshaw, or maybe somebody from the Crown's office, you know, the prosecutor. Do you understand?

"Well, all you have to do is say nothing to them. Nothing. You just tell them I'm your lawyer, they want to know something, they ask me. Here's my card, you just show it to that sergeant or whoever.

"And the most important thing, when they tell you they'll send a doctor to see you, you say no. And if they send one anyway, you don't talk to him. Remember this, because you have a right to say no to their doctor, they can't do anything about that. And even if they try to tell you the doctor only wants this, that or the other thing, you just say no."

Well, and his crooked lawyer didn't have to worry about that, Kazmer forgetting how to say no to a doctor. If not seeing doctors was all a person ever had to do to keep out of jail, he wouldn't have to look at any jail from the inside for too long. But then the lawyer had a piece of advice that made no sense, for he added, "You are going to see the doctor I bring in here myself, and no one else." And this meant that he did have to see a doctor after all, if not Sergeant Gorshaw's, then the crooked lawyer's. And maybe it made a difference, though Kazmer couldn't see it.

"What is that for, sir, that doctor?" he asked, but the young lawyer just smiled and said that if he asked Kazmer to make him a table, he wouldn't stand around his workbench asking what this tool or that tool was for; and maybe that was true enough. And it wasn't as if he hadn't seen a doctor on his own anyway, and Petrona was seeing a doctor, too. Maybe doctors were just part of this glass-and-metal world, people just kept on seeing them, no matter whether they needed them or not.

It was better to be thinking about what it would be like, that day in court, if the crooked lawyer was telling the truth. Because then, for once, it wouldn't be a day to remember in shame. Then people would listen as Kazmer explained what the law did to him—to him, and to Petrona, too, because didn't she say, "It's not the way the lawyers said it was going to be, Mr. Harcsa, I want you to know that"? And then people would understand. They'd say, "Well, *who* is this law good for, proving lies, squandering children's property, when it's no good for the husband or the wife?" That's the way it would be, nor would there be any jail at the end of it, if that young lawyer were only telling the truth.

And maybe he *was* telling the truth, because not even an hour had passed after he left, and there was Staff Sergeant Gorshaw asking to speak to Kazmer, just as the lawyer said he would be. And the big gray-haired man next to him was a doctor, no less; and they wanted Kazmer to let the doctor speak to him too. Well, and if the sergeant thought that Kazmer would, just for his say-so, he should use a sharper knife to carve his notions out of his brain with.

"What's the matter, Kazmer?" Sergeant Gorshaw asked. "You afraid he's gonna stick a needle in you? He's not that kind of doctor, you know."

Well, a big pinch of salt it mattered what kind of a doctor he was, for Kazmer just shook his head, that was easy enough to do. And they would have had to get up much earlier in the morning, those doctors and policemen, if they wanted to goad him into saying something he shouldn't, now that for once he had good advice and his own son-of-a-bitch lawyer working for him.

And he was working all right, the lawyer, there was no doubt about that, because he came to see Kazmer the very next day. Nor did he come all by himself; and the man he had with him, a sad little man with yellow fingers brushing cigarette ashes from his lapel, he looked like someone Kazmer had seen somewhere before. And no wonder he did, because he was that doctor Mr. Perkins had sent him to, whatever his name was, that Dr. Witstein!

"You see, I did a little *research*, Uncle," the lawyer said, "and I thought you might feel more comfortable seeing an old friend again."

Well, Kazmer thought, back home people liked sharing a little more bacon than he ever did with Dr. Witstein before they'd go around calling him a friend. But it didn't matter much, so Kazmer just listened as the lawyer explained how he had spent a day talking to all the people who knew Kazmer, even neighbors and such, and how Mr. Perkins told him about *persuading* Kazmer to see Dr. Witstein. And it was a hell of a good thing that Mr. Perkins told the young lawyer about that, it seemed, because Mr. Witstein was just about the smartest *expert* there was in the country on people being Section 16, which was what the lawyer wanted Kazmer to be, too. And it was just a lucky *coincidence* that Kazmer had gone to see him about his troubles, of all the doctors he could have gone to see; and luckier still that they could get wind of it before the opposition, meaning the police, could. Because this way Dr. Witstein was going to be *their* expert now, and no one else's.

And the crooked lawyer, he said most of this in English, except the last bit, which he said in Hungarian. And then he added, still in Hungarian, "His nose is a little out of joint because maybe he should have spotted you for a Section 16 when you first went to see him; but never mind, he'll spot you for one now. And even if he doesn't, I've got plenty of other doctors; and the main thing is that since we got to him first, the prosecutor won't be able to call him against us. That's the beauty of the law."

That was good, except the lawyer might as well have said it all in English, for all the sense he was making to Kazmer. But he was happy if his lawyer was, and if it meant spending an hour with Dr. Witstein for fifty dollars, fine, it wasn't as if he hadn't spent an hour with him before. Nor had it been such a bother, that hour, because the little doctor had caused him no pain with his hands or with his words and it was even good perhaps, getting some of his troubles off his chest, even if he had felt ashamed about it afterward. For what kind of a man would have to bend another person's ears with his sorrows? As if all people weren't visited by the world's grief, if not in spring then in winter, if not all at once, then bit by bit. It all came to the same thing in the end.

Except it didn't, because that talk with Dr. Witstein after the crooked lawyer left, well, it was very different from what it had been the first time. Not that the doctor talked any more, because he didn't; he only asked questions again and listened. But the questions he asked were not the same kind. And it was hard for Kazmer to tell at first what kind of questions they were.

For instance, Dr. Witstein would suddenly ask him *where* they were, as if he had forgotten that they were in the visitors' room in jail. Or he would ask Kazmer if he could remember the days of the week, and if he could, was it all by himself or only when the *voices* in his ear were whispering them to him? And Kazmer was still puzzling this question over in his mind, thinking that maybe he didn't understand the doctor's English, when he'd turn around and ask if it was against the law to shoot a person, which any fool would know it was, not only here and there but all over the world. But Kazmer just said yes it was, as if it hadn't been a foolish question; and he even explained why he thought the police had put him in jail when the doctor asked. And it was only when the doctor pretended to forget how many months were in a year that Kazmer got angry.

"What for you ask like this," he said, "you think I crazy?"

And no sooner did he say it than it dawned on him, for that's what it was and nothing else, and how could he have been such a fool. *That Section 16, that was for crazy people!* That was the excuse the crooked lawyer had in mind for him, making out that Kazmer was crazy. No wonder he could promise that he'd never have to go to jail. That place where they put crazy people is not called jail, whatever it's called, and that's where that crooked father's crooked son was conniving to put him!

And that's what Kazmer was to be taken for in court if he said that shooting Mr. Loeblich wasn't wrong, the way a crazy person would say it, one who didn't know right from wrong at all. And then his lawyer would call Dr. Witstein to prove it, the smartest expert on crazy people; and if he wouldn't, some other doctor would. And the law, it wouldn't let Dr. Witstein tell people not to believe that other doctor, because the crooked lawyer spoke to him first. And then it wouldn't matter anymore what Kazmer said, when it was his turn at the witness stand.

For who listens when a crazy person speaks, and never mind if he's speaking the truth. Even a sheep isn't worth the shearing once it begins to go around and around. A man is no better, he's best forgotten; feed him water and bread. No wonder his crooked lawyer would let him speak; he could speak all day if he liked, for who would listen? Who would listen in that court to a man the doctors said was crazy? People would only sleep, or maybe smile at the voice of the truth speaking about husbands and wives and the bad law; and who could blame them? Who could blame people sleeping or smiling when the doctors say the truth is crazy, Section 16, can't tell how many months in a year. And then, if that son-of-a-bitch lawyer had his way, what lesson is there for people to learn from Johnny's and Borbala's house padlocked, or even from Mr. Loeblich's lifeblood in the hallway? Nothing. A crazy man. Nothing.

And he, he might as well have run like a bandit after firing that gun, if it was for nothing; because nobody would have stopped him in that courthouse. There was no need for Uncle Harcsa to come all that way, if it was for nothing, or to order Kazmer to wait in that little room. He had crossed tougher borders than the one between Buffalo and Fort Erie, nor was Mexico at the end of the world for a man with a thumb and a good pair of legs. As for not seeing Johnny and Borbala if he ran to Mexico, well, he wouldn't be seeing them for a long time anyway. He wouldn't see them in the madhouse, and he wouldn't in jail. But it was to tell people something that he didn't run; and ten crooked lawyers would be ten too few to stop him from telling it now!

And Kazmer got up from the table, nor was it hard to see from the way he did it that he wouldn't be sitting down again on his own. And he said to Dr. Witstein, "You go now, thank you. You send me bill, I pay. But no come again. I need no more doctor and no more lawyer."

Then he turned his back and looked at the green wall, and it was only from hearing the door close that he knew that Dr. Witstein was gone. But it wasn't even a second or two later when he heard the door open again, and it was the crooked lawyer coming back in, just as fast as his legs would take him.

"What's the matter, Uncle?" he asked. "Why did you send Dr. Witstein away?"

Kazmer didn't answer, just looked at him.

"Come on, what's wrong?" the lawyer asked again, impatiently. "Have you gone crazy, or what?"

And in spite of himself Kazmer had to laugh because it was funny, but it wasn't a good laugh all the same. "Crazy?" he said. "It would be a lucky day for a crooked lawyer, because then he wouldn't need a doctor to prove any lies."

"Oh, so that's what it is," said the lawyer, turning his eyes to the ceiling and sighing deeply. "Well, you heard another bird-song, now just sit down and let me show you another bird.

"Maybe you're crazy, maybe you're not. I don't know and it isn't my business. But you'd better pray to God that you were crazy when you shot that lawyer. Because if you weren't, then you killed a man in cold blood. That's the name of that bird, and do you know what it fetches at the fair these days? It fetches a mandatory twenty-five years in jail, which means twenty-five years even if the judge is your uncle.

"But if the doctors say you're crazy, you go to a nice clean hospital where they feed you honey for breakfast. And when in two years, four years, six years the doctors see that you're not crazy anymore, you go home. And if you can't tell the difference between six and twenty-five—well, then you *are* crazy, Uncle, and who needs a doctor to prove it."

And that crooked lawyer, wasn't he full of good replies; but even the devil wouldn't be much without his tongue. And it was true, because two or four years would pass, and even six wasn't the end of the world, but in twenty-five Johnny would be thirty-six years old and even little Borbala would be thirty-four. And he himself, well, there was no point in trying to figure out how old he would be or what he'd do if they ever let him out alive, and perhaps it would be better if they didn't.

But if that's what it was all about, the time he'd have to spend in jail, he could have run from that courthouse. If he had just wanted to shoot Mr. Loeblich to get even, he could have waited for him around some dark corner one night, and then who would have known that it was he who did it? Then it wouldn't even be any two, four, six years in a madhouse, only people saying in the shop, did you read about that lawyer who got shot, wasn't it terrible, and who could have done it? But it wasn't at night, because he killed Mr. Loeblich in broad daylight; and not around some dark corner, for he did it in the Supreme Court of justice.

And if he was crazy to do it, or if he let a crooked lawyer pretend that he was, then it was crazy for any man to stand up for his family. It was crazy for a father to protect his children's

house, and crazy for a husband to stop a young man from grabbing for his wife's skirt. Then marriage was only fuck me and
make your mouth real hard, and it'd take a crazy man to say
that it was more. Then husbands weren't husbands, nor were
wives wives; and they weren't fathers and mothers either, only
those private spaces Petrona was going on about, persons in
their own rights fulfilling their potential, watching Johnny
Carson on the color TV. And children weren't children but
orphans, never mind if their parents died of the Spanish flu or
not. Orphans, and lucky to have some mature adult to look
out for them, like Judge Winkler or Mr. Schuldig, after the
man who begot them and the woman who gave them birth
got through their no-fault divorce.

But he wasn't crazy; whatever the law said, Section 16 or all
the other sections before and after it. Because the world did
not begin when the first magazines were printed for women to
read under the electric hair dryer, or for men either; and in
that long world that had gone before, people had lived for
their families and they died for them, too. They lived and they
suffered and they died when they could have run away; and
any person who gave up the family for no reason *was* at fault,
nor was a blue truck any reason and neither was a hard mouth.
For what was a person's fault, if making a promise to God and
then trading it for whatever caught his or her fancy at a shop
window wasn't? And if the law was setting up to make it easier
for such persons to prove lies about their husbands or wives
who had kept their promises, it was the law that was crazy.

But Kazmer said none of this to the crooked lawyer, and all
he said was, "Well, sir, I shot the wrong man the other day after all. Because all he was trying to steal from me was my skin,
but you are grabbing for my head, and it's lucky for us that I
caught you in time."

"You *are* crazy," the lawyer said. "Let me tell you, Uncle . . . ."

"I'm not your uncle, either," Kazmer said. "If I was your uncle,
I'd rip off your ears and fry them."

And the way Kazmer said this, well, it would have made most men back off even if he didn't raise his voice. But the crooked lawyer wasn't a man to let go of his courage in his pants, whatever else was wrong with him, and he only laughed at Kazmer.

"You ride a high horse for a pauper," he said, "and maybe you could have ripped off a lot of ears twenty years ago, but not today. Today you need a gun to do any harm to anybody, and you haven't got one because the police took it away from you. So don't tell me what you'd do with my ears, just try and take the wax out of your own. You just chew on this for a minute, because after that jury comes back into that court-room, wherever *you* will be going and for however long, *I* will be going home."

"Well, and what are you saying?" asked Kazmer. "That I'm a crazy man?"

There was a little silence after that, because first the lawyer opened his mouth as if to say something, but then he closed it again. In the end he made up his mind, though, and he said, "What the hell, I'm going to tell you the truth.

"No, I don't think you're crazy at all. I think you're just a guy who got fucked around a bit, first by your wife, then by a lot of other people, until you got tired of it and decided to do a little fucking of your own. So you went out and picked one of them and rained on his haystack but good.

"Well, I don't happen to think a man has to be crazy to do that. It's human nature. Everybody out there is trying to bend the law to get their pound of flesh, and they'll always get it off the back of the fellow who can't bend the law his way. And they sure had their knives in your back, but when you saw what the game was about, you just changed the rules on them a little. Hell, I admire you for it.

"And not only that, but I thought you played it smart," the crooked lawyer continued, "because you didn't run. People who run only get caught sooner or later, but when I read in the paper that you stayed put, I thought, well, that's a smart man, he's giving himself a chance. This once he might be able to bend the law his way. Maybe, just maybe he could get his own back and get away with it. He could end up a winner, and that's what life is all about, Uncle, isn't it?"

"If you say so," Kazmer said. Then, seeing that the other man was expecting to hear more, he added, "You're the one for carrying big books in your briefcase."

The lawyer chuckled, thinking that it was settled. "Well, now that that's settled," he said, "what do you say I go out and call Dr. Witstein back?"

And Kazmer was aching to say yes, because he was thinking of the twenty-five years. Twenty-five of them, one after the other, oh Petrona! Every last part of his body wanted to say yes, perhaps even his big toe. But God must have given him strength because what he said was no.

The lawyer's face fell.

"Maybe I'm wrong," he said, "and you really are crazy."

"May be," Kazmer replied.

"This is a big case," the lawyer said, almost as if he were speaking to himself. "It's on the front page of every newspaper. It's a big case and I think I could win it."

"Hell, sir," Kazmer said, because he couldn't bear to see a soul in such torment, not even a crooked lawyer's, "there'll be other big cases. Maybe I can send you some from jail."

"Go to hell," the lawyer said. "Why can't you just do as I tell you? I'm your lawyer, you hired me."

Kazmer nodded, because it was true. "I did hire you, I guess," he said, "and that's why I'm firing you now." And because there was nothing more to say, he turned his head toward the green wall again, waiting for the door to close.

But this young lawyer, he wasn't like Dr. Witstein, he didn't just go quietly when he was told to leave. He came around to the other side of the big table instead, and sat on the bench beside Kazmer. "Listen," he said to him, "you send me away, and the court will only give you another lawyer. And that other lawyer, he'll try the same thing I'm trying. You have no other defence, the facts are facts. So who do you want for a lawyer, Uncle, some eel who can't even speak your language?"

Well, and that young man had finally run out of good replies, and Kazmer was glad to see it. "Hell, sir, you're an eel yourself," he said. "You don't speak my language just because your father taught you a little Hungarian."

And then he added, "Even back home they are eels these days, painting posters," though he wasn't sure if the lawyer could understand that.

Whether he did or not, he did get up from the bench and walked all the way to the door, not that he could walk through it without a last word. "Well, when they stand you up in court," he said, "the clerk will ask you if you plead guilty or not. And when he does, you might as well say guilty, because it'll all come to the same thing."

These were the crooked lawyer's parting words; but whatever it was coming to, it wasn't coming to it very fast, because it took three more months for a black-robed old man to stand up in court and put that question to Kazmer. True, it wasn't his first time in court since he had become a smoking gun, because they had taken him there before, not only once but twice, except it was only for deciding how soon they would be taking him back again, which was called an *adjournment*. But this was to be the real time this time, there was no doubt about that.

And it happened to be an April morning, the streets slushy and slick, as Kazmer could see from the window of the little room where they had put him to wait for his court-appointed lawyer. It was on a day like this that Petrona had left her note on the kitchen table five years ago, nor had the April clouds in the sky changed much, whatever else might have changed underneath them for better or for worse. She never came to see him in jail; and he would not have seen her if she had, but she never even tried. He'd see her in court, though, as a witness;

that's what the court-appointed lawyer said. Not that it mattered one way or the other.

That court-appointed lawyer was a quiet, older man, and he might have been a good man. Except, as people used to say back home, St. Paul could not have turned his back more quickly on a bunch of Rumanians than Kazmer would turn his back on him whenever he appeared, so who could tell if he was a good man or not. Kazmer talked to him only once, and that was when they had met for the first time; and even then he talked to the lawyer only because of another trick someone had warned him about the night before in jail. It was this man in his cell, a forger of some kind, who wasn't a fool though he stammered badly, who had told Kazmer about this trick, and it was a good thing that he had. It was when they were talking about lawyers, and Kazmer said he had fired *his* because he was trying to make out that Kazmer was crazy, nor would he speak to another lawyer again; and this was when the forger said, stupid, that's the worst thing for what you want. Because they'll just say you are crazy if you can't *instruct* your counsel. So Kazmer said to the court-appointed lawyer as soon as he laid eyes on him, "I can instruct you good, but I no want to," and that took care of that.

And he said no to the doctors who came, whether they came from his new lawyer or the police, though he was careful to say it politely, and not the way a crazy person might. "Thank you that you come, but goodbye," he'd tell them, "because what I say, I say to all people in court." And he must have done it right, because even the judge agreed with him the time the police took Kazmer to court for an adjournment. "What do you want me to do?" the judge had said to the police lawyer who had complained about Kazmer not talking to the doctor. "I did order a psychiatric assessment, but I can only order a horse to be led to the water, I can't order it to drink."

And then he also added, "Anyway, I suppose he's entitled to his day in court."

But now that the day was here Kazmer's heart grew faint because what if he couldn't prove himself to be equal to it? What if they let him talk and he could say nothing but little things? What if people wouldn't understand him, no matter how hard he tried; and then he would not get another chance for twenty-five years, if he ever got one again. Then how would anyone ever know? Because it wasn't easy, explaining everything that happened, not even for lawyers or doctors in books, let alone a man like himself, trying to do it all in one breath.

And if he couldn't explain it, he wouldn't end up a winner, that was for sure; and if ending up a winner was what life was all about, as the crooked lawyer had it, *his* life wouldn't be about very much at all. A man of next to fifty, no wife, no house, no children, and for a future maybe nine thousand nights in a cell with Mr. Loeblich's ghost. Not much, if life was all about winning; but maybe it was lucky that Kazmer had never carried big books in his briefcase so he could never tell for sure what life was all about.

The courtroom was full, but all the faces in it belonged to strangers, all except Mr. Perkins's face, which belonged to Mr. Perkins and no one else; and Kazmer would never have thought that he'd be glad to see it in that courtroom, but he was. Petrona, well, they must have kept her waiting elsewhere because Kazmer couldn't see her, though he had looked twice. He even looked a third time, just after they motioned him to stand, because the old man in the black robe was standing up, too, reading from a piece of paper, putting his question to Kazmer. "That on or about December the 2nd," the old man said, peering at him over his glasses, "you did kill Garry Loeblich, a human being; and how do you plead to that charge, guilty or not guilty?"

And what Kazmer thought was why not say guilty, because his heart was growing faint. Why not give in, if he could not explain it anyway? Why bother if no one would understand him, and he'd be just a pity to see struggling, like a fish on the rocks trying to breathe? Why not say guilty and have it done with, take the crooked lawyer's parting advice, that it would all come to the same thing. Except it wouldn't, because he wouldn't let it; and hell, he might as well have gone along with that son of a bitch, pretending that he was a crazy man if he was ready to give in to all these shadows in their black robes now.

And as Kazmer looked up in defiance his heart nearly stopped, because there, in the jury box, sitting among the twelve people who were to be his judges; there, where he would least have expected it, he saw a familiar face. And he knew right away whose face it was, for he would have recognized that man anywhere! Oh, the doubts, the fears he could have saved himself from with a spoonful of faith, if only he had not sat there with his glance nailed to his shoes like a fool. Because that man was chosen for his jury in front of Kazmer's very eyes, if he had only opened them to see.

And now it was all right, because when he started talking, that juryman would understand him, and knowing it would raise his words and give them wings. That fat, friendly, decent man from the color TV, the only one he ever liked, the one man who could strip wood and repaint it like Kazmer himself, with calm and easy strokes. The only good visitor from Petrona's evil world of shadows on the color TV, the one spirit the two of them might have even shared, had he but had the chance to ask her about him. Except he never had, and now it was too late.

But it was not too late to tell people why, and it was easier with a friend to watch him tell it. And not just to watch Kazmer, but to help him out a little when he needed it, because a TV man would speak the shadows' language, and in a glass-and-metal country it was smart to have a glass-and-metal friend. Well, just let the old man in the black robe wait for his answer, for now it was time for Kazmer to steady his voice so that it might be quiet and deep, a man's voice and not a fool's. And so it was, a man's voice; and hearing it, Prince Csaba himself might have allowed his horse to pull up in the sky and shake a satellite or two out of its mane, while he listened with satisfaction to his servant Kazmer reply: "Not guilty!"